# Safe Refuge

Newport
of the
West Series
BOOK ONE

## Pamela S. Meyers

Scrivenings
PRESS
Quench your thirst for story.
www.ScriveningsPress.com

Published by Scrivenings Press LLC
15 Lucky Lane
Morrilton, Arkansas 72110
https://ScriveningsPress.com



Paperback ISBN 978-1-64917-014-9

eBook ISBN 978-1-64917-015-6

Library of Congress Control Number: 2020940028

Cover by Diane Turpin, www.dianeturpindesigns.com

(Note: This book was previously published by Mantle Rock Publishing LLC and was re-published when MRP was acquired by Scrivenings Press LLC in 2020.)



All Scripture used is from the King James Bible.

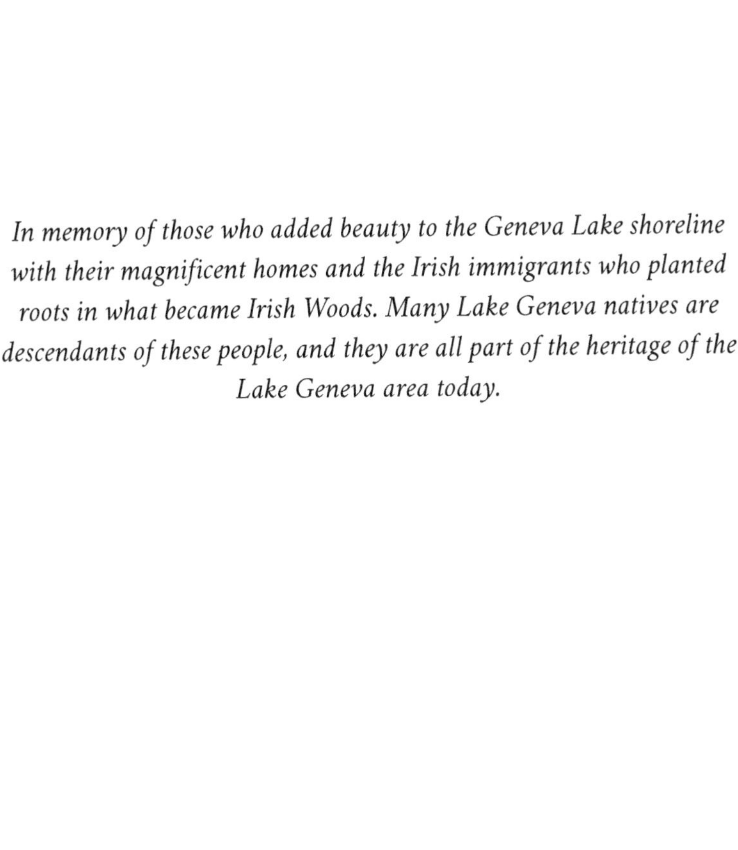

*In memory of those who added beauty to the Geneva Lake shoreline with their magnificent homes and the Irish immigrants who planted roots in what became Irish Woods. Many Lake Geneva natives are descendants of these people, and they are all part of the heritage of the Lake Geneva area today.*

# ACKNOWLEDGMENTS

A book never is brought to completion and publication on it's own. And *Safe Refuge* is no exception.

Without the provision of resources provided by the Lake Geneva Public Library and the Geneva Lake Museum, many details of the area that add authenticity to the historical snapshot of the town that is now called Lake Geneva would be lost forever.

Thanks to Bethany Souza, former owner of the Maxell Mansion. While attending her workshop on the Baker House, another historical property in Lake Geneva, I learned about a set of diaries written by Mrs. Charles Baker, an early resident of the town. For a number of years she kept a yearly diary that included the goings on about town as well as details about her family and friends. I spent a wonderful day at the Wisconsin Historical Society archives at the University of Wisconsin-Whitewater where these diaries are stored. The 1871 and 1872 diaries were a huge help to me.

Thanks also to Patrick Quinn, the town historian, and someone I've known since high school. He provided valuable information on Irish Woods. I also want to give special thanks to Helen Brandt of the Geneva Lake Museum. Helen is always a wealth of information regarding Lake Geneva history, and she provided me extensive notes on Irish Woods that I was able to use.

No book of mine can be written without good critiquing and prayer. When it comes to both, my Penwrights online writing group fills the bill. Also my crit group, Sharpened Pencils, spent hours critiquing this story for me. I also must thank my dear friend and writing buddy, Ane Mulligan. With her hard crits and brainstorming about this story, she helped me more than she probably realizes.

My life group always prays for my writing and I feel every one of those prayers. Thank you Sue, Judy, Betty, and Catherine. You guys are prayer warriors and I am so blessed you have my back.

I couldn't ask for a better publishing team than those at Mantle Rock Publishing. Thanks to Kathy Cretsinger, the publisher and those who work under her. Erin, your editing helped make this story more polished and strong, and Diane, your creative abilities shine with this cover. Thank you for wrapping my book in such a beautiful package.

Last, but never ever least, I thank my Lord and Savior Jesus Christ for inspiring me to write and for being my source of strength to get through tough deadlines. He is ever-present in my life each and every day. To Him be all glory.

# CHAPTER ONE

*October 7, 1871*
*Chicago, Illinois*

"Glad I caught ya before you be leavin'."

At Rory Quinn's comment, heat filled Anna Hartwell's cheeks, and it wasn't because of the unusual fall heat wave Chicago was experiencing. She turned from the family carriage and shielded her eyes with her hand. The Illinois Street Mission janitor and general handyman, leaned against the mission school's doorframe, shirtsleeves rolled up, his muscular arms folded across his chest. A dimpled grin filled his face.

She pressed her hand against her flip-flopping stomach. Why did seeing him always produce that reaction? Maybe because despite the only thing he ever wore was a well-worn shirt and denim pants held up by black suspenders, Rory was more handsome than any man who frequented her usual social circles.

She should look away, but she needed to make sure the memory of his face was forever etched in her mind. "I was about to search for you. I only came out to give Patrick my bag." She swallowed against the lump in her throat that felt the size of a small boulder and forced out her next words. "I need to return to the classroom before I leave." Guilt replaced regret. To tell him the truth would only result in questions with answers she'd rather not share.

Rory stepped across the wood sidewalk until he stood close enough to cause her stomach flutters to reawaken. "If I get my way, I won't be back in time for the service tomorrow night. I hope to spend the evening with me family. So don't look for me." He rubbed the horse's nose. "Too bad you can't attend Illinois Street Church on Sunday mornings."

Anna's chest tightened as she ran the toe of her right boot along the edge of the wood sidewalk. All the more reason to memorize his face now. "I'm blessed Mother allows me Sunday nights there." She looked into the deep pools of his blue eyes. "Speaking of peace, it sounds like you're planning on attempting amends with your dad again."

"Yes. I want to talk to him about the place in Wisconsin where my Uncle Denis lives. You remember me talking about Irish Woods, don't you?"

How could she forget his descriptions of virgin forests and rich farm soil? "What lake did you say the area is near?"

His eyes lit up. "Geneva. You know it?"

Her already spiraling world came to an abrupt stop. The irony of it all. "My father purchased some shore property there. It sounds wonderful. Maybe you'll be our neighbor someday."

His rich hearty laugh she enjoyed so much rose on a wind gust. "I doubt that. Any land me be buyin' won't be on any lakeshore. I'll be toiling the earth while you enjoy your paddle boat rides."

"Father says the village there is small. We're bound to bump into each other, at least in passing." Feeling like she was acting in a play, she had to stop this nonsense talk. "I was just going to get water for the horse and fill a cup for Patrick before I leave. I'll walk you back inside."

"You tend to Patrick and your belongings. I'll get Goldie some water."

As she stepped into her classroom the temperature rose at least ten more degrees. She lifted the metal cup, ready to dip it into her water supply.

"I've been thinking."

She spun around as Rory stepped into the room. His deep blue-eyed gaze never left her face. "If we both end up living near Geneva Lake, you're probably right about seeing each other. If that happens, I'd enjoy that. Even if it be only for a moment."

Anna slipped her hand that held the empty cup behind her back to hide the sudden tremble. "I would, too, Rory." She needed to say something to not get his hopes up, leaving out that by sunset she would be on a train headed as far west as her savings could take her.

Free from being forced to marry a man she didn't love. How could she when she'd seen a different Lyman Millard than her parents had? One who, as a child, had been cruel to his pets, and, as a man, hurt her physically and emotionally. Surely, she'd never be welcome in her family's new summer home after today. She stepped closer and tilted her head back to look him in the eyes. "Rory, there's something you should know ..."

He looked down at her expectantly.

The words "I care for you more than you'll ever know," sat poised on her tongue. But she could never say them. "I'll pray for you and your talk with your dad tomorrow. You'll be in every thought and prayer."

A soft smile filled his face as his gaze dropped to her mouth. "My bonnie lass. If you only knew how much I—" He leaned down.

Pulse racing, she angled her head back.

He came closer, his breath teasing her lips. Yearning to feel his lips against hers became an insatiable need. She raised up on her toes and closed her eyes. A soft brush of what felt like butterfly wings tickled her lips.

"Miss Anna?"

They jumped apart.

Patrick stood in the classroom door, eyes wide. "I was concerned when you didn't come back."

For the second time in a quarter hour Anna felt her face heat. "I'll be right out."

The chauffer's brows rose, and he turned and headed toward the front door.

Rory's face was as red as hers felt. He hoisted the bucket of water from where he'd set it on the floor to his shoulder. "Goldie's waiting. See you outside." He turned and headed toward the door.

She opened her mouth to call out asking to him to not go, but the slam of the door to the street told her she'd waited too long.

She didn't move until her racing heart calmed, then, using measured motions, placed her hat on her head and tied its ribbon beneath her chin.

As she stepped outside, carrying her cape and Patrick's filled water cup, Rory was lifting the bucket up to Goldie. "Here we go old girl." Goldie's nose dipped into the water, and she went after it as if she'd not had a drink in days.

Anna handed Patrick his drink and was rewarded with a huge smile. Relieved he seemed to have recovered from his shock, she regarded him while he gulped the refreshment. Why, except for a long coat in winter, hadn't she noticed before how his uniform never changed? His wool jacket had to be uncomfortable.

Patrick handed her the empty cup. "Thank you, Miss Anna."

Her gaze drifted to Rory, letting the sound of his soothing brogue wash over her as he spoke to the horse. The man was a natural with animals and children. The kind of father she'd want for her own youngsters. The kind of man she'd never have.

"If you're ready, Miss Anna, I think Goldie and I are set to drive you home."

Anna startled and faced Patrick. She'd not noticed him climbing down from his bench. She nodded. "I'm ready. But I need to be dropped off at a friend's near the railroad station. No need to wait. I'll take a trolley home."

Patrick's eyes widened. He opened his mouth, then shut it. "Yes ma'am."

She couldn't get anything past him. He probably knew exactly what she was doing, and after walking in on she and Rory, he probably thought they were both running off together. If only that were true.

"Miss Hartwell, Claire wanted to say goodbye."

Anna turned. Mrs. Monahan and her daughter stepped closer. She'd forgotten the woman had asked to speak to Mr. Rollins, the school's director. Had he told her that this was Anna's final day?

"I'm taking Claire out of school." Mrs. Monahan's voice caught. "We be moving to the south side tomorrow. I got me a cleaning job down there. The school is too far."

Anna frowned. "I thought you had a position working for the Vanderarks."

"I wasn't able to arrive at six a.m. because I needed to drop Claire off at school first." She stared at her well-worn boots. "They let me go. Without that pay I can't afford our rooms in Kilgubbin."

Anna placed her hand on the woman's arm. "I'm so sorry. Do you have a new place to live?"

She shook her head. "I saw a small apartment I liked, but they want a five dollar deposit. I don't think I'll ever have that much money all at once." She held up a pair of dollar bills. This is all I've got right now. We'll stay with my cousin until I can find something."

Anna shifted her weight from one foot to the other. The last train west left in less than an hour. Her hand went to her pocket, and her fingers brushed against the ten one-dollar bills she'd managed to save from her weekly allowance. She'd given so much to the children and their families already. Couldn't she be selfish this once?

"I'll miss you, Miss Hartwell."

The child's voice broke through Anna's reverie. She hunched down, not caring if the dust from the wood sidewalk dirtied her skirts. She drew the little girl into a hug. "I'll miss you too, sweet Claire." Shocked at the feel of the child's bones beneath the fabric of her dress, Anna's heart fell. The bills in her skirt pocket felt as though they weighed much more than the paper they were printed on. They held her ticket to freedom. She'd heard teachers were needed in Denver for the miners' children. But what about the child standing in front of her?

She wrapped her fingers around the bills and glanced up at Patrick. Even he was better off than the Monahans. There must be a different way to break off the engagement. The Lord would help her sort it out. She stood and drew the money from her pocket and pushed it into the frail woman's hand. "For your deposit and some to keep you going a while. Go get that apartment."

Mrs. Monahan's mouth fell open. "Lord have mercy, Miss Hartwell, I can't accept this."

Anna pushed the woman's outstretched hand away. "It's my going-away gift."

"You've already done enough by teaching my wee one to read and learn the Bible." She thrust the money toward Anna.

She clasped her hands behind her back. "It's for Claire. I've no need for it." She peered down into the girl's eyes. "You enjoy your new school, Claire. And obey your mama."

The child bobbed her head. "I will Miss Hartwell."

Anna smoothed the straps on the little girl's threadbare apron that covered an equally frayed dress. The child had so little and she and her sister had so much.

Settled on the carriage seat, Anna rearranged her skirts while Patrick returned to his bench and lifted the reins.

"I've changed my mind," she said. "Let's go straight home. It's much too hot to be out in this heat. I don't mind if you want to take off your coat. You must be sweltering."

The man glanced over his shoulder. "Thank you, Miss Anna, but I would never dream of removing my coat while on duty."

"You mean you wouldn't dream of Mother catching you without your uniform in proper order. I understand."

Although Patrick didn't respond in words, Anna detected a knowing look in his gray eyes before he faced forward.

"Goldie drank the whole thing. I'm not surprised." Rory said. "It's hot enough out here to cause anyone to thirst."

She looked at Rory who stood a few feet away from the horse, holding the empty bucket. So distracted by what she'd done, she'd nearly forgotten he was still there. His eyes went to Anna, and they held each other's gaze a moment longer than they should.

"I'll see you Monday." He grabbed his broom from where it leaned against the building. "Got to finish my own work so I can go home too." Broom in one hand and the bucket containing the empty cup in the other, he whistled an Irish tune as he stepped into the mission.

Anna's heart squeezed. The last view she had of the only man she would ever truly love was of him walking away. How fitting.

RORY'S WHISTLE faded as he returned the empty bucket to where he found it near the school's back door. He started down the hall that stretched through the building toward the front. Was he fooling himself in thinking Da would hear him out about his idea for a fresh start for the family? He stopped and leaned against a wall.

*Am I chasing an impossible dream?* He'd not had a civil conversation with Da since Easter Sunday two years ago when he'd stumbled upon the Illinois Street Church's Easter services, a lost and confused man. He heard D.L. Moody preach and two hours later, stepped outside, a changed man. He couldn't wait to get home and tell his family so they, too, could experience the same joy.

That day, Da declared Rory as good as dead unless he returned to the family's church. The same one that left him unsettled and confused. No matter how much Ma had begged his father to change his mind, Da refused. Tomorrow, he hoped to appeal to Ma's heart and let her work on Da. Two years was a long time to not see your family. His niece probably stood a half-foot taller.

Folding his arms over his chest, he stared at the ceiling.

*Are you there, God?*

Seeing nothing but cobwebs and only hearing the drumming of his heart pounding in his ears, he headed down the hall. As he passed Anna's classroom, he felt a smile stretching his face. Not an Irish drop of blood in her, but with her reddish brown hair and eyes the color of emeralds, she sometimes looked more Irish than some Irish women. He'd wanted so much to kiss her earlier, and her upturned face assured she wanted his kiss. They'd come so close. The tickle of her soft lips as he brushed his own against them burned in his memory. Maybe, when the time was better, they would have their kiss and it wouldn't have to be done in secret. Ha! What a dreamer he was.

Just as well he wasn't going to be at church tomorrow night, especially if Da didn't welcome him. Putting on a smile and acting as if the joy of the Lord was in his heart had become more and more difficult—even at church. How could he have joy when he was estranged from his family and had come to love a woman he couldn't have?

# CHAPTER TWO

Sunday afternoon, Rory stepped off the streetcar, then removed his cap and raked his fingers through his damp hair. He stared up at the unrelenting sun. The family apartment had to be stifling. No matter the weather, Ma always cooked a big Sunday dinner then made it stretch for several days.

He turned onto his family's street. On either side, apartment buildings lined the road. So many families crowded into tiny apartments. As a child, when his world only reached about four blocks in any direction, he had no idea of anything different.

Da worked hard at the lakefront all day, loading and unloading boats that came from the east coast. But, he never made enough money to move the family out of the old neighborhood.

*Please, God, let Da listen to me. Irish Woods can be a good start for all of us.*

Rory strode past the apartment building his sister Maureen and her family lived in and approached a three-story building several doors down.

A hunched over woman shuffled toward him. Old Mrs.

McIntosh seemed even more bent than the last time he'd seen her. "Mornin' Mrs. McIntosh. How be you this morning."

She raised her head. The same deep lines crisscrossed her face as they always had. Recognition lit her eyes and she offered a toothless smile. "Rory Quinn. Have you and your da made up?"

Heaviness filled his chest and he stared at his feet. "I'm afraid not. I'm here to make peace."

She held out a hand, gnarled with arthritis. She patted his arm. "I'll pray your da is willing. No one should live apart from his family."

Inside the building, he took the stairs to the second floor, breathing in the aroma of chicken, potatoes, and onions along the way. He approached his family's door and his brother-in-law's hearty laugh, followed by a child's small voice penetrated the wood. A familiar ache filled his chest. He raised his fisted hand then let it drop. Maybe he should forget trying. Make a new life for himself. But, If he didn't do this today, he'd always wonder what might have happened. He drew in a deep breath and rapped on the door. The laughter halted.

"Who can that be?" Ma asked.

"We don't know unless we answer it." Da's voice sounded as strong as ever. The floor beneath his feet shuddered as heavy footfalls came closer.

The door swung open.

Rory ran his gaze over Da's lined face as Da did the same with him.

His father's lips twitched, then flattened into a thin line. Anger flashed from his eyes. "What are you doin here?"

"I came to see you." Rory stretched to peer past Da's broad shoulders.

Ma scurried up and their gazes met. "Rory, my boy. You've come home." She thrusted an arm around her husband.

Da pushed her back. "Not our boy anymore." He glared at

Rory, his blue eyes almost all black. "Are ya comin' home to your church?"

"No, but . . ."

"Then you are still as good as dead to me. Now go on and get out of here."

"Da, I know how to get all of us out of this place for good. We can start—"

The crack of wood hitting wood echoed in the hall. Loud shouts filtered out from the other side of the door.

"Lord have mercy, what is goin' on out here."

Rory turned and stared at a woman peeking through a partially opened door. "Sorry for the commotion. We're okay."

"Then, keep it down."

Ma's sobs came from behind the apartment door and he pounded his right fist against the palm of his left hand He had half a mind to force his way in. Da had no right to stop him from seeing the rest of the family. He angled his body and planted his feet.

"Enough, Doreen. He's not our son anymore."

"Lord have mercy on his soul, I know."

Rory wiped the sting from his eyes and turned away.

SUNDAY EVENING, Anna plopped on the old swing by the service porch's back door. It had been a long while since she'd sat where the kitchen help gathered to shuck corn or to take a few moments' break. She set the swing in motion, its squeak evoking the same comfort she'd felt as a toddler when she snuggled up against her nanny's ample chest.

During tonight's worship service, her focus had drifted countless times to the fifth row from the front where Rory usually sat. She should have moved elsewhere to not be reminded of his absence, but she couldn't get herself to change seats. Somehow, being able to see where he normally sat made her feel closer to him even in his absence.

The backdoor flew open and whacked against the outside wall. Mother stepped onto the porch, her lips downturned in the same perpetual frown. "There you are. It's bad enough you insist on attending that other church on Sunday nights, and now that you're home you still avoid us. Calista and I have been waiting to go over last minute details for the wedding dinner."

Anna stiffened and stilled the swing. "We've already discussed the menu at least a dozen times."

Mother rested her fists on her hips. "If you hadn't been at church, you'd know that we're changing to some foods that hold up better in heat. Now come inside. Your sister is waiting."

Mother's stare met hers. The stubborn woman wasn't moving until Anna agreed. "You need not go to all the trouble because I plan to call off the wedding."

Her mother gaped at her. "That is not for you to decide. Everything is set and you and Lyman are getting married day after tomorrow."

"But I don't love him."

Mother rested a fist on her hip. "Of course, you don't. Time will take care of that. Do you think your father and I loved each other when we married?"

"Mother, he hurts me."

"What do you mean hurt?"

"He pinches me until I bruise and one time he punched me in the stomach. Took the wind right out of me." Mother raised her chin. "I've never seen a bruise on you. If that were true I would. He's always the perfect gentleman."

"Of course he is when others are around. When he hurts me, he's careful to do it where bruises don't show."

"You're lying, and lying won't get you out of the marriage." Mother turned and stepped inside.

The screen door shut with a loud *bang* as if putting a firm period on Mother's statement. Anna inhaled through her nose and hoped the smoky smell wasn't from a fresh fire. It took hours to extinguish that inferno, and the firemen would be too exhausted to fight another. She sniffed again. The smell was too pungent to be from last night.

She said a silent prayer for rain and stood. May as well get the dinner menu discussion over with. A waste of time because by tomorrow night she would be on a train headed west even if she had to crawl to the railroad station on her hands and knees.

Finally, after a laborious discussion about food she never planned to eat, Anna stood in the middle of her dressing room as Jane, the personal maid she shared with Callie, loosened the laces on her corset. She let out a whoosh of air. "I don't know what I'd do without you to get me out of this contraption."

Jane answered in the Irish accent Anna loved. "Knowing you, Miss Anna, I suspect you would find some way to loosen it yourself." The maid's words echoed in Anna's thoughts. If she had the reputation of getting the impossible done, she surely could manage to be on the next train west tomorrow. She'd find the necessary funds somewhere. The corset fell away, and Jane dropped a thin cotton nightgown over Anna's head from behind.

She spun around, enjoying the feel of her loose nightgown lifting from her clammy skin. Eyes closed, she wrapped her arms around herself and whirled out of the dressing room and into the bedroom, imagining she was dancing with Rory in Irish Woods. The scent of the outdoors and smoke from a campfire tickled her nose. Her eyes popped open. That smell wasn't part of her imagination. "There must be another fire."

The door to the hall opened, and Callie burst into the room, her dressing gown barely closed over her nightgown. Her brunette hair, already released from its combs, lifted from her shoulders. She raced to the open window and leaned out. "It is true. The sky *is* on fire." She turned, her face ashen. "What if it comes this way?" Her shrill voice echoed off the bedroom walls.

Anna hurried to the window. To the southwest, a red glow filled the otherwise dark sky.

"There, you see it?"

Anna gulped and draped an arm across her sister's shoulders, keeping her focus on the scene outside. "It's a long way off. They'll put it out before it comes this far north. Just like they did with the fire last night. And don't forget. We're north of the river."

A ball of fire erupted over the city and exploded. Callie shrieked. Small orbs of flame shot out and dropped to the ground, reminding Anna of the fireworks she'd watched last Fourth of July. She pulled her trembling sister closer.

A bell's frantic cadence rode the hot wind through the window.

"There's the courthouse bell." Anna worked to put confidence in her voice. "Now more firemen will help. They'll get it out." The bell had rung out notice of a fire somewhere in the city many times, but never had it sounded so frantic.

*God, help us.*

A wad filled her throat. The Chicago River would halt the flames from advancing north, but Rory's family lived beneath the enflamed sky. Was he still there or had he returned to his rented room in Kilgubbin? She turned away from the window and put her hands over her ears. She could avoid looking, but she couldn't stop from hearing that infernal bell.

*Please, Lord, protect Rory and his family.*

Mother marched into the room wearing a dress she usually reserved for weekdays at home. "Girls, get dressed." Her hard dark eyes flicked from Callie to Anna. "The Vanderark's butler reported that the fire is out of control and their entire household is evacuating to the north. Your father left for his office a while ago, and we're to pack up our valuables and load them into the carriage to be safe." She spun toward the door, her skirts swirling. "Be downstairs in five minutes."

"I'll never be ready that fast." Callie waved her hands in the air. "On a good day it takes that long to get my corset tightened. Why the hurry? The fire is a long way away."

Anna peered out the window and winced. The red sky appeared closer. What if the river didn't stop the flames? She turned and squared her shoulders. Fear could not, would not paralyze her. She scurried to the armoire and opened it. "Forget the corset, Callie. Put on the roomiest dress you have." She reached for the dark gray dress she often wore for teaching because it was looser around the middle.

"But all my dresses are tight without a corset." Callie's voice rose at least two octaves. "They were made for finishing school and my coming out socials. How am I going to carry them all if we have to leave?"

"You won't. Just take one or two day dresses. We'll probably be back tomorrow after the fire is out, and you'll still have your party clothes." Anna waved a hand at Jane. "Go help her. I'll be fine by myself. There's no time."

Jane's lips trembled as her gaze darted to the open window. "Yes, ma'am."

An ache filled Anna's throat, and she rested a hand on the maid's shoulder. "You're worried about your family, aren't you?"

The young woman nodded. "My ma and sister. They be all I have."

"I know." Anna whispered. "Go find your family. Bring them here if you can. Callie will have to manage on her own. If we have to leave, we'll likely head north and wait it out. Hopefully, we'll meet up later."

Creases formed between the young woman's blond brows. "But when your mother realizes I've left, I've lost me job."

"Your family's welfare is more important. I'll deal with Mother about your position."

Callie tugged at Jane's arm. "Let's hurry. I'll help you slip out the side door. With all the commotion, Mother won't realize you've gone."

Anna raised her gaze to the ceiling as tension released itself. Praise God her sister had come to her senses. Callie and the maid darted into the hall, and Anna threw off her nightgown and tugged the chemise she'd discarded moments earlier over her head.

Minutes later, she grabbed her packed carpetbag, then gave the corset where it lay on the floor a swift kick and headed for the door.

Servants crisscrossed the circular, marble-floored foyer as Mother shoved a large landscape in a gilded frame into the hands of Henry Gibson, the family's newest servant. "Take this out to the carriage, and put it with the other artwork I gave you."

"Is there going to be any room for us, Mother?" Anna came the rest of the way down the stairs. "The carriage is only so big."

Mother threw her shoulders back and raised her chin. "Really, Anna, you have no respect. Your father worked hard to pay for our collections. If he isn't able to rescue the papers from his office, we may have to sell our artwork and silver. You girls can sit on each other's laps if necessary." She studied Anna's carpetbag. "Surely you didn't squeeze your wedding dress into that small thing."

"I've only room for two day dresses and some undergarments. If we're gone longer, I need daywear, not a wedding dress. It will be here when we come back."

Mother hustled to the stairs and took the first two steps. "I'll carry it. You have no regard for how much that gown cost. You'll still have to dress appropriately on your wedding day, which will happen soon."

Anna gaped at her mother. "Isn't our safety more important?" She dropped her bag to the floor, then crossed the room and picked up an alabaster vase. "Father isn't back yet?"

Mother's mouth twisted into a grimace. "No. The streets are full of people walking north, and I'm sure he's having a difficult time maneuvering around all that riffraff from the south side."

Anna ignored her mother's insensitive remark. "How did Father intend to get to the office with all the people coming the opposite direction? I can't imagine driving a horse and carriage through a mob."

"He took Maverick and went on horseback." Her face red, as if she would burst any moment, Mother glanced up the stairs. "Where is Calista?" She ground the words out between clinched teeth. "If that sister of yours is preening in front of the mirror again . . ."

For once Mother wasn't condoning Callie's girlish preoccupation with herself. Had her sister gotten Jane out the side door as planned? "She probably is preening, Mother. You've always encouraged her that way."

Mother rolled her eyes. "Well, not tonight. Go get her."

"I'm sure she'll be along. I'll check Father's library for valuables." Anna darted toward the library, crossing over the inlaid floor medallion that filled the center of the room, and stepped into the wood-paneled room. She rushed over to his massive desk and opened the top drawer. A photograph of a woman with a small girl lay on top of some business papers. She picked up the photo. The child looked to be Callie, but who was the woman? Somewhat attractive with dark blond hair and wearing a plain dress, she looked like no one in the family. Perhaps some English cousins Anna had never met. She tucked it into her pocket and focused on what she came here for.

The old tarnished watch rested in its usual place. She lifted the timepiece and ran her thumb over the intricate scrollwork on its cover.

When she was small, she used to crawl on Father's lap while

he held the watch and told her how as a young man in England he'd scrimped and saved to buy it. Now he could purchase a million watches, but he always kept this one to remember where he came from.

"Anna, get out here. We need to keep working."

She flinched and slipped the timepiece into her dress pocket next to the photo. As far as Anna was concerned, other than the Bible, already tucked into her carpetbag, nothing else was worth saving. She'd already lost the locket Father had given her on her sixteenth birthday. She wasn't losing his pocket watch. "Coming."

A thick envelope caught her eye and she picked it up. Without writing on the outside she had no idea what it was. She gently broke the wax seal and gasped. She quickly flipped through the bills and mentally calculated. There had to be a thousand dollars. She closed the envelope and folded it in half before stuffing it in her pocket with the picture and the watch.

In the main room, Callie stood next to Mother, her dark brown hair swept up onto her head in a haphazard sort of way. Her dress pulled tight at the seams across her midsection. A second carpetbag sat on the floor next to Anna's. Callie caught Anna's eye. "Mother wants us to go to the kitchen and make sure the servants aren't helping themselves to the silver they're supposed to be packing."

"Let's go." Anna gripped her sister's arm and pulled her toward the stairs that led down to the kitchen. In the stairwell, she whispered. "Did Jane get away okay?"

"Yes, that's what took me so long. We had to wait for the back hall to clear so she could escape without being seen. Where does Mother think we're going to sit with all the things she wants to take?"

"I have no idea, but more to the point, where does she think we are going to escape to?"

Callie stopped and looked at Anna. "Didn't she tell you? We're going to the Millard's."

Anna stiffened. From the fire to the pit of hades as far as she was concerned. "I suppose they are far enough north and west to be spared."

"I wish Father would hurry. I'm really scared. His office is where the fire seems to be. What if he . . . "

Anna wrapped her arms around Callie. "I'm sure he's hurrying as fast as he can. God will protect him. "

"If God cared, He'd stop the fire." Callie fumbled in her dress pocket, then apparently not finding a handkerchief, wiped her nose with the back of her hand.

"God promises to never leave us." Anna gave Callie a push. "Come on, let's get to the kitchen before Mother comes looking for us and discovers Jane is missing."

By the time the women arrived in the kitchen, the servants had filled several pillowcases with the family sterling. Anna peeked into one of the makeshift bags a maid held open and recognized a silver tea set. She nodded and waved her toward the door.

Another maid came up and opened a pillowcase. Anna peered at the chafing dish and candlesticks on top of several other things. How did Mother expect her to check everything? If she wanted every piece accounted for, she'd have to stay and inventory them herself.

She took the bundle then asked the servants if they had loved ones they needed to check on. All but Henry said they did, and she sent them on their way. She assured Henry he could come with the family, as would Patrick.

As she was about to find Mother, Patrick burst in the door. "The red sky is coming closer."

"Callie, Mother, and I are coming—also Henry. And," she gulped hard. "Father, if he makes it back."

Patrick frowned. "There's only room for three in the carriage because of the bags of silver."

Anna shook her head. With Maverick gone, they were down to Bella, the sorrel mare and Goldie. "I was afraid of that. Let's hitch Bella to Father's phaeton and load some belongings in that one." She looked at Henry. "Can you drive the smaller carriage?"

He stared at the floor. "I don't know. I've ridden horseback as a boy, but never drove a carriage."

Anna pressed her lips together. The poor man was probably afraid they'd leave him behind if he weren't useful. Mother wasn't going to like it, but there was no time to worry about trivial things. "Then I'll drive." She looked at Patrick's startled face.

"Don't you remember letting me take the reins when I was a child?"

The middle-aged man, nodded. "Yes, but we agreed to not tell your parents."

She offered him a sympathetic look. "Don't worry. As to who taught me to drive, the secret is still safe." She glanced at Henry. "Please help Patrick transfer some of the belongings to Father's phaeton. You'll ride with me." Carrying the filled pillowcase she still held, she followed the men outside.

A cacophony of shouts and children's wails assaulted Anna's ears, and she turned to the street outside the gate. Even though it was now past midnight and the gas street lamps had gone dark, the column of people moving north was easy to be seen.

Anna breathed in the stench of smoke and her nostrils burned. Was the fire *that* close? She put the pillowcase in the carriage then started for the house.

The backdoor opened and Callie scurried through, her arms laden with a bundle of clothing.

Anna met her at the steps. "I'm going to find mother and convince her that she needs to stop packing. The carriages are full."

Callie pushed the garments into Anna's arms. "I'll get Mother." She headed for the door.

Anna let her go. Her sister would be able to persuade their mother to leave her precious treasures easier than she could. At least if Anna drove the smaller carriage, she wouldn't have to listen to Mother's continuous complaints.

She gave the bundle in her arms a quick glance and sighed. She'd told Mother that saving the wedding dress was a waste, but she didn't listen. Anna stuffed mother's day dresses in the large carriage then ran into the barn and tossed the wedding dress in Maverick's stable. If it didn't burn, let the horse trample on it.

A few moments later, Anna climbed into the phaeton and glanced at a pair of oil paintings that sat on the passenger-side floor. She supposed the Trumbull was of value, but the other one by an obscure artist, she wasn't sure. Henry was going to have a difficult time placing his feet.

Across the way, Patrick worked at making room for his passengers among the collection of Mother's favorite things, while anguished shouts and baby wails from the passing mob outside the gate increased with each passing moment. She sighed. Even Solomon would have a difficult time convincing Mother to make a choice between her family and her possessions.

She could only hope it didn't come to that.

# CHAPTER THREE

Mother marched through the back door, carrying another bulging pillowcase. Callie plodded behind her with the carpetbags.

Had Anna's brain become so numb she'd forgotten their personal belongings? She pointed at the larger carriage. "Put the bags in there."

Mother stared at Anna. "What are you doing in the driver's seat?"

"Driving."

"Aren't we going to wait for Father?"

Anna ignored her sister's question because she had no answer.

"Where is Henry?" Mother's demanding voice rose against the roar of the wind. "He can take the reins."

Anna squared her shoulders and faced her mother. "He's never driven a carriage before. I'll be fine." She peered toward the street. The mass of people moving north stretched from one side of the road to the other. Some carried possessions on their backs, and others a child. Seeing adults in such despair was one thing, but children were another matter.

She turned away. Chances were her family would be able to return in a day or two, but the people out there had probably lost everything except what they could carry.

Someone yelled Anna's name and she turned toward the voice.

Father emerged from the throng and plodded across the gravel drive, his tie hanging around his neck, shirtsleeves rolled up, and a large metal box on his hip.

Anna gasped. "Father, what happened to your face?"

"Thank goodness you're all safe." He looked over his shoulder at the reddening sky. "This inferno is a monster. Maverick spooked and bucked me off on LaSalle Street, and I banged my face into a hitch. By the time I got to my feet, the boy was gone. I hoped he'd headed back here." His gaze flicked from Goldie to Bella, and his shoulders sagged.

Anna swallowed hard. "He hasn't shown up."

"I was afraid of that. He served me well." Father held up the metal box. "At least I recovered what's important before the blaze ate up the office building." He looked at Patrick then Anna in the phaeton. "Good heavens, are we down to Anna driving?"

"I've driven before, Father."

He marched to the phaeton. "I'll take over. Go ride in the other carriage with Calista and your mother. Henry, come with me." He looked around the turnabout and raised his voice. "Where are the other servants?"

"I told them to leave if they needed to make sure their families were safe," Anna said.

Mother pinned a glare on Anna and opened her mouth.

Callie's eyes widened. "Don't yell at her, Mother. They were desperate to find their families." She tossed her head and stomped across the yard, handed the carpetbags up to Patrick, then climbed into the carriage.

Anna scrambled out of the phaeton. While Father took his place in the driver's seat, Mother placed the stuffed pillowcase next to him. "This is the silver coffee urn the Field's gave us on our anniversary. We can't lose it."

Father grimaced. "What's more valuable?" His voice rose. "Someone's life, or an urn we never use? He lifted the pillowcase and dropped it to the ground. "Henry, get up here."

Inwardly cheering her father on, Anna marched to the carriage and settled next to her sister.

Mother let Patrick help her onto the seat across from Callie and Anna. "It's bad enough we're leaving Anna's wedding gifts. There's probably a lot of silver in those boxes."

Anna shrugged. She didn't dare speak her mind lest she be replaced with the coffee urn.

Father brought the phaeton next to the carriage. "Patrick, you go first and I'll follow. Bella snorted and shook her head. She lifted her front feet, causing the packed phaeton to tip back. Father scrambled out of the carriage and used his bare hand to knock a burning ember from the animal's back. "That's okay, girl it's gone." His soothing voice calmed the horse.

"The wind is carrying embers right toward us. We need to leave now!" Father climbed in the phaeton.

Patrick gave Goldie's rear end a soft slap with the reins and clicked his tongue. "Let's go Goldie."

The carriage lurched ahead then came to a stop. The wall of people, some limping, others riding in wagons and carriages, their shouts and moans more elevated than earlier, appeared impenetrable.

An elderly woman collapsed in front of Goldie, and several people cursed and stepped over her limp body. Anna prepared to jump from the carriage, but stopped when a pair of men helped the lady to her feet. One picked her up and carried her.

Anna prayed for the woman, then for Patrick and Father. Though they were both experienced drivers, the horses had never faced anything like this.

Goldie took a step backwards. "Come on, girl, be aggressive.

There's a break." Patrick clicked his tongue again. Goldie gingerly stepped forward and Patrick maneuvered the horse and carriage into the moving stream.

Anna turned to make sure Father was behind them. Behind her father, angry tongues of flame scampered across their home's shingled roof and licked the tree branches that hung close to the house. A limb caught fire and dropped, smacking against a chimney. Sparks flew into the air as huge flames ate up the roof like a choice roast of beef. Good riddance as far as she was concerned. Too bad all the dark memories related to those walls couldn't disappear from her recollections at the same time.

"I thought the river would stop the fire." Callie moaned. "My beautiful dresses."

A fireball exploded and heated air enveloped the street. The mass of people sped up, some scampering ahead of the carriage. Anna tried to study each man who passed them. Wouldn't it be a miracle if one turned out to be Rory?

She forced her thoughts to the present. What was wrong with her that she'd think such a thing right now? Was this the end? She shut her eyes to wait for God to take her. A moment passed and the heat lessened. She opened her eyes, surprised they'd moved nearly a block past the inferno. But would they outrun the flames?

Mother shifted on her seat and held a handkerchief to her mouth "This smoke is horrid." She glanced at the dresses that were tucked around her feet and gasped. She bent and clawed through the clothing. "I gave Anna's wedding dress to you, Calista. Where is it?"

Callie's eyes widened. "I gave all the dresses to Anna."

Anna straightened and threw her shoulders back. "There wasn't enough room for all of them. Mother would need her clothes before I'd need a wedding gown. I left it in the barn."

Mother glared at Anna. "That dress was a silk original from

Worth of Paris. If you think not having the dress will prevent the marriage from happening, you're wrong. I can have another day dress made anytime. Why would you even think to do such a thing?"

Anna grimaced. "I already told you I won't marry Lyman Millard. The dress had little value to me."

Mother's lips pressed into a thin line. "You will marry Mr. Millard, and after what you've done, you can do so in rags."

Anna took a deep breath. The smoky air caught in her throat and she coughed until she thought she'd expel a lung.

Callie handed her a handkerchief.

Anna put the hanky over her mouth, then took it away. "We need to be thinking about Father and how he'll have to deal with his business and find us a new place to live before anything else."

Callie's lower lip trembled. "I heard Father say he's going to telegraph Mrs. Maxwell up in Geneva and see if we can stay with her. I didn't know the Millards have their own telegraph line."

Anna coughed into the handkerchief. "A lot of the people in their neighborhood got them last year." For once Anna was grateful for the Millard's penchant for always being the first to acquire a new invention.

*Thwap.* The carriage rocked.

Anna peered over the side. Next to the carriage's back wheel, a man lay unmoving in the street. Another man halted next to him and gave him a shove with his foot. "Get up, man. You be trampled on if you keep laying here."

"Patrick, stop!"

At Father's shout, the carriage halted.

Henry jumped out of the phaeton and came beside him. "Get up quick. I can't keep the crowd from steppin' on ya long."

"My knee won't hold me. I tripped over her sack." The man pointed up ahead.

Several feet in front of them a woman, carrying a big sack, disappeared into the crowd.

The man struggled to stand on one leg, using the carriage and Henry's arm as braces. He took a step and fell against Henry. The two of them nearly toppled over.

Mother jumped up and shook a live ember from her dress. "We're going to be burned if we don't move." Callie stomped on the glowing cinder.

Behind them, Father's wounded face filled with compassion. "You can ride in the bigger carriage."

"We've no room for him," Mother shouted.

"Yes, we do, Eleanor." Father hollered instructions to Patrick to give the loaded pillowcase on the seat next to him to someone in the crowd then help the new passenger onto the bench.

"You don't even know what's inside that bag." Mother's complaint went unheeded.

Within a heartbeat, the crippled man sat beside Patrick. He called out to Father, "Thank you, sir. May God bless you for your kindness. I was one of the last ones to make it across the river before the oil in the water caught fire. A river burning. Strangest sight I've ever seen."

The men got the horses moving and the carriages jostled forward.

Mother crossed her arms and jutted her chin, her face set as though made of stone.

Anna closed her eyes against the sting from the smoke. At least with them shut, she could pray for safety for the mission children and Rory.

"We're nearing Lincoln Park." Patrick called out. "Looks like this is where most of the people are stopping. Should we keep going?"

Mother cleared her throat. "Of course we'll keep going. We're not about to sit in this godforsaken place and let the flames force us into the lake. We have a nice refuge at the Millard's."

Jolted out of her daydream, Anna opened her eyes. How long had they been on the move? Lincoln Park was normally a fifteen-minute carriage ride from home, but at the pace they were moving, at least a half an hour must have passed. She drew in a breath. Was that horrible odor from the fire or everyone's clothing? At least now, the only noises besides the wind were the *clip-clop* of horse's hooves, and a baby's wail up ahead. The still leafy trees that canopied over their heads created a shield between them and the red sky. If one tried hard enough, it would be easy to pretend nothing was wrong—except for all the people.

Off to her left, like a mother hen, a nun stretched her arms around the shoulders of several young children. Claire Monahan's sweet face emerged in Anna's thoughts. Was the child okay? What about her mother? Father said he thought Kilgubbin was spared, but Mrs. Monahan said they were moving to the south side today. Or was it already tomorrow? Anna bit her lip. Saturday seemed like a year ago.

An hour later, Patrick guided the carriage into the Millard's circular drive. At the sight of the gas-fed lanterns' glow on either side of the double-door entrance, Anna's chest tightened. Fire had taken all she knew. And now, she'd been brought to a place that only spelled more distress. Ever since they left Lincoln Park, she'd focused on Geneva Lake, using the imagery of its surrounding forests and clear blue waters as Father and Rory had described. Was it wrong to think that God was showing her the safe refuge He planned to provide?

*Please, Lord, may it be true.*

"Thank goodness that street person wanted off in the park. I don't know what we'd have done with him if he'd come here."

Anna gaped at Mother. "What would you have us do if he'd stayed? Tell him to find a place in the stable with the animals?

He wasn't a street person. I heard him tell Patrick he's an accountant at Marshall Fields."

Mother cleared her throat for the umpteenth time, but Anna ignored her and scanned the sky. For the first time the redness seemed far away. She then focused on the Millard's Greek Revival mansion. The Millards had emigrated from England a couple years before Anna's parents. Mrs. Millard had quickly become fascinated with the South to the point Anna suspected she secretly had favored it during the Civil War.

Patrick brought the carriage to a stop, and Anna braced herself. She had at least one day of enduring the presence of Lyman Millard before they could escape to Wisconsin.

"You poor dears, bring yourselves inside at once." Hortense Millard's affected southern drawl blended oddly with her natural British accent, causing her to sound even more insincere than she probably was. She came down the mansion's front steps, looking as though she was about to head to a ball. Nothing ever disturbed the woman's attempt at always appearing perfect. She probably slept standing up so not to disturb her coiffure of curls and tendrils.

Anna gathered her skirt and waited while Patrick assisted Callie out of the carriage, and Father attended to Mother.

"My goodness, you people look like you just came from a war."

Father turned a watchful eye to the south. "We did, Hortense. I don't know what started this inferno, but I hope it will soon be under control."

He turned his back on Mrs. Millard and inspected his horse's hindquarters. "Look's like that cinder back there didn't do you any harm, girl."

Their hostess regarded Anna, and her mouth twisted into a grimace. "You poor dear. You must have borrowed one of the help's dresses in your rush."

"It is my own dress. I wear it when working with the children at the mission."

"Oh. Yes. Your charity work. Well, once you and Lyman are married, we'll find something more suitable for a woman of your position." She offered a stiff smile to Mother. "Lyman and his father left hours ago for their office to rescue anything they could. They should be back soon." Her smile faded. "Won't it be nice for our young people to spend time together, Eleanor? It will be like old times when they were children. We'll have to reschedule the nuptials as soon as possible. Perhaps out here at our church."

"Anna has to marry in our family's church." Mother looked at Patrick. "Bring our belongings inside please, then see the horses over to the stable. After that take a rest. You must be exhausted." Mother's sugary tone—reserved for when outsiders were around—grated against Anna's ears.

"We can discuss wedding plans later," Mrs. Millard said. "I'm sure we'll have plenty of time since the city must be in ruins."

If your telegraph line is operating, I'd like to wire Mrs. Maxwell in Geneva and ask if we can stay with her for a few days until we can locate a place of our own."

Mother let out a long sigh. "Leonard, I can't imagine where you think we're going to find appropriate shelter. It's nothing but wilderness up there."

"I hear the lake is pristine," Mrs. Millard patted her perfect curls. "One of the Sturgis brothers has already purchased a gorgeous home there. We've been talking about building a summer villa ourselves. This city gets so hot in summer."

"I'm sure it's lovely. Nothing is sitting right with me now. Our beautiful mansion is gone, and we're homeless." Mother reached in her reticule for a handkerchief and dabbed her eyes.

"You poor dear." Mrs. Millard draped an arm across Mother's shoulders. "Let's get you inside." The women headed to the front door, with Anna and Callie following.

"I'm sure Leonard wouldn't take you to a place like Geneva without some kind of lodgings, although I doubt a home can be built quickly with winter around the corner." Mrs. Millard continued to talk. "Perhaps this disaster has him not thinking rationally. As I said, y'all are welcome to stay as long as necessary."

Mother returned her handkerchief to her bag. "Leonard has said Mrs. Maxwell has a large home, but I abhor staying in another person's residence."

Mrs. Millard raised a brow. "Well, I hope you won't be too put out staying here."

Mother waved a dismissive hand. "I didn't mean you, Hortense. Why we're like family we've known each other so long."

"And we soon will be family with our children marrying soon." Mrs. Millard paused on the veranda and offered Anna a smile. "I'm sure you aren't looking forward to living in such a primitive place like Geneva. You can stay with us. I'm sure Lyman would love to have you here."

Anna's stomach soured. She'd rather live in a teepee than spend a day in Lyman Millard's presence. "Thank you, but I think after such a loss it's better for all of us to stay together as a family." Anna walked past the older women and stepped into the large foyer. The others followed close behind. She stared up at the thousand-light chandelier that Mrs. Millard had ordered from a company in Atlanta before the war.

"Girls." Mrs. Millard crossed to where Anna and Callie stood. "I've set aside the guest room that faces the back of the house for you two. Feel free to go up any time. One of the maids is preparing a bath for you." She looked at Anna and dipped her head. "Unless you want to wait up with me for Lyman and his father. There's no telling when they'll get back, and I'm a bit concerned."

All Anna wanted was to close her eyes against this horrible

night and sleep for a month. She stifled a yawn. "Thank you. But I'm exhausted, as I'm sure my sister is."

Mrs. Millard rested a shaking hand on Anna's arm. "Are you sure don't wish to wait for Lyman?"

Tension crawled down Anna's spine. As Lyman's supposed fiancée the correct response would be to wait up with Mrs. Millard. She issued a silent prayer for the right words.

Father stepped over. "You girls go on. I'll wait up. I'm too riled after what I've gone through to sleep." He faced Mrs. Millard. "I need to send that wire to Mrs. Maxwell if the telegraph is operating. I want my family out of this catastrophe as soon as possible."

"As far as I know it's working." Mrs. Millard stepped over to an embroidered bell pull and yanked. "I'll have the butler show you where it is."

Anna smiled her thanks to Father and followed her sister up the circular staircase. She would pray the rest of the night that Mrs. Maxwell would respond positively to Father's request and the trains would still be running. She'd board that train for Geneva Lake and never ever come back.

# CHAPTER FOUR

An empty feeling in the pit of Anna's stomach had her wishing she hadn't given her sandwich the Millard's cook had made for her to a crying toddler. They'd only been in route for less than an hour, and it would be at least two hours, before they'd sit down to lunch at Mrs. Maxwell's.

The family had managed to secure the only facing seats in the car. Mother sat kitty-corner from Anna, straight as a fence-post, her lips set in a straight line. Next to her, Father, slumped in his seat, staring straight ahead and looking as if the light had gone out in his soul. His eyes misted over and he blinked rapidly. Anna ached for him. He'd risked his life to get his papers before they burned, was thrown from his beloved horse, and then got the family off the property in the nick of time. Now, here they were homeless, but alive. In time, Father would be grateful for that.

The repetitious *clickety-clack* of the train, along with the constant hum of chatter and a baby's wail, helped to drown out Callie's moaning over the loss of her ball gowns and Mother's complaints about losing most everything else. Despite the anguish and sadness, Anna, couldn't help but rejoice. She'd prayed for a way to stop the wedding and as bad as the fire had been, here she was on what was to have been her wedding day being taken mile after mile away from Lyman.

She shut her eyes and let visions of beautiful Geneva Lake, as Father and Rory had described, occupy her thoughts. If Rory had survived the fire, chances were he'd head to Geneva—maybe with his whole family. She'd made a vow that morning to the Lord that she wouldn't give up looking for him.

"Geneva, Wisconsin. Final stop."

Anna opened her eyes and focused on the rotund conductor standing at the front of the car. A loud hiss sounded outside the open windows, and the train braked to a stop. A portly man stood from his seat across from the Hartwells, wearing dress pants but no matching jacket. He finger combed his gray hair then wedged himself into the already filling aisle.

"Hey. Wait your turn," a tall man behind them shouted.

More passengers crammed into the aisle—mothers with babies on their hips, whining older children, and a few elderly people who tried to maintain their balance despite being jostled. Was this small village large enough to accommodate everyone? At least Anna's family had a place to go—a lovely home on the lakeshore.

Mother regarded the throng and clucked her tongue. "Let's sit until this motley crowd clears the aisles."

Outside the window, several peoples' eyes flicked back and forth, searching the train windows, their eyes full of concern. In front of a barnlike structure across the way, two men laughed as they wiped down a fire engine wagon. How odd to see firemen enjoying themselves while down in Chicago, their counterparts were spent and exhausted.

"Here, let me help you. You can't manage the child and your bag at the same time."

Anna turned. Father stood in the aisle next to a young woman wearing a wrinkled day dress. She propped a baby boy who looked to be eight or nine months old on her hip, and in the other hand she held a bulging satchel by its handle.

Father took the woman's bag, and she shifted the child from one arm to the other. "Thank you so much."

At hearing the familiar Irish lilt in her voice, an ache filled Anna's chest. Would she ever be able listen to the Irish accent without wanting to weep? She could be at peace if she knew Rory and the mission school children had survived the fire. Perhaps even some of her students were somewhere on the train. She scanned the crowd, but the adults made it difficult to see any one shorter than five feet.

"Leonard, how are we going to carry our *own* bags?" Mother's icy comment snapped Anna out of her thoughts. She stepped into the aisle then squeezed around a man and nearly gagged at the putrid smell of smoke and body odor. She smiled at the young mother and chucked the small boy under his chin. "All I have is one small bag. I'll be happy to hold your baby until we're outside. That way you can carry your bag and my father can tend to my mother's things."

The worry lines on the petite woman's forehead dissolved "Thank ya, miss. But you can't carry both your bag and the baby can you?"

"My sister can carry my bag. Hers is small like mine." Anna glanced over her shoulder at Callie whose mouth hung open. "You don't mind, do you?"

"Of course she doesn't mind," Father said.

Callie's smile didn't extend to her eyes. "I'm pleased to help."

"Thank you, Callie. I'll meet you and Father on the platform."

Father offered Anna a smile. "That's my girl. Thank you."

She took the child into her arms and ran a palm over his silky curls. "My name is Miss Anna, little one. What is yours?"

"His name is Phin Cassidy, just like his father." The mother's lower lip trembled.

Someone jostled Anna and she fell forward. A hand came

around her waist and pulled her upright, the child still nestled safely in her arms. "I've got you, miss."

Anna called out a "thank you" to someone she couldn't see. "We need to move before we're trampled on." They shuffled down the narrow aisle behind a family of four, the two children wearing nightclothes, and alighted onto a wood platform.

Anna hummed a soothing lullaby to the boy as they wove through the throng. As long as he could see his mama ahead of them he stayed quiet. They paused on the edge of the crowd, and Anna faced the woman. Although the tightness around her eyes said otherwise, the young mother couldn't be more than twenty years old "I'm Anna Hartwell. I'm so sorry about your husband."

"Rose Cassidy. You are a blessing Miss Hartwell." The boy whimpered and reached for his mother. Rose took the baby then surveyed the crowd. "My brother is to meet me. I guess he's not here yet."

"I'll be happy to wait with you until he comes." If Mother complained about waiting, Anna would walk to Mrs. Maxwell's. In this small village, the home couldn't be far. Surprised at the brazen thought of moving about a strange town unchaperoned, Anna stifled a smile. "Where did you live in Chicago?"

"Conley's Patch, near where the fire started. Almost every building in the neighborhood is gone."

Anna's heart quickened. "Would you happen to know a Quinn family who lived there?"

"I knew people by that name who lived in an apartment building across the street. An older couple. Do you know the man's first name?"

Rory only referred to his father as Da. She shook her head.

"Their daughter was married and had a little girl." Rose pressed a kiss to her little boy's head.

What did she mean by *had*? "Do you know if the older couple had a son?"

"I've only seen the daughter. No son." She swallowed hard. "I heard the entire family perished."

"All of them?" Anna's words came out in a whisper.

"Aye. There's nothing left of anything on our street. We escaped our home by the grace of God." The woman's chin trembled. "Except for my husband and the old woman who lived in the apartment next to us. He went back in to bring her out." She glanced at her son cuddled against her chest. "For him, I need to go on. Be strong."

Anna's face heated. What was she thinking, asking all these questions? "I'm so sorry. I had no business fretting over my concerns when you just lost your husband and your home."

"I understand. We're all trying to locate someone, aren't we?" She surveyed the mass of people. "My brother and his family live near here in Irish Woods. I sent a wire from the train station. I hope he received it."

Anna's pulse quickened. Did she dare ask her to be on the lookout for Rory?

Rose shot her free hand into the air and waved. "Here I am, Steven. Over here." She glanced at Anna. "What a relief. He's come for me."

A man scurried up. "Rose. Thank the good Lord you and Phin are okay. He grabbed up her bag and stared at Anna. "Sorry, miss. I didn't notice you at first. Are you with my sister?"

She shook her head. "My family is here. I helped Rose and Phin off the train."

"Thank you again, Miss . . . Anna." Rose looked as though she would burst into tears. She faced her brother. "Let's go." The pair disappeared into the milling crowd.

"There you are." Father hurried up with the rest of the family following behind. He gestured toward several carriages off to his right. "Mrs. Maxwell's driver is probably waiting over there."

Anna trailed behind the others toward the carriages. If the Quinn family Rose spoke of were Rory's kin, was he with them when the fire started? He wasn't in church that night so she had to presume he was. Pain filled her throat and she tried in vain to swallow it away. It was one thing to accept she may never see him again because they were in different places, but to think of him as dead was quite another. The fire didn't start until evening. Perhaps he'd already left by then.

"Ah, I recognize Charles." Father picked up his pace and the women hurried after him.

The Maxwell's landau carriage was able to hold the whole family and their belongings, which amounted to more than what they'd carried from their home. As much as Anna felt Hortense Millard was more interested in herself than others, she'd been touched when the woman insisted the three Hartwell women take two dresses a piece from her extensive wardrobe. Hoping she'd find a teaching job in Geneva to support herself, Anna selected two that had the least amount of adornments. Not easy to do with Mrs. Millard's penchant for baubles and anything that shimmered.

Mrs. Maxwell's driver settled his sturdy form onto the high bench and snapped the reins. "Giddy up, Sally. We need to get these people home." He glanced at Father, beside him. "We should be at Mrs. Maxwell's within fifteen minutes."

The carriage rumbled past a two-story wood frame hotel. A livery sat next to it, and on the other side, a wood-frame one-story building that looked like a feed store.

Mother grunted. "Really, Leonard, I feel like you've taken us to the Wild West. There's nothing here."

Father waved a hand at a stately three-story home. "Look at that house, Eleanor. Almost as fine as the ones in our old neighborhood."

Mother lifted her chin so high Anna wondered if a bird would mistake it for a perch. "There is no comparison."

Father faced the front, his back as straight as a board. "When you see the lake, you'll change your mind."

Mother frowned. "Chicago has a lake too." She fanned her face with her hand. "It's as hot here as it is at home. I thought it was to be cooler."

Father heaved a breath. "Compared to what's left of the city, Geneva looks like Paradise to me."

Anna glanced at Callie. The girl's lower lip stuck out like a quivering shelf, but for once she'd kept quiet.

A wagon approached, heading toward the depot. As it passed, the driver waved and called out to Charles. "Looks like you got a carriage full."

Charles nodded. "Sure do."

She glanced from one side of the road to the other. Nothing but wood frame buildings, most of them feed stores or liveries. For once, Anna found herself agreeing with her mother. The town *was* depressing.

"There it is, everyone." Father turned and grinned. "The lake is up ahead." He shifted his body so Callie and Mother could see.

Callie leaned over the side of the carriage. "I think I see it. Anna, you have to look too."

She peeked around her father. A short distance ahead, the road dipped and beyond that, blue water stretched out to a tree line a good distance away. This is what she'd been waiting for. "I do see it, and it's lovely."

Mother tisked. "You act like you've never seen a lake before. Just a puddle compared to Lake Michigan."

Anna held back her words. No matter how wrong the woman was about something, she always managed to get in the last word.

Several women walked along the wood sidewalk and paused in front of a window display of simple, but attractive dresses. A sign over the door said, "Seamstress-Millie Austen." Anna made a mental note. She and Callie would have to soon order dresses more suitable than Mrs. Millard's garments.

They reached an intersection. "This is the center of town."

Charles indicated a three-story building on the corner to their left. "That's the Lake House Hotel. We've got another one closer to the lake called the Geneva, but they just started using it as a student residence for the girls' seminary."

The driver took the carriage through the intersection, and Father spoke up. "When we come to the lake, Charles, would you stop a moment so my family can take in its beauty?"

Charles nodded. "There's a spot the other side of the bridge where we can get a good view. The trees are beginning to turn. If you catch the view on a calm day, the reflection in the water is like none other."

As the driver guided the carriage around a slight curve, he waved his hand in the direction of the land to their left. "Plans are for a big hotel to go up over there. More people from Chicago are hearing about our lake and want to come here now that the train track is finished."

Cool air caressed Anna's face, reminding her of Lake Michigan's onshore breeze. The afternoon sun cast a swath of shimmer across the blue-green water. Trees lined the shore in an unbroken stretch of green except for an occasional splash of orange, giving a hint of the coming autumn. Set back in a clearing across the bay and next to a large three-story home stood a huge windmill. That had to be the Sturgis home she'd heard so much about.

Sally's hooves clip clopped across a wood bridge. "This here is the White River where the lake flows out," Charles said. "When the hotel is complete, they plan to dam up the water to construct a lagoon." He guided the carriage off to the right, and they halted a few feet from the water's edge.

"Just ahead is the village dock." Charles pointed to a long pier that jutted into the water. "Mr. Sturgis must be in town. That's his steamboat. You can see Maple Lawn across the bay. Got himself a nice house. The townspeople aren't too favorable about his windmill, but it's helped irrigate the property during this draught. I hear more of his family escaped the fire and is staying at a boarding house down the way."

Anna shielded her eyes from the late afternoon sun and studied the white boat that bobbed at the city dock. Long and sleek with a cabin at its rear, it looked large enough to live on. She surveyed the shoreline on either side of the bay. Where was Mrs. Maxwell's house? Perhaps trees secluded her property.

"Our land is about two hundred yards down from Maple Lawn," Father said. "I'm hoping to get the tree clearing started before winter sets in. In the spring we'll build a home at least as magnificent as Maple Lawn." He looked at Mother. "Are you starting to feel a bit better about Geneva, Eleanor?

"Only if we could buy Maple Lawn and not have to endure being homeless for so long."

Father's smile dissolved.

"I love it here, Father."

His eyes brightened. "I think so too, Anna."

A warm feeling came over her as it always did whenever she countered her mother's criticism of something Father had done.

"Can we get to Mrs. Maxwell's soon, Leonard?" Mother patted her face with a handkerchief. "I've had enough of this heat."

Charles clicked his tongue and gave the reins a shake. The carriage continued along the dirt road with the lake lapping at the shore off to their right. "We're almost there, Mrs. Hartwell. It looks like we may be getting some rain at long last. That should help cool things down." At the next road he turned the carriage away from the lake. "Mrs. Maxwell lives just up this hill."

Anna's heart fell. Not a lakeshore home after all.

At the hill's crest, they turned into a circular drive, and Anna stared at the rather plain white house. Nothing like Maple Lawn. More like a large farmhouse.

Mother sniffed. "Well, at least it's got a roof, and it's clean."

Poor Father. He was doing his best for them and, as usual, it wasn't enough.

The carriage halted before the small porch that covered half of the home's front. The door opened and a plumpish lady, her dark hair pulled back into a chignon fashioned from braids, stepped out. Clothed plainly by either Mother's or Mrs. Millard's standards, she hurried down the steps.

Father was already on the ground and walking toward her. "Jerusha, it is so kind of you to open your home to my family."

She took his offered hand. "It will be nice to have the house full of people again. If only Philip were still alive to help. The news coming from Chicago sounds horrid. At least all of you are safe." She looked toward the carriage. "You ladies must be exhausted. Please come in, and we'll get you settled." She turned toward the house and called out, "Maria, Sarah, come quickly to help our guests."

A young woman who looked to be about Anna's age, her dark blond hair pulled back into a snood-covered bun, came onto the porch. She wore a plain gray dress protected by a black apron. "Sarah will be along. She's upstairs preparing the rooms."

Anna accepted the driver's assistance as she stepped down from the carriage. She approached Mrs. Maxwell and waited while Father introduced her as his oldest daughter.

Anna nodded and held out her hand. "I echo my father's appreciation for allowing us to intrude upon you. I'm afraid after a few days of four extra people in your lovely home, you'll be wishing for some peace and quiet."

Mrs. Maxwell accepted Anna's hand and offered a soft smile. "After all you have been through, it's the least I can do. I can't imagine the horror you've all experienced. You may consider this your home for as long as necessary."

Anna liked the woman immediately. Maybe staying here wouldn't be so bad after all.

Mrs. Maxwell turned to greet Mother and Callie as they

approached. She gave a slight nod to Mother. "Mrs. Hartwell, what a dreadful time you've had, losing your precious home and coming up here so suddenly. I'm sure Geneva must seem like you are out in the wilds."

Mother fussed with her reticule, probably working to come up with a response that wasn't snippy. "I have to admit, Mrs. Maxwell, it's going to take some time getting used to all this quiet. The city is so vibrant and noisy. I'm sure you are used to the inactivity here."

"Please call me Jerusha." She glanced toward Callie and Anna. "That goes for you girls too." She looked back at Mother. "I spent most of my years living in Chicago and watched it grow from a town not much bigger than Geneva. I've only lived here a short time. It took some adjustment, but now I can't imagine living anywhere else. My poor husband only lived two years after we moved here. He loved it so much."

The door to the house opened and a young woman no older than Callie stepped out wearing a similar dress and apron as Maria. A lock of curly brown hair had escaped the bun at the back of her head. She looked at Jerusha "The bedrooms are ready for our guests."

"Thank you, Sarah."

A tight smile filled Mother's features. "Sarah appears to be quite young. I don't believe in children working, even as domestics."

Jerusha's eyes narrowed. "Maria is my housekeeper, and Sarah has been with me since she was a child. Her parents worked for my husband and me when we lived in Chicago. They both died in a bad accident, and I took Sarah in and raised her as my own. At sixteen she did a few chores as I would have any child of mine do, but I insisted she finish her schooling. She's eighteen now and at her request, only started working for me this past year." She turned abruptly. "Maria, show our guests to their accomodations as we discussed earlier. And make sure there's fresh water in each room."

"I already took care of the water." Sarah looked at Anna, and then Callie. "I'd be happy to help you two settle into your room."

Not knowing if she should agree without Jerusha giving her approval, Anna rested a hand on Callie's arm and held her back, waiting to see what the lady of the house would say.

Jerusha waved her hand. "Girls, go on. You don't have to wait for my okay. Maria will show your parents to their quarters. I'll have Charles bring your bags up when he returns from tending to Sally."

With all the visiting, Anna hadn't noticed that the bags were sitting at the end of the walk and the carriage was gone. She followed her sister up the stairs and into the house. She could imagine the words her mother would spew out at Father once they were alone. She'd probably insist Father find them a place to rent rather than stay with someone who treats her help like equals. She could only pray that the fire damage would keep Lyman at bay long enough to plan her permanent escape.

# CHAPTER FIVE

*I*nside the rather austere but tastefully furnished entry hall, Anna trailed behind the other two women to the stairs. Unlike the circular staircases she was accustomed to seeing in homes of people of means, this one wasn't open at all. Simple stairs that led to the second floor. At the top of the stairs, they walked single-file over the wood-planked floor and entered a room halfway down the narrow hallway.

She crossed to a pair of windows. "We may not be on the water, but the view is as impressive. Callie, come look expanse of lawn. One of the trees is already a beautiful orange."

"Trees are trees." Callie crossed to one of the two beds. "I'll take this one. It's farther away from the windows. Not as drafty."

Sarah stepped farther into the room. "This house is well heated. We have two wood stoves downstairs, and the heat rises nicely to the second floor." The pretty girl smiled. "And when winter sets in, we have an ample supply of goose down comforters and quilts."

Callie waved a hand. "I doubt we'll be here that long. I'm sure Father will find us adequate housing in the city."

Sarah frowned. "I thought Miss Jerusha said your new home here in Geneva couldn't be built until spring and you would be with us until then."

Callie stared at Anna, surprise written in her eyes. Callie would likely say something about Sarah's brazen behavior of contradicting the one she was serving once they were alone. But, Anna found it refreshing.

She worked to put a positive tone in her voice. "Father will restore our home in the city sometime in the future, but his office is destroyed, and I'm sure he'll want to get the business up and running first. I understand he intends us to stay here for at least a year. After our home on the lakeshore is built in the spring, we'll transfer over there." She smiled at Sarah. "The down comforters sound wonderful. I can't think of anything better than snuggling into a feather bed under a goose down comforter."

Charles came to the open door with Callie's carpetbag in one hand and Anna's in the other. At Anna's bidding, he stepped into the room and set the valises on the floor. He gave a slight bow. "If there is anything else you need from me, please let me know."

In a whisper of a moment, the man was gone, and Sarah looked from Anna to Callie. "Do you wish help with your unpacking?" She indicated a carved wood armoire snug against the wall opposite the beds. You can keep your things in there. It's empty."

Anna took a step toward Sarah. "Thank you. We don't need any assistance. You've already been a wonderful help."

After Sarah left, Callie dropped onto her bed and arranged her skirt. "Did you really mean we aren't going to be home by winter? If we don't return to Chicago by December, I'll miss the cotillion." She bit her lower lip and turned away.

Anna counted to ten. When she was Callie's age she hadn't been excited about her coming out festivities and viewed them as something to be endured. She'd already begun her freshman year at college and was more interested in her studies and enjoying the freedom from living under Mother's angry disposition. But her sister was different. Mother never treated Callie in the same mean-spirited way she had with Anna.

"We have to take each day as it comes, Callie," Anna said. "You saw the horrible devastation on our way to the train station. I hardly think debutante balls are on the minds of anyone right now. It would do you good to think about your blessings. Thank God we escaped the fire without injury, and that we have such a nice place to stay."

Callie turned from Anna and pressed a fist to her mouth. "We could have stayed with the Millards. There's plenty of room there."

Anna placed a palm over her heating stomach. "This is a far lovelier place to wait. Think of that horrible smell and the depressing sight we'd have to see whenever we went somewhere."

"You just don't want to be around Lyman. You're luckier than you realize, Anna. You'll be set for life marrying him."

"Set for a boring life without much love."

"Don't you think marriages with love are only in fairy tales?"

Anna swallowed. "It does seem that way doesn't it?" She sat next to her sister. "Callie, you don't have the mantle of an arranged marriage hanging over your head. You have the freedom to find love. Go. Do it. Don't settle for mediocre or marry for money."

Callie's eyes searched Anna's face. "Is Lyman that bad? I mean, he's so handsome and has a good future with his father's company."

Anna sighed. "Looks aren't everything. I've seen a side of him the rest of the family hasn't."

"What are you talking about?" Callie leaned closer. "You can tell me. I won't tell anyone."

Anna stared at her lap. Should she tell what she'd kept to herself for years? It would feel good to confide in someone, but could she trust Callie to keep quiet? She raised her head and looked at her sister. "What's inside a man is what is important. Like Rory." She snapped her mouth shut. Never had she said his name out loud at home.

Callie's eyes widened. "Rory? Who is Rory?"

Heat crawled up Anna's neck and over her face. "No one special. A man at the mission."

Callie grinned. "From the ten shades of red your face has become, it seems this Rory has turned your head."

Anna jumped to her feet and returned to the window. She had to choose her words carefully. "We're only friends. Good friends. Patrick has met him." She faced her sister. "Don't you dare breathe a word. If mother finds out I was even carrying on a conversation with the mission janitor, an Irish immigrant, she'd insist on my marrying Lyman immediately. And I have no intention of ever marrying that man."

Callie pressed her clasped hands against her chest. "But you would marry Rory if you could. I see it in your eyes, sister dear. Maybe he's descended from an Irish knight. That would smooth Mother's feathers."

What ever possessed her to say his name? Anna shook her head. "No signs of royalty or knighthood in his family." She dropped her gaze. "I should probably be speaking in the past tense. I fear Rory may have died in the fire. He was to visit his family in Conley's Patch where the fire started."

"But you don't know for sure, do you?"

Anna shook her head and swallowed against the knot of emotion in her throat. "No. But with the mission burned to the ground and Illinois Street Church likely gone, I've lost my means of finding out." She shrugged. "I'm sure my friendship with him is a thing of the past. Except for one slight hope."

"What's that?"

"He always dreamed of moving here to an enclave west of town called Irish Woods. On the day of the fire, he planned to convince his father to bring the family here to live. I need to find this Irish Woods and see if he's there."

Callie jumped to her feet. "I'm suddenly feeling a whole lot better. Tomorrow we'll start looking for Rory."

# CHAPTER SIX

The next morning, Anna settled in the carriage next to her sister for the trip to the seamstress shop. She lifted her heavy skirt to position it better, and it thudded over her legs. The brocaded frock had to weigh at least ten pounds. As eager as she was about searching for Rory, ordering new clothes took first priority.

"I'm sorry your mother isn't joining us." Jerusha arranged a blanket over her knees.

Anna wasn't sorry. Excursions were always far more enjoyable without Mother. "I'm sure she'll be fine. She prefers shopping alone."

The carriage began rolling, and she inhaled the crisp air. All around, spots of bright yellows and oranges peeked out of still-green trees. She'd always loved fall and, despite their catastrophe, she was determined to enjoy this one.

"In another week, the entire park over there will be a riot of color." Jerusha pointed to a small common off to their right.

Callie stared across the park. "What's that building in the middle of the trees?"

"That's the ladies seminary." Jerusha tucked her hands under her blanket. "We should have taken the enclosed carriage. I had no idea it was so chilly." She glanced in the direction of the school. "I have a wonderful idea, Calista. I'm sure they'd let you enroll there. It might be a way for you to pass the time while you're here."

Anna felt Callie stiffen, and rested her hand on her sister's arm.

Callie frowned. "Thanks for the suggestion, but I graduated from finishing school last spring. Aren't those girls younger than me?"

"I suppose so," Jerusha said. "But, it may be a way of meeting girls close to your age."

"I'll give it some thought."

Anna wanted to hug Callie for her restraint. Despite her moments of childish behavior, her little sister was growing up.

They stopped in front of the same seamstress shop Anna had noticed when they first arrived. How had she missed the red window boxes of geraniums that still bloomed despite the drop in temperatures? No woman would be able to resist such an appealing place.

Charles assisted Anna from the carriage, and she stepped onto the wooden sidewalk. She turned toward the sound of approaching boot heels. A woman wearing a simple dress and carrying a basket of groceries smiled and said "hello" as she passed. Anna returned the greeting, and a warm feeling washed over her. Mother may consider the village too small, but if small meant friendliness, she preferred here to there any day.

Inside the shop, bolts of fabric stacked on counters lined either side of the long narrow store. How easy it would be to choose material by the way they were arranged by color and fabric type. Anna turned to her sister. "I think we just arrived in a dream. There are more choices here than our seamstress in Chicago ever had."

"I agree. I love that one." Callie pointed to a garnet dress with lace trim around the neckline that hung on the wall. "Oh, and look." She scooted toward a wire mannequin that peeked out from behind a stack of bolts at the end of a counter. "This is almost like my debut gown. I can't believe it."

Anna stepped closer. It was very similar to the dress Callie lost in the fire, except the silk was a richer blue. Almost like Geneva Lake when it reflected the sky. She pulled her sister into a side hug. "You do realize, don't you, there may not be a cotillion this year? The site where the dance was to be held has likely been destroyed."

Callie's face contorted, but thankfully, no tears accompanied it this time. She nodded. "Yes. But I'm hoping they'll find a new location in an area that didn't burn."

"Do you think people will make a fancy dance more important than rebuilding the city? I expect some of those who planned the ball lost their homes and possibly their lives."

Callie nodded. "You're right. I'll hold off ordering a new gown until we know for sure."

Anna gave her shoulder a squeeze.

"Ladies, I didn't realize you were already here." A sprite-like woman with salt-and pepper gray hair swooped into a bun on the top of her head scurried toward them.

"Here you are right on time, and I'm so busy sewing in the back I didn't hear the bell." The woman's French accented voice carried Anna back to childhood when she attended a private school.

The seamstress came closer and the scent of rose water filled the air. While she greeted Jerusha with an air kiss and slight embrace, Anna admired her tan two-piece dress. She loved how the small bustle was covered by a peplum that flared out from the buttoned up jacket. The design was perfect for a seamstress who required freedom of movement—and also for a teacher.

Millie looked from one sister to the other. "Jerusha's note told me of your plight. My heart goes out to you girls. You pick out two dresses—any style—and I'll charge you only for the materials. *oiu?*"

Anna's heart melted. "Miss . . . ."

Dimples appeared on her round cheeks. "It's Mrs. Austen, the former Millicent Le Blanc until Mr. Austen wooed me thirty years ago. You can call me Millie. Everyone else does."

Anna inwardly startled. How odd it felt to be treated as though she were a needy person. "Millie. You are so kind to offer a discount, but we may have lost our home, but we aren't penniless. We'd rather you offer the discount to someone who can't pay."

Millie nodded. "That's very generous." She pulled at the tape measure draped around her neck. "Let's get you two to the dressing rooms so I can take your measurements."

After the measurements were taken and fabrics and styles chosen, Jerusha opened Millie's door to the street, causing the overhead bell to jangle. "Those two hours flew by and I'm hungry. The Lake House Hotel has a nice little restaurant. We can stop there for a light lunch before we go home."

Anna's stomach growled. "Lunch out sounds wonderful."

Creases formed between the older woman's brows. "I must warn you that a hotel restaurant in Geneva is a lot different from one in Chicago. That may change when the Whiting Hotel is built, but for now the Lake House is a bit more . . . um, shall we say rural?"

Anna laughed and waved her hand. "I don't care as long as they have good food."

The women walked three abreast toward the hotel, stopping every so often when Jerusha greeted someone. Impressed that a woman of such a high position in the community would stop and chat, Anna decided maybe it was better Mother hadn't joined them.

They arrived at the intersection of Main and Broad and stopped under an overhang.

"Here we are."

"Howdy, Miss Jerusha."

Startled, Anna looked down at a grizzled man sitting in a rocker next to the hotel's entrance. He grinned at the women. She wanted to turn away from his tobacco-stained teeth, but to do so would be rude.

Jerusha stepped toward the man. "Why, Jerome Watkins, how have you been? I haven't seen you at church in a long while." The man pushed his hat back on his head. "Been laid up with some kind of stomach ailment. This is the first week I've felt good enough to be out." He glanced at Anna and Callie. "Who are these pretty ladies you got with you?"

Jerusha introduced the girls who nodded a hello.

"I reckon I'll be in church this Sunday. Maybe I'll see all of you there."

Jerusha laughed. "I hope so, Jerome." She took a step toward the hotel door. "Shall we go in, girls?"

They entered a small lobby that contained a counter and two straight-backed chairs arranged against a wall with a small table between them. To their right, through a wide entry, several people sat at tables, chatting quietly. The attire of two of the men reminded Anna of Rory, while a third man wore a suit. Anna's heart rate quickened. If Rory were at Irish Woods, perhaps they *would* cross paths. Was it only last Saturday they'd had that conversation? Not even a week ago? It seemed like a year.

A waiter showed the women to a table with a view of Main Street. After they ordered sandwiches and hot tea, Anna stared out at the street. If Rory were in Geneva, what would it be like to run into him? Perhaps she'd be on the sidewalk and see him going by on a wagon. She'd call out his name. Seeing her, he'd break into the dimpled grin she loved, then leap off the wagon and run to her. There, in the middle of the street, they'd hug and—

Anna forced her thoughts away. She had to stop having giddy dreams about a man who quite likely perished in the fire or could be anywhere but here. And to imagine them kissing in the middle of the road like that.

"Anna, what are you thinking about?"

At her sister's words, her neck warmed. "Nothing." She stared at the cup of tea the waiter must have set in front of her while she was in dreamland. She had to get her thoughts back to reality or she'd never be able to eat her lunch.

Jerusha shook out her napkin and placed it on her lap. "Calista, I know you aren't too interested in attending the seminary, but Geneva can become very quiet during the winter. Outside of an occasional theatrical production and church events, there isn't much entertainment. After the lake freezes, the young people do enjoy ice-skating. But that's still months away."

Anna straightened. "Callie, I think you should look into the seminary. You can at least meet some other girls."

Her sister leaned back and crossed her arms. "And what are you intending to do with *your* time, sister? Other than look for Rory."

Jerusha's brows went up. "Who is Rory?"

Anna hoped her cheeks weren't as pink as they felt. She shrugged and rearranged her napkin on her lap. "Just a friend I met at the street mission where I taught."

"You're blushing again." Callie snickered. "Seems to me he's more than a friend."

Their hostess paused her teacup halfway to her mouth and peered at Anna. "Wasn't your wedding postponed by the fire? Is Rory—"

"No." Anna's ears burned so hot they must have glowed. "I'm sorry for interrupting. The man I'm supposed to marry by arrangement is Lyman Millard. Rory worked as a janitor at the mission school." She swallowed a growing mass in her throat. "The blaze began in the part of town where Rory's parents lived, and he was to visit them that day. He and his family likely perished."

"But you don't know for sure, sister." Callie turned to Jerusha. "Maybe you can help her."

The older woman frowned. "Is there a reason to think he might be in Geneva?"

"He's mentioned Irish Woods several times and hoped to move there with his parents." Anna slumped, her arms suddenly feeling heavy. "He has an uncle who lives there. It's all I have to go on."

The waiter arrived with the food and refreshed their drinks.

Jerusha took a nibble of her sandwich and set it down. "Irish Woods is several miles west. If I want to go to Williams Bay—a few miles farther down—I go by boat, so I've never seen Irish Woods. Do you know his uncle's name?"

She shook her head. I'm not sure. It might be Quinn the same as Rory's or something else if he comes from Rory's mother's side."

"Sarah volunteers at the school there on Mondays. I'll have her ask if anyone has met a new man by that name."

Anna stared at their hostess. "There's a school in Irish Woods?"

"Yes. Lots of families live out there."

Anna's mind spun like a child's top. If she were teaching at a school there, she'd be able to look for Rory more easily. She could barely make herself stay seated. "I'd love to find another position like I had at the mission school."

"There's only one teacher, and it's a one-room school at that. Let me think."

Jerusha stared toward the window for at least a minute before she faced Anna. "I heard the Sturgises and Rumsey's are both staying at Mrs. Tamlin's boarding house down Main. Between the two families there are quite a few children. Perhaps you could help as a temporary companion of sorts. It's not Irish

Woods, but maybe it would be something temporary you can do to stay busy. As soon as we finish lunch, let's walk down to Mrs. Tamlin's."

"How awful it must be for those little ones to have lived through the fire and find themselves suddenly away from everything they know. If I can help, I'm available." Anna picked up her sandwich and took a large bite. Suddenly, she was hungrier than she'd been in days.

Rory sat on his bed and held Anna's pendant he'd found in the mission school rubble that morning. She'd been very upset the day she lost it, and he felt terrible he wasn't able to find it for her. Wouldn't she be surprised when he gave it to her—*if* he ever found her?

Was he hoping against hope? Her house was nothing but a pile of ash and a pair of chimneys. He hadn't been able to bring himself to go to Conley's Patch to see the remains of what had been the family apartment. "God, why didn't I go to them sooner about moving to Irish Woods? Why, God?" As always, no answer came and eventually his tears dried.

He rubbed his thumb over the locket and pressed a tiny lever. It popped opened. He held the open pendant next to the gas lamp and his heart seemed to fall clear to his toes. She'd never mentioned anyone special, but the man looked too young to be her father.

He closed the locket then stuffed it into the nightstand drawer. Resting his elbows on his knees, he stared at the floor. The ministry was gone, the church was gone, and his family was gone. Anna may as well be gone—perhaps in the company of the man in her locket. How foolish he'd been to fall in love with her. To even dream that one day she'd fall in love with him.

God was in control, but if He had a lesson in all of this besides learning to lean on Him, Rory had no idea what it was. He'd committed to help with cleanup for the next week. As soon as he finished his obligation, he'd do what he planned all along. Join his uncle in Irish Woods and carve out a new life. There was nothing left for him in Chicago.

"Miss Jerusha, will you be wanting to use the carriage later today, or should I take Sally down to the stable and get her settled?"

At Charles's voice, Anna roused from sleep. They were turning into the circle drive in front of Jerusha's home. How had she managed to nod off? It had been a full day from being fitted for dresses, then the lunch before a stop at the home where the Sturgises were staying, only to learn there wasn't a need for a children's helper. As nice as Mrs. Sturgis was, Anna was relieved. Teaching was what she was called to do and a means to support herself when she refused to go through with the wedding.

She straightened. "I must have dropped off. I hope I didn't miss an important conversation."

Callie sighed. "Just more discussion about the seminary." The carriage rolled to a stop and she gathered her skirts and stood. "I may consider it."

Anna followed the others into the house as Mother came down the stairs. "It's about time you returned. I hope you haven't been all this time spending your father's money."

Anna bottled a sigh. "Father's money is safe. We had lunch at the Lakehouse Hotel Restaurant, then stopped in at the boarding house where the Sturgis and Rumsey families are staying."

Mother's eyes widened. "Both families are living in a boarding house? They can certainly afford better living circumstances than that."

"I suppose, if any were to be had in this small village." Jerusha removed her hat and hung it on a hall tree hook. "The Sturgis family spent last summer at Mrs. Tamlin's, and they seem quite content there."

"Well, I'm thankful for your hospitality, Jerusha. This is surely a much better arrangement." Mother looked from Anna to Callie. "Your father has taken the train to the city to get his office reestablished in temporary quarters." She gave Anna a hard stare. "You'll be pleased to know we received a telegraph from Lyman. He and his mother plan to take the train here on Monday and will stay until Thursday. They want to begin planning your wedding."

# CHAPTER EIGHT

Anna stared at her image in the bedroom mirror. The tautness around her mouth and eyes that hadn't been there the past day had returned. How could it not when all through dinner Mother talked about the wedding plans and if they should arrange for the ceremony to be in Geneva, or at the Millards' church in the city. Mother supposed the Millards' church would have to do since no church in Geneva was large enough to hold the guests.

She plucked hairpins and combs from her chignon until her reddish brown waves fell past her shoulders, then picked up a brush and stroked it through her hair.

Callie lay stretched out on her bed, the comforter up to her chin. "The way you're attacking your hair, you won't have any left on your head. Maybe if you do that, Mother will have to postpone the wedding until your hair grows back." She laughed. "I'm glad our parents didn't arrange a marriage for me. Not with their taste in men."

"Didn't you say the other day you thought Lyman would make a wonderful husband?"

"That was until you told me about Rory."

Anna faced her sister. "I was barely a month old when the wedding plans were sealed. You know all that." She faced the mirror and resumed her brushing.

"I still wonder why Mother treats you so much worse than me. And, of course, she treated Richard the nicest of all."

Anna stopped brushing and stared at the mirror. She barely thought of Richard anymore. When she did think of her little brother it became too painful. He'd died on his tenth birthday and Mother was inconsolable for weeks, blaming Father as the cause. If he'd lived he would be seventeen and preparing to head to college, probably to Yale or Harvard.

"Aren't you listening to me?"

Anna expelled a breath and set her brush on the dresser. She stared at her sister's reflection in the mirror. "I guess I wasn't."

Callie had pushed herself to a sitting position. "I asked what you were going to do about finding Rory? If he's still alive, you can't marry Lyman."

"What you don't understand is whether Rory is alive or deceased, I'm not going to marry Lyman ever." She needed to start asking questions. Would it be so hard to locate his uncle? "I need to get to Irish Woods. That's the only place to start."

"Then ask Charles to take you there."

Anna tied off the end of her braid with a ribbon. "It's probably a wild goose chase. But it's the only place I know to start. My mind has a hundred things rumbling around in it. How will I ever fall asleep?"

Callie slid back under her covers. "Think about Rory after you get in bed and then you'll dream about him all night."

Anna laughed at the girlish suggestion. She climbed into her bed then doused the lamp. Callie was right. She'd think about Rory's handsome face and imagine how his kiss would have felt if Patrick hadn't interrupted them.

THE NEXT MORNING, Anna had just finished dressing for the day when Sarah came to the bedroom. "I'm here to make your beds, if that's all right."

Anna nodded. "Of course. If you don't mind me staying, I was about to read my Bible. I can sit over there out of your way." She indicated a flowered upholstered armchair next to one of the windows.

Sarah's dimples deepened. "No bother. I'm happy to see you read the Bible too. If I don't, my day feels empty."

A bubbly sensation flowed through Anna. "You're a believer?"

Sarah nodded. "Yes, Miss Anna. I am."

"Well, then, that makes us sisters. Please call me Anna. I've been told you volunteer at the Irish Woods School. How would I find out if a friend of mine is living there? He may have gone there after the fire."

Sarah pulled the top sheet tight then the comforter over that. "I volunteer at the school every Monday. I'd be happy to ask for you."

"Do you think Charles could take me out there today?"

Sarah fluffed a pillow and set it in place. "He's already taking Miss Jerusha and your mother to our church. They're preparing boxes of clothing for the victims of the other fire up north in Peshtigo. With Chicago getting all the attention, that small town is hardly getting the aid they need."

Anna frowned. How did she miss the news about a second fire? Mother had hardly considered the plight of the refugees from Chicago's conflagration, and now she was going to help aid people from another fire? She smiled to herself. Maybe some of the church peoples' desire to help others would be good for Mother.

Sarah fluffed the second pillow and set it next to the other one. "Why don't you ride out to Irish Woods with me on Monday? You mentioned you taught at a mission school in the city. The teacher might appreciate your help with the new refugee children. Then you can inquire about your friend at the same time."

Lyman and his mother wouldn't arrive until Monday afternoon. If she didn't welcome them right away, would that matter? "That's a marvelous idea. I think you are an answer to my prayers."

Sarah grinned and picked up the water pitcher from the dresser. "I love being an answer to prayer. We'll leave at seven-thirty Monday morning."

"I'll be ready." Anna opened her Bible to where she had left off reading in the book of Psalms. Mother wouldn't like it one bit if she weren't there to greet the Millards when they arrived on Monday, but finding Rory was more important.

She only had to get through the next two days. She stared at the ceiling. Finally, she was going to find Rory one way or the other.

"I THOUGHT the greatest blessing of the fire was that with the mission school of yours burning down, you could focus on what young ladies of your position are expected to do. And now you want to teach more immigrant children here? I thought you'd left all that silliness behind."

Anna glanced away from Mother's penetrating scrutiny. Today had been a perfect Sunday with church and a nice meal around the table with another family Jerusha had invited. With guests in the house, Mother had been stifled. But now they were alone in the parlor with everyone else retired for the night.

Anna took a step toward the front hall. "I have to do as I'm called, Mother, and if there's a need at the school, I will stay to help. If there isn't, I'll return home with Charles."

"It's that church you attended in the city. The idea of the

reverend expecting young unmarried women to mix with such riff-raff, even if it is just children. I don't think most of them even bathe but once a month."

Anna sent God a silent prayer for her mother's hardened heart. "The children are the ones who might bring the rest of their families out of the trap they're in when they go home and tell them about God's love."

Her mother shuddered. "Your fiancé is coming tomorrow. He and his mother deserve your full attention. I'm thinking maybe the wedding can be at Jerusha's church if we're here longer than a few months."

"I thought you didn't care for that church. All you did was complain about it after we were alone." Anna would love to have her wedding in that lovely little church, but the idea of marrying Lyman in any church was an abomination. He had no more use for God than a snake.

Mother flinched. "It's not my first choice, nor my second for that matter. But since the fire, we must all sacrifice something. It could be months before our own church is rebuilt" Mother's mouth twisted and she gave a dismissive wave. "Go. But no more plans until the Millards leave on Thursday."

"I wish you'd told them the trip is a waste of their time because I have no intention of marrying that man. Ever." Anna trudged up the stairs. If they didn't need her help at Irish Woods School, she'd find some other way to find Rory, even if she had to meet every train that arrived from Chicago.

onday morning, Anna covered a yawn with her hand. She brought the carriage blanket she shared with Sarah up to her chin as the horse pulled the small buggy up a steep grade west of the village. Waiting until bedtime to inform Mother of her plans for today wasn't a good prescription for a full night's sleep.

"Turn around, Anna. You'll never see a view as pretty as this one."

They'd reached the hill's crest. Anna twisted around and peered over the back end of the carriage. The steeple of the new Catholic church that crowned the hill east of downtown glistened like a precious jewel in the early morning sun. Vivid orange and yellow leaves sprinkled across the valley, seemed to glow in the sunlight. "Oh, I wish I were an artist and could capture this. Charles, can't we stop a while and take this in?"

"We could, Miss Anna, but Miss Sarah has to be at the school in fifteen minutes."

Anna settled back in her seat. "Of course. That was selfish of me not to remember the schedule. I suppose we'll see it again on the return trip. Which for me may be a half an hour from now."

Sarah laughed. "I doubt that."

Anna gave her attention to the passing rows of dried corn-stalks tied together in bunches and an occasional field of hay bales waiting to be stored for the winter. Her nanny's stories of growing up as a freed slave on a Missouri farm had served her well to know something about farming. "Who owns all this property?"

"The people of Irish Woods mostly," Sarah said. "Many helped build the first railroad out from Illinois. When they got to the end of the line, they saw land was available and staked their claims. Since then, others settled here too.

The driver guided the carriage into a turnabout drive in front of a clapboard schoolhouse, much like the one-room schools Anna had seen in the east where she attended college.

Children of assorted ages played on a swing that hung from a thick low branch of a tree large Oak tree, while older boys played with a ball a distance away. "Miss Anna," Charles said. "I'll carry the box of food Mrs. Maxwell donated inside then wait here until you find out if you're needed."

She followed Sarah and Charles toward the school door. Before they reached the steps, a plump middle-aged woman stepped out and strode toward a bell hanging from a hook. She spotted the women and paused. "Good morning, Sarah." Seeing the box Charles carried, her face lit up. "We will appreciate Mrs. Maxwell's donation today. I expect more refugee children from the fire to join us." She opened the door. "Charles, please leave it on the table at the back of the room."

He nodded and stepped inside.

"Mrs. Cleary," Sarah said. "This is Anna Hartwell. Her family is staying with Mrs. Maxwell. She taught at a mission school in Chicago until the fire, and I thought maybe you could use some extra help."

Anna stepped forward. "I know this is quite unexpected, Mrs. Cleary. I would truly love to help if I'm needed."

Mrs. Cleary clasped her hands and grinned. "You are an answer to my prayers. I expect at least ten new children this morning, and I hear more are coming by week's end. I can certainly use you."

Anna restrained herself from bouncing on her toes like a child and silently thanked God for the blessing. "Yes ma'am. I'll let Charles know he can leave without me."

A few minutes later, as the Maxwell buggy headed out of the school property, Mrs. Cleary handed Anna the bell rope. "I'll let you do the honors. Give it about eight hard tugs. Then we stand by the door to greet the children."

Anna yanked at the rope, careful to count the pulls.

On the second ring, the children began racing across the grass. Before she could sound the eighth ring, the boys had lined up on one side and the girls stood in a parallel line a few feet away. Several children huddled off to the side looking unsure of what to do.

An older boy with dark hair faced the children not in line. "This is what we do first. You boys get behind me. You girls line up there, behind Becky."

The children did as he directed.

Mrs. Cleary gave the young leader a look of approval. "Well done, Liam. Thank you for helping this morning." She surveyed the children's expectant faces. "This morning we welcome some new scholars." She went on to read the names of the new arrivals from a piece of paper then glanced at Anna. "And to help us with our classroom today is Miss Anna. I want you to listen and obey her the same way you do with me and Miss Sarah."

Anna surveyed the children, but let her focus linger on the new students. Made homeless by an angry fire, she was no different than they. She took a step closer. "I've also lost my home and the school where I taught in the fire, and that's why I'm here. I'm happy to be of help to Mrs. Cleary."

"Do you know when we can go back home?" A small girl with eyes as big as silver dollars kept her hopeful gaze on Anna.

Her heart ached and her shoulders sagged. "I don't know. It will be awhile before they can clean up what's left from the fire and rebuild. It's hard starting over isn't it?"

The girl nodded, a solemn expression on her face.

Mrs. Cleary clapped her hands. "Time to get inside, children."

Anna and Sarah waited until the children followed their teacher, and then they stepped into the classroom. Orderly rows of desks filled most of the space along with a couple of wood tables and chairs at the back. Today's day and date was printed in large letters on the blackboard, the same way Anna had done in her classroom. A well-worn potbelly stove sat in a front corner. By the room's warmth, either Mrs. Cleary or someone else must have arrived a long while ago to get the fire started. An ache filled Anna's throat. Rory always got the fire going in her room before she arrived. She had to find out if he were alive or dead.

She approached the teacher. "Mrs. Cleary, I'm wondering if you know a family by the last name of Quinn. A friend of mine might have come up here. He said his uncle lived in Irish Woods. My friend's name is Rory Quinn."

The older woman paused as if thinking. "I can't say that I have. My husband and I are past having young children in the home. That's the way most families get to know other families in the area. My daughter-in-law is expecting their first child soon. That will be the first youngster in our family in quite a few years. Do you know if his uncle has school-age children?"

She shook her head. "I'm thinking not. They've probably already raised their family."

"Well, keep an eye out while you're here. You are free to ask around." She scanned the room. "It looks like all the children are here now. Until we can locate desks for our new students, they'll have to use the tables at the back." Mrs. Cleary said. She went to her desk at the head of the room and rang a bell. "Children, as I call a new scholar's name, raise your hand and I'll assign you one of the tables."

Within a few minutes, the new students had been divided between those in grades five through eight and one through four. While Sarah assisted with the regular scholars, Anna spent the morning working at the tables with the new children. She had just finished helping a little girl with reading and was about to move on to the boy next to her when a timid voice interrupted.

"Miss Anna, I'm scared."

She faced a boy named Timmy who couldn't be older than five or six. She pushed his reddish blond hair from his eyes. "What are you scared of?

His lower lip trembled. "That fire in the stove. I can see it through the grate. What if it jumps out into the room and burns the school down?" Tears trailed down his cheeks.

Anna wrapped her arms around the child and pressed his head to her. "Since the big fire, I have fears like that sometimes, but then I stop and think about what I'm afraid of. The grate keeps the fire inside the stove. It won't jump out into the room as long as the grate is closed."

"But nothing stopped the fire before."

What could she say that would comfort him? Sometimes fear was so irrational yet so hard to dispel. "God promises us He will always be with us and He won't let anything happen that will permanently hurt us." She leaned back and looked at his sweet face. "Do you have chickens where you are staying?"

He nodded.

God asks us to imagine him like a mother hen with her chicks and tells us that when we are afraid we can find shelter under his wings." She placed her hands on both his shoulders.

"When you start feeling afraid, imagine yourself crawling under God's wings and letting Him protect you."

He rewarded her with a gap-toothed smile. "I can do that, Miss Anna." She gave him another hug. "Good boy."

"It's time for us to break for lunch, children." Mrs. Cleary walked to the exit. "For those of you who didn't bring a lunch, Mrs. Maxwell donated some food that will make a good meal. Miss Anna and Miss Sara can you help me, please?"

For Jerusha's donation, Maria had sliced the roast beef from yesterday's Sunday dinner and also included some ham and a loaf of bread. Most of the regular students had their lunch pails with them, but only two out of the half dozen new students brought lunches.

Once the children were eating, the three women settled at a table with their own meals.

Mrs. Cleary looked at Anna. "I can see how much help you are to these refugee children." She nibbled at her sandwich. "I know you only thought to come today with Sarah, but do you think you could be here every school day until things settle down?"

Anna's bite of ham sandwich stuck in her throat, and she reached for her cup of water. Being there everyday gave her purpose. A way to keep an eye out for Rory or perhaps find his uncle. And a reason to stay away from home. Saying yes to the request would bring on Mother's indignation, especially with the Millards in town, but the children needed help and stability during this crisis.

She smiled at the teacher. "I'll be happy to return tomorrow and however many days I'm needed. She had all afternoon and the ride home to pray for the strength to stand up to Mother.

After lunch, while the children played outside, Anna printed the last word in a list of spelling words on the blackboard and stood back to check her work.

"Excuse me, I hope I'm not interrupting anything, but would you have a place for this child?"

Anna turned. A stocky woman, her dark hair streaked with gray, stood by the door. A little girl that reminded Anna of Claire from the mission school stood beside her, Her dress hung on her tiny frame like a large tent. She clung to the woman's hand as if it were the only thing keeping the little one alive. Anna resisted the urge to turn away from the sadness in the child's eyes.

The woman took a step into the room. "I'm Fiona Devine and this is Katie Hanrahan. She's the only survivor in her family, and friends of my husband and me brought her here with them. They couldn't keep her, so we've taken her in. They only arrived this morning." She gulped and ran her free hand over Katie's head of red hair. "I know we should have waited until tomorrow to bring her to school. But, I thought if she could be with other children, it would help her day to go better. She's had such a fright, and we have no other children at home."

Mrs. Cleary scurried down a narrow aisle between two rows of desks. "Of course, Katie can stay. Being in school half a day will make it easier for her tomorrow when she comes for the whole day." She bent and chucked the small girl under her chin. "We're happy to have you, Katie." She straightened and faced Anna. "Miss Anna, why don't you sit with Katie while I get the information I need from Mrs. Devine?"

Anna approached the child, then hunched down and looked into blue eyes that reminded her so much of Rory's. "I'm happy to meet you, Katie. Do you want to come with me to the table? We can draw some pictures or just talk."

The girl nodded.

Anna led the child to a table at the back. She had no doubt this is where she was to be and not sitting in Jerusha's parlor planning a wedding she would not be attending.

"You'll do no such thing, Anna. I was humiliated that you weren't here to greet your fiancé when he arrived." Mother crossed her arms and lifted her chin. "You will not be going anywhere the rest of this week unless it is in Lyman's company."

Anna stiffened and faced the bedroom window. "Why isn't Lyman in Chicago helping restore the city instead of wasting his time planning a wedding that will never happen?"

"Stop talking that nonsense. He has been helping his father."

"Doing what? I can't imagine that it was anything that would dirty his hands."

"Really, Anna, you should be grateful your father and I arranged for you to marry into the Millard family and it's time you stop this charade about not marrying Lyman."

A sour taste rose in her throat. "I'm not in love with him and I'm certain he's not in love with me. There will be no wedding."

"What does love have to do with anything? Turn around and look at me. I will not carry on this conversation speaking to your back."

Anna faced her mother's granite-like face. "Love should have everything to do with it, but you wouldn't know about any of that, would you?" She stared into pupils so large they reminded her of shiny black beads

"Life isn't a fairy tale." Mother balled her hands into fists. "We have an appointment at the seamstress shop tomorrow morning to discuss your wedding dress and I expect you to be there."

Anna sighed. "I have a commitment to the school and the children. Many families less fortunate than we have no place to go since the fire. Or they've squeezed with other families in homes that are already too small. Children suffer the most. They've been uprooted, and they don't understand why. If I can help the little ones there find some comfort in their new surroundings, that's what I intend to do tomorrow morning."

Mother heaved a sigh. "I'll order Charles not to take you to that school." She said "school" as if it were poison on her tongue that needed to be spit out.

Anna bit back a spiteful remark. "Charles is under Mrs. Maxwell's supervision. I told Jerusha of my plans, and she agreed that Charles can take me to the school the rest of this week."

Mother huffed and turned toward the door. The sound of her skirts whipping back and forth accompanied by her foot-falls filled the room. "You have no idea what you are doing to this family, Anna. It is your fault we have to have another dress made. If you'd not left it in the barn, this could have all been avoided. You will marry Lyman, and you will marry him before the year is out. I'm sure in time you will grow fond of him."

A hard *click* sounded.

Anna faced the window, arms crossed, and scowled. "I'll disown this family before that happens."

She shut her eyes. "Lord, You've commanded me to honor my parents, but does that mean marrying a man who is nearly as mean as the devil? I'll meet with Lyman now, but unless you show me I'm wrong, I will go back to the school tomorrow."

She turned and flounced across the Oriental rug to the armoire, then took out the gaudier of the two dresses Mrs. Millard had given her and held it up. There had to be at least a dozen layers of ruffles on the skirt. Never had Anna seen such a garish pink. And if she didn't wear a bustle, the skirt would drag on the floor like a ball gown.

She returned the dress to the armoire and took out the second one. At least it was a decent color and didn't require such a large bustle. She laid it across the bed then worked her way out of the clothes she'd had on since before dawn. What irony that the only clothing she had, aside from the two day dresses she'd packed, were gowns from a woman she disliked almost as much as the woman's son. Millie promised to have at least one of the frocks she'd ordered ready by late next week.

As Anna was attaching a hairpiece to the back of her head, Callie wandered into their bedroom. Her mouth twisted into a smirk. "You sweetheart is downstairs."

She rolled her eyes. "Please don't tease. You know how I feel about the man." She fastened a decorative clip into her hair to hold the hairpiece in place.

"How do you know it's not Rory?"

At Callie's mocking tone, Anna glared at her younger sibling. "Wipe that silly smile from your face, little sister. For all I know, Rory perished in the fire. It's not funny."

Callie's expression dissolved into one more serious. "Sorry. I'm just so tired of everything being so somber."

"Didn't you go to the seminary for classes today? I doubt the atmosphere there was very subdued."

"I went." She sat on the foot of her bed. "Those girls peppered me with questions about the fire. That's the last thing I wanted to discuss."

Anna picked up a hand mirror and checked the back of her

hairdo in the dresser mirror. "I'll never make my hair look as nice as when Jane styled it." *Did Jane and her family survive the fire?*

"Anna, are you listening to me or thinking about Rory again?"

She faced Callie. "Maybe you should ask them questions first, such as what kinds of things they do to entertain themselves."

"Why? What they like to do won't appeal to me. Those girls are younger and seem babyish."

"You can't be more than a year or two older."

"But I've been to finishing school and *am* debuting this year."

Anna rolled her eyes. "We've already had that conversation. The children I met today are the *real* fire refugees. They had little before the fire, and now they have even less. If Mrs. Maxwell hadn't sent food with us this morning, some wouldn't have even had lunch."

A sharp rap sounded and the door opened. Mother stepped inside. She glared at Anna. "Lyman is waiting."

Anna lifted her hands in surrender. "Yes, Mother. I'm coming."

Mrs. Millard brushed scone crumbs from her skirt. "I suppose you young people would like some time alone. She stood from the sofa and looked around the parlor. "Ah, there's the door. I get so confused in a new place. After dinner, Eleanor and I want to discuss wedding plans. Tomorrow, Anna will see the dressmaker for a fitting." She gave a slight lift of her chin. "I'd feel much more comfortable if my own seamstress were here, but I've been assured that Millicent does wonderful work."

Anna stiffened. "I can't go to Millie's tomorrow—or for the rest of the week."

Mrs. Millard's blond eyebrows arched. "Oh? Whatever plans could you have in this godforsaken place? You've only been here a few days."

"I'm helping at a school west of town. Many children who escaped the fire are there, and the teacher can't tend to all of them."

Lyman's smile didn't reach his eyes. "Anna, your charity work is very commendable, but there must be others who can help while Mother and I are here. All Mother has talked about is our wedding."

Anna shrugged. "Perhaps, but there's one thing I have that others don't."

He frowned. "What?"

"I'm a refugee too. I understand what it feels like."

"You're no such thing, Anna Hartwell. We're only temporarily displaced." Mother stepped into the room. "Sorry I was detained. Were you discussing the wedding plans?"

Lyman stood. "Mrs. Hartwell. It's so good to see you again. We had just begun the discussion."

Mrs. Millard threw her shoulders back. "Anna insists she can't take time to be measured for her dress tomorrow because of helping some orphans."

Mother stared at Anna, managing to keep a tight smile on her face. "I thought we settled this. You'll have to rearrange your schedule, Anna, and let someone else help with those raga-muffins you seem to like more than your own family."

Jerusha stepped into the parlor and offered a friendly smile as she looked at each of her guests. "I'm Jerusha Maxwell. I'm glad to see you've made yourselves at home."

Lyman stepped over to Jerusha and took her hand. "Mrs. Maxwell, it is my pleasure to meet you. I've heard many wonderful things about your late husband. He contributed much to the cause during the war."

Jerusha's eyes lit up. "Thank you for your kind words, Mr.

Millard." She looked at Mrs. Millard. "Sorry I couldn't be here when you arrived. I was working at my church, packing boxes for the sufferers from the fires. We're gathering donated clothing and giving it out faster than people can bring more in."

Deep lines formed between Mother's eyes. "Fires?"

"Why, yes. There were other fires the same day. Peshtigo is the place we collected clothing for the day you went with me."

Mother threw her shoulders back. "I thought that was for the Chicago fire."

Jerusha nodded. "It's easy to get confused. It's up north. Another happened across Lake Michigan in a town called Holland. I haven't heard about the refugees in Michigan, but I'm sure many suffered loss there as well. My church is sending supplies to both Peshtigo and Chicago. I suppose Anna has told you about her day with the refugee children. Such a wonderful thing she's doing to help." She turned toward the door to the entry hall. "Sorry to have interrupted your conversation. I just wanted to introduce myself to our visitors. Dinner will be served at six p.m."

Lyman pulled out a pocket watch and checked it.. "Anna, my dear, it looks like we have time for a brief tour of the town. All I've seen so far is the short distance between here and the Swenson's guest cottage across the street."

Anna stood and worked to keep an even tone to her voice. "Of course. How impolite of me not to offer."

A short time later, Anna climbed into the buggy and pressed her body as tight as she could against her side. She pulled the blanket over her legs and tucked it around herself.

Lyman regarded her with an intense stare.

She held his gaze, wondering how the left side of his brow could furrow while the other side stayed smooth. Not only was it strange, but it made him appear even more menacing. She had half a mind to leap over the side of the carriage and run back to the house.

The buggy rolled onto the road, and Anna inhaled the crisp air, determined to enjoy the ride despite the man beside her.

They reached the bottom of the hill and made the turn toward town. Lyman stared past Anna at the water. "Geneva is a beautiful lake, but it's too remote for me. After we're married we won't be spending much time here."

Anna stiffened. The first words out of his mouth, and he couldn't find anything positive to say. If she were a man she'd like to push him out of the carriage and tell him to go back to Chicago. She mentally counted to ten and gave him a practiced smile. "To the contrary, I find the area to be quite refreshing with the lake, trees and clean air. And the people here are very nice."

Lyman angled back and gave her a pointed stare. "You must be jesting. Whoever heard of having dinner as early as six o'clock? You're no more the same as these people than me. I haven't decided where yet—either in your old neighborhood or maybe on Prairie Avenue—but I plan to build us a magnificent house that rivals any of those that burned down, including yours. Prairie Avenue escaped the flames. Maybe that's the better location. Of course, you'll be accompanying me to social functions, and many are being held in that part of town these days."

Lyman's monotone voice grated against Anna's ears like an out-of-tune soprano. She closed her eyes and pressed her body against the side of the carriage. Maybe if she showed Lyman how incompatible they were, he would insist they not marry. Let him break it off. "I prefer the earlier dinner hour. That way my food is digested by the time I go to bed. Otherwise I'm up several times."

She ignored Lyman's startled look at her discussing such things so openly, and pointed to the shore on the opposite side of the bay. "Father is building a home over there, just down from the Sturgis estate. I love the primitiveness of the shore. It wasn't long ago Potawatomi Indians lived there. I hear some of them are still around, living in those woods. I would love to have a house on Father's property. If we lived here, I could continue teaching—."

He pinned a stare on her, so cold it could have frozen the lake. "We'll live in Chicago."

"Chicago is nice, but what if God wants me here in Wisconsin?"

A vein in Lyman's neck throbbed. "The Bible says the wife must submit to the husband. There's no need for further discussion." He tugged at his coat sleeves and shifted his weight.

They crossed over the bridge spanning the White River and angled onto Broad Street. At the intersection with Main Street, Lyman glanced at the wood frame buildings that occupied the four corners. "Most every building is of wood construction. All this could go up in flame if someone's animal kicked over a lantern like what happened in Chicago."

Anna stared at him. "Is that how the fire started?"

"Right there in that godforsaken Conley's Patch. It's not yet been confirmed publicly, but that's the speculation." He uttered an ugly chuckle. "Could happen here too."

"Perhaps. But if it does, I'm sure a new village will spring right up, same as Chicago." Anna crossed her arms. "I'm not planning to live anywhere but here. If we fulfill that nonsensical agreement between our parents and go through with this marriage, there's no reason I can't live here and you stay in the city during the week. That's how it will have to be, Lyman. Or there will be no marriage at all."

His eyes burned hot, and he tipped his head back. A laugh like a mongrel's bark rose from his throat. He glared at her. "You're the feisty one today. Enjoy that attitude you little she-devil," he said through clenched teeth, "because once you are Mrs. Lyman Millard I won't tolerate impertinence of any kind."

He tunneled his left hand under the blanket and grabbed her

fisted hand, then worked his fingers under hers and forced them back. Despite the mounting pain, she fought against the pressure until it felt as if her fingers would break. She squeezed her eyes shut and held her breath until her strength drained out and she slumped.

Lyman took hold of her hand and squeezed hard then brought his mouth to her ear and whispered "Much better."

The smell of liquor tickled her nose. Tears filled her eyes and she willed them not to spill over.

He sat back, still keeping her hand in his firm grasp. "Now let's enjoy the romantic ride our mothers are hoping this to be."

Memories of Lyman as a thirteen-year-old boy pushing a servant's son into a wall when no adults were around flashed into Anna's mind. He'd pushed so hard the boy's body had made an indent in the plaster. At the boy's scream, Mr. Millard had burst into the room, but instead of telling the truth, the boy said he'd fallen against the wall when he tripped. After Mr. Millard took the crying boy from the room, Lyman laughed and said he doubted the punk servant's boy would bother him again.

It was clear he included women in the same category as servants. She would never be his punching bag. She pulled against Lyman's grip, using her full body weight. He didn't budge. Without warning, he released his hold and her shoulder slammed into the sideboard with a *thud*. Pain traveled across her shoulder blade. Tears erupted and she blinked at them.

Charles whirled around. "What was that?" He looked from Lyman to Anna. "Everyone okay?" He stared at Lyman, looking as though he wanted to kick the man to the moon.

Anna refrained from rubbing her left shoulder and averted her eyes from his gaze. "I'm a wee bit clumsy today. Almost slipped off the seat."

A skeptical expression filled the driver's features before he faced forward.

Lyman chuckled under his breath.

Oh, how she loathed the man.

# CHAPTER ELEVEN

The next morning, Anna waited until Callie left their room then went to the mirror and slipped her dressing gown off her left arm. A huge blue and yellow bruise covered her shoulder and trailed several inches down her upper arm.

Tears stung her eyes. What had she done to deserve this? Was God that displeased with her? She raised her arm, and pain shot through her shoulder blade. She'd only raised it an inch or two. How would she manage at school without letting on she was hurt? She'd have to concoct a story. If anyone found out the truth, she'd die of embarrassment.

She let the dressing gown drop to the floor, grateful she'd kept her chemise on all night to avoid the pain of working her way out of it. She reached for her day dress. At least it buttoned all the way down the front and she could easily slip it on.

The door opened.

Anna's right hand went to her left shoulder and she turned her back to her sister. "I thought you were having breakfast."

"We received a message that the girl I usually ride to the

seminary with is sick, so Charles is taking me. He's waiting for us out front."

"Now, you've told me. I'll be along shortly." Anna slipped behind a screen set up in the far corner of the room.

"What's wrong? What are you hiding?"

Why did her sister have to always be so curious? "I'm not hiding anything." She realized she'd dropped her dress when she covered the bruise with her hand. "Can you hand my dress around the screen, please?"

"Only if you tell me what's wrong." Callie's soft footfalls on the plush rug that took up the center of the room came closer. "You may as well tell me, Anna. Turn around."

Her sister's voice was behind her now. Anna swallowed hard. It was impossible to hide anything when they shared a room. She dropped her hand and turned.

Callie's gaze went directly to Anna's bruised shoulder, and her mouth fell open. "Where did you get that?"

Anna forced a chuckle. "You know me. Always clumsy. I tripped over a doorstop at school yesterday and fell into the doorframe. I had no idea it had turned such an ugly color."

Callie tilted her head and stared at Anna. "You always were a bad liar. What's the truth, sister?"

Anna winced as she worked her arm into the dress's left sleeve. "Just what I said."

"I don't believe you for one minute." Callie took hold of the dress and brought it over Anna's shoulder then let her slip her good arm into the other sleeve. Before Anna could try, Callie started buttoning the dress.

"Thank you."

Callie stood back. "Your hair's a mess. Let's get it restyled. You may not want to tell what really happened right now, but you know I'm not going to settle for a lie. I'll get it out of you one way or another."

They met Charles outside and he gave Anna a wary look as if

to say, *"Are you okay?"* She feigned interest in a pair of squirrels chasing each other across the lawn. She'd have to be especially careful around him not to show discomfort with her shoulder or he'd put two and two together. She held out her right hand and he assisted her into the carriage.

Grateful for the silence once Callie was dropped off, Anna forced her thoughts onto the children. Would that sweet cherub named Katie return? Anna's heart wrenched at the thought of the child losing her entire family in the fire. How could she complain about her trials when Katie's were so much worse?

Several children already played in the schoolyard when they arrived. Mrs. Cleary came down the porch steps and scurried over. "Anna, I'm so relieved you're here. I just received word six more scholars will enroll today along with the seven that entered yesterday."

Anna walked with her to the porch steps. "I'm glad to be here. I thought about Katie almost the entire ride and prayed she wouldn't balk at coming back today. She seemed in shock yesterday."

Mrs. Cleary stopped and nodded. "I've been hearing terrible stories like Katie's. Entire families gone or others separated. Many children are missing." Her voice caught on her last words. She pulled a handkerchief from her pocket and dabbed at her eyes.

During Anna's trip up Dearborn Street through the mass of humanity the night of the fire, she'd seen several children scurrying along not seeming to be with anyone. She'd presumed their parents were close by, but how many of those wee ones were orphaned like Katie?

She followed Mrs. Cleary inside and assisted with preparing the tables to accommodate the new students, grateful none of her tasks required her to lift her arm above her shoulder. The teacher had been assured that new desks were being built by the men of the community and should be done the following week.

Meanwhile, an additional table and chairs had been placed at the back of the already crowded room.

At exactly eight-thirty, Anna stepped onto the school's front stoop. She faced the schoolyard and scanned the children. Her spirits sank. No Katie. Why did the little redhead seem more important to her than the rest? Was that fair to the others? She sent up a short prayer that Katie was okay then pulled on the bell rope with her right hand.

The children stopped their play and stampeded toward Anna. There seemed to be more than six new ones today. How would they manage to teach them all? She shooed the children inside and turned to follow in their wake.

"Miss Anna, Miss Anna, wait."

Anna spun around.

Fiona Devine scurried up. A chalky hue had replaced her rosy cheeks of yesterday. "I can't get Katie to come to school. She's still laying in her cot and says she doesn't want school, she wants her ma."

Anna's heart felt like it had moved into her throat. "Come inside with me."

Mrs. Cleary stood at the front of the room directing the students to their desks and tables.

Anna waited until the children were settled then went to the teacher and whispered, "Can we step outside a moment? There's a problem."

The teacher asked the children to stay quietly in their seats and put an eighth grade girl in charge.

Outside, Mrs. Devine repeated to the teacher what she'd told Anna. "Can one of you come with me and convince Katie to come to school? Last night all Katie talked about was her time with Miss Anna." She looked at Anna. "She's quite taken with you, it seems."

She felt like smiling for the first time that day. "I was taken with Katie as well."

The woman looked at her with pleading eyes. "Perhaps if you came home with me, Katie would agree to come to school."

"I'd love to, but we have so many children. Too many for one person to handle."

The teacher waved a dismissive hand. "I can manage anything for twenty or thirty minutes. The child needs to be here. Go."

Mrs. Devine did most of the talking on the way to her house. She'd met her husband twenty years ago in Chicago. Ten years later, they moved to Wisconsin and staked a plot to farm in Irish Woods. They had two sons, fifteen and seventeen, who helped with the farm. She loved having a little girl around, but she couldn't take on her care for much longer.

As much as Mrs. Devine's story was interesting, the nonstop talking made Anna's skin feel like it was crawling up her back. Concern for Katie and the constant ache in her shoulder were about all she could handle.

Relief washed over Anna when Mrs. Devine led her down a lane to a tidy white farmhouse. Inside the front door, Anna surveyed the small living room—no larger than the pantry had been in her Chicago home.

The older woman's gaze surveyed the room, probably seeing it through a visitor's eyes. "I know it's not fancy, but it's ours."

Anna offered the woman what she hoped was a supportive smile. "Mrs. Devine, this is one of the coziest living rooms I've ever been in."

She rolled her eyes. "That can't be true. I can tell you come from wealth by the quality of your dress and your manners."

"I'd rather spend an afternoon here than in a fancy mansion. Let's find Katie and get her up."

Mrs. Devine glanced toward an open door. "Katie's cot is in the add-on at the back of the house. It's our oldest boy's room. We moved him upstairs to share with his brother." She crossed to the door and Anna followed her through a small dining room that held a round oak table and four matching chairs, along with a fifth one that didn't match.

If the Devine men were large, they would have little elbowroom with a small child squeezing in between them. Katie had to have family somewhere. Someone must be frantically looking for her. If there was a way to find them, Anna had to try.

They stepped into a small kitchen and Mrs. Divine went to an open door. "Katie's in here."

Anna came up beside her and let her eyes adjust to the dimness. "Can we bring some light in here?"

"Of course." Mrs. Devine took a match from her pocket and lit an oil lamp that sat in the middle of the table. She carried the lamp into Katie's room, and the small space came to life. Katie's small figure lay stretched out face down on the mattress. Anna sat on the edge of the bed and rubbed the little girl's back. "Hey, lassie, time to wake up. Miss Anna wants to see you."

The child muttered something into her pillow.

"I looked forward to seeing you all the way to school and was very disappointed when you weren't there. So disappointed I had to come here to find you."

Katie slowly rolled over, but her eyes remained closed.

"Can you sit up, so I can see you better?"

Her small chest rose and fell several times then her eyes fluttered open. She stared at Anna, her face as expressionless as the china doll Anna had as a child.

She pushed Katie's bangs from her eyes then rearranged her long braids across her chest. "Do you feel sick?"

Katie shook her head.

"Are you sleepy?"

"No."

"I know you miss your ma and da, and it's very hard to do normal things. But would your mother want you to not go to school today?"

"No." Katie's voice remained a whisper.

"Then why don't you get dressed and come to school with me?"

She turned her head to look at Anna. "Will you stay with me while I'm there?"

"As much as possible." She hoped the other new children wouldn't demand as much personal time.

"Okay."

By the time Katie dressed, Mrs. Devine had prepared a lunch pail for her. She also handed Katie a bundle wrapped in wax paper. "You can eat the bread and jam for breakfast while you walk."

During their trek back to school, Katie told Anna about the night the fire burned her entire neighborhood and how she had stayed with another family like Ma told her to do. Later she waited for her ma or da to come for her. They never came and after a train ride, she was here. "Miss Anna, do you think my Ma and Da know where I am now so they can find me?"

Anna's heart nearly broke in two. She didn't want to give the child false hope. She squeezed Katie's hand. "I'm sure they will find you, if they are able. I do know God watches out for all children, and He is watching out for you now."

A hint of a smile touched Katie's lips and Anna mentally thanked God for what seemed to be the right words. Today would be a good day after all.

# CHAPTER TWELVE

Anna all but flew down the school steps and approached the waiting carriage. A man sat in the passenger seat, his back to her. He slowly turned and her stomach seized.

"Good afternoon, my love."

Hairs lifted on the back of her neck and she took a step back.

Lyman opened the door to the passenger compartment. "I thought we could take a look at your father's property and choose a place for our home."

She didn't believe him for one moment. "That would be difficult since there's no way to get there by road. Besides, I thought you didn't want to live here."

Lyman narrowed his eyes. "This place is more primitive than I prefer, that is true. Only trying to keep peace, my love."

"I have a few stops to make on the way home. It may take me a while."

He rolled his eyes. "What kind of stops?"

"The seamstress shop. Then after that, the church to—"

"Can't you do those things another day?"

"No. Katie needs new clothes as soon as possible."

The skin around his mouth drew taunt. "Who is Katie?"

"An orphaned refugee from the fire. She lost her entire family."

"Can't these immigrants take care of their own?"

She had half a mind to ask to sit next to Charles. If he'd been Patrick, she would have. "They don't have the means."

Charles jumped down from his seat and held out his hand to her.

She placed her hand in his and pain shot through her arm. She winced before she could stop herself. "Please drive me to Millie's."

"Yes, ma'am." His face gave no clue what he must be thinking as he helped her into the carriage.

Anna nestled into the corner of the passenger seat and tucked her hands underneath her legs. Awkward, but at least Lyman couldn't grip her the way he had before.

He glanced at her. "No blanket?"

"I'm fine." *I'd rather be cold than have you abuse me under the covering.*

She closed her eyes and feigned sleep. The *clip-clop* of the horse's hooves pounded out a lullaby of sorts and on a normal day would have lulled her into sleep, but she needed to remain alert.

"You think you're so smart, Anna. But, you'll have your comeuppance soon. Mark my words."

At the whisper, Anna's eyes opened. Lyman's face was inches away, his pupils so large they made his eyes an unsettling black. A shiver slid down her back—the kind that a warm blanket couldn't cure.

She shut her eyes and whispered. "Don't be so sure whose comeuppance will show up first. Mine or yours." She waited for one of his caustic remarks and when none came, she slowed her breathing the way she learned years ago to fool Mother into thinking she was asleep.

"We're almost to Millie's, Miss Anna. Do you still want to stop?"

She opened her eyes. Lyman sat on his side of the seat, staring out into the street.

"Yes. I'll try to be quick. Please wait." She glanced at Lyman. "Unless Mr. Millard wants you to take him to his guest quarters while I'm inside."

He gave her a vacant stare. "I've nothing better to do in this godforsaken place. I'll wait."

Charles assisted Anna from the carriage. She held his gaze a moment before turning toward the shop entrance. Oh, how she missed Patrick.

Anna stepped inside the seamstress shop and the overhead bells jangled. She glanced around. Millie had received some lovely wools for winter since she was last there.

"Miss Hartwell, were we supposed to have a fitting today?" Millie scurried from the back of the store, her cheeks flushed. Loose tendrils that had escaped her bun framed her face She glanced over her shoulder toward the dressing room. "If we did, I must not have noted it. I have a client here now."

Anna shook her head. "This will only take a minute. I'm not due for a fitting until next week. I apologize for not sending word before my arrival, but my reason for coming came up unexpectedly." She explained Katie's plight then said, "I'm hoping maybe you have a sample dress I could purchase for Katie. Perhaps I can return tomorrow when you have more time?"

Millie drew a lace-trimmed hanky from her jumper pocket and dabbed her eyes. "That poor child. No need to wait. I may have some sample dresses from last year's styles. Let me get them." She hastened toward the back of the store.

Anna stepped to the window. Charles sat on the carriage driver's bench staring straight ahead while Lyman sat stiff as a board inside the carriage and scowling at his pocket watch. If the man didn't want to wait, why didn't he walk back to the Maxwell home? It wasn't *that* far.

"Here are two dresses that might fit the child."

Anna turned as Millie laid a pale blue frock across her cutting table. "This one has a eyelet lace trimmed pinafore to go with it. I intended it to be for church or special occasions."

She walked to the table and looked at the dress. "It's lovely."

"And then there is this one." Millie laid a dark blue and black checked dress beside the pale blue one. "This style is perfect for school. *Oui?* Do they look like they would fit the little girl?"

She nodded. "Oh, yes, they're perfect." She opened her reticule. How much are they?"

Millie gathered up the dresses and began to wrap them in white paper. "I wouldn't dream of charging you. My contribution to the cause." She tied string around the package and finished it off with a bow. "I've been thinking. If Katie is in such need, so must the other children too. I'd like to help."

She wanted to hug Millie and twirl her around. "What a perfect idea. I can bring you their measurements and as you have the time, you can sew the dresses." She was almost bouncing on her toes.

"Millie, did you forget about me? Can't you plan charity work another time?"

Anna cringed and looked over Millie's shoulder.

Mother stood outside the changing room wearing a day dress still in need of a hem. "I should have known Millie was talking to you, Anna." She looked at Millie. "I apologize for my flighty daughter interrupting your day."

Millie's mouth fell open, and she quickly closed it. "Oh Mrs. Hartwell, I don't consider Anna's interruption an intrusion. In fact, I'm excited to be able to help with the refugee children.

Mother's angry expression dissolved. "Of course, I'm always pleased my daughter is concerned for the less fortunate."

"Nothing brightens one's spirits like new clothes, and not ill-fitting hand-me-downs. Anna and I are finished now." Millie faced Anna with her back to Mother and mouthed. "We'll talk later."

"Thank you, Millie." Anna picked up her package then met her mother's stare. "See you at home, Mother."

Outside, Charles assisted Anna into the carriage. "Where to now, Miss Anna?" Charles asked.

"It's too late to stop at the church. Home." She glanced at Lyman. "Unless Mr. Millard prefers going to his guest quarters to rest before dinner."

He gave a dismissive wave. "The Maxwell home is fine."

After Charles climbed to his bench, Lyman glared at the precious package on her lap as if it were poison. "We have plans to make before dinner, don't we, my dear."

She stiffened. "The only plan I have is to take a nap. It's been a tiring day."

"We'll see about that." Lyman's clenched jaw and lowered voice made it difficult to hear him, but Anna didn't miss a word.

She held back a sigh and kept her focus on the side of the road. Ten more minutes and she could escape behind her bedroom door until dinner.

At the house, Anna hustled to the front door and let herself inside, not waiting for Lyman. She was shrugging out of her cape when he entered. She hung the garment on a hook and retrieved her package from where she'd set it on a straight-backed chair. "I'll see you at dinner." She took a step toward the stairs.

Lyman grabbed her upper left arm and squeezed. "I didn't dismiss you."

Heat filled her stomach. "I don't have to ask permission to leave your presence."

"As my fiancée, you do." His hold tightened.

Pain shot through her arm, but she fought to keep her face placid. "Fiancée according to our parents, but not to me. I have no intention of marrying you." She yanked her arm from his grip and stomped up the stairs. At the top she glanced back. If he was still in the entry hall, he stood out of her line of sight. Good riddance.

She marched toward her room. Lyman came around the corner from the opposite direction and stood between her and her door. His lip curled. "You must have forgotten there's a back stairway from the kitchen."

How dare the man. Had he no scruples at all? She glared at him and spoke through clenched teeth. "Get away from me. You have no business being on this floor."

He took a step toward her.

"Come any closer and I'll scream."

"Go ahead. There's no one else in the house except the maid and the cook and they're in the kitchen.

She raised her voice, "I mean it Lyman. Leave me alone."

Her bedroom door flew open and Callie stared at both of them, eyes wide. "What's going on?"

# CHAPTER THIRTEEN

"Anna, you've got to tell Mother about Lyman." Callie paced in front of their bedroom's small sitting area.

The heat of shame crawled up Anna's neck and into her cheeks. She turned away, then unbuttoned her dress and let it fall to the floor. Without looking for her dressing gown, she crumpled into an upholstered chair and nibbled at her thumbnail.

*It's all my fault.*

She knew better than to provoke Lyman. So why did she do it? Pressure built behind her eyes. "Please don't say anything to anyone, including Mother or Father. I just have to learn to keep my mouth shut around him and it will be fine." She attacked her thumbnail, and gave in to the release of pressure the gnawing sensation gave her.

Callie knelt in front of Anna, then gripped her older sister's hand and pulled it from her mouth. "It isn't your fault, Anna. Our parents need to know about this so they can end this stupid arrangement." She looked at Anna's thumb then all her fingers. "Your fingernails have always been so beautiful and now look at them. They're down to the quick. If you don't tell, I will."

She pulled her hand away. "Charles knows."

Callie sat back and stared at her. "How?"

"When Lyman shoved me against the side of the buggy it made a terrible sound, and he asked if I was okay. I made up an excuse for the noise, but I saw by his expression he didn't believe me. I hope he follows the servant's code of being invisible to their masters and keeps it to himself. It will only bring embarrassment on Father if this gets out."

Callie shook her head. "You're wrong, Anna. If you don't tell, what *can* you do?"

"What I said. Watch my tongue and don't provoke him." She stared at her lap. "Perhaps in time Lyman will start acting like a gentleman. Either way, he and his mother are due to leave in a couple of day's time. I'm going to lie down for a while."

A LOUD RAP jarred Anna from her sleep. She raised her head from the pillow and blinked. What time was it?

The bedroom door flew open and Mother stood in the dim hall light. "Is sleeping all you girls have to do? It's almost time for dinner. You'd better get dressed." She lit a gas lamp that sat on the dresser then glared at Anna. "I hope you've thought about how rude you were interrupting Millie's work today."

Anna rubbed sleep from her eyes and sat up. "Millie didn't say it was an interruption."

"Of course she didn't. She's a polite woman. I forbid you to go back to that school anymore this week. You'll spend the day tomorrow with Mrs. Millard and me, discussing wedding plans and getting measured at Millie's."

Anna flung her blanket off and leaped to her feet. "I can't stay home tomorrow. I have the dresses Millie donated to take to Katie. How can you be so cruel to a child, Mother?"

Mother snapped her chin upward. "Charles can deliver them to the school. I'm not that heartless."

"Why is it so important for me to marry a man like Lyman? He thinks nothing but of himself, is a bore, and—"

"He mistreats her."

Mother's gaze went to Callie who still lay in her bed. "What do you mean?"

"Look at her bru—"

"Callie means he's boorish." Anna folded her arms across her chest, making sure her hand covered the bruise and gave her sister a pointed stare. "I still refuse to marry him."

"You *will* marry him, Anna Hartwell. If you don't, you'll hurt your father deeply."

She narrowed her eyes.

"Don't you mean it will hurt you, Mother? You relish being linked to the Millards, hoping their celebrity will rub off."

A knock came and Mother answered the door. Maria held out an envelope. "Mrs. Hartwell, a messenger just dropped this off and said you were to read it at once."

Mother closed the door then removed a square white notecard from the envelope. She handed it to Callie. "Read this."

Callie scanned the note. "Hortense and Lyman have been called back to Chicago. They're leaving on the morning train and won't be at dinner tonight because they have to pack."

# CHAPTER FOURTEEN

Anna sat up and blinked. "Can you repeat that, Callie?"

Mother's brows shot upwards. "You heard her. The Millards are leaving in the morning. They're not even coming for dinner. Something dreadful must have happened. I hope Mr. Millard hasn't taken ill."

Anna sent a silent prayer of thanks heavenward. "And I'll be at the school tomorrow as I promised."

A deep V formed on Mother's brow. "Just because the Millards are leaving doesn't mean I'll permit you to work at that school."

Anna clinched her jaw. If she had to sneak out before dawn like before, she would.

"Mother," Callie said. "If you won't permit Anna to go to the school tomorrow, I'll go in her place."

She opened her mouth to protest, but mother spoke first. "Are you girls forgetting that the Bible says you are to honor your parents?"

"It also says to not provoke your children to wrath." Anna draped her blanket over herself to conceal the bruise. "I am an adult and over the age of twenty-one. I'm going to the school tomorrow. I need to get the girls' measurements for Millie."

"Oh do what you want."

The door shut behind her swishing skirts.

Callie giggled. "You put her in her place, sister. And it was a long time coming."

"It doesn't mean what I said was right. After all, she is our mother. And as long as I am living under her roof ..." Anna tipped her head. "Did you really mean you'd go in my place if I couldn't? I'm sure we could use the help."

Callie stiffened. "I'm no good with children. That's only your calling."

She offered her a soft smile. "Maybe, maybe not."

THE FOLLOWING MORNING, Anna settled into the buggy, the paper-wrapped dresses on her lap. She drew in a breath and exhaled a white cloud into the air. Charles had put the buggy's canvas roof up, but she'd need the wool blanket around her legs today.

Last night at dinner, Mother had monopolized the discussion by hypothesizing over why the Millards left so suddenly. When Anna suggested perhaps Lyman had changed his mind about the wedding, all color drained from Mother's face and she ordered Anna to never say such a terrible thing again.

A dark thought threatened to burst Anna's bubble of joy. Was there truth in what Mother said about a cancelled wedding hurting Father? She shook off the question. Both families were well off, although Mr. Millard's net worth was substantially more than Father's. She knew this because of a conversation she overheard last year—something about some extra expenses Father had. What they were, she had no idea.

She closed her eyes and silently thanked God for the day, ending her prayer with the same request she'd made daily since the fire—that Rory was okay and that somehow she'd learn of his whereabouts. She spent the rest of the ride daydreaming about finding Rory in Irish woods and how they would embrace and kiss. If only Patrick hadn't interrupted them that day back at the mission school. At least then she'd know how it felt to have his lips pressed against hers. Much better than imagining it.

Charles drove the buggy into the schoolyard as Fiona Devine scurried down the school steps and walked with determined steps toward her home.

Anna called out to her. "Mrs. Devine, please wait!"

The woman halted and turned.

Anna gathered the package of dresses in one arm and held her other hand out to Charles. He helped her from the carriage, and she hurried across the patchy grass to the woman's side. "I'm so happy to have caught you. I have something for Katie."

The woman frowned as she studied the package. "I just told Mrs. Cleary that Katie wouldn't be here today. The child has an upset stomach. I don't know if it's something she caught or if she be afraid to come. I don't want her here if she is really sick."

Anna thrust the package into the woman's hands. "Then you must give this to her. They're new dresses that the seamstress in town has given her."

The woman's mouth fell open. "Are you sure?"

Anna laughed. "Yes. Very sure. I was ready to buy them, but after I explained about Katie's circumstance, Millie insisted she *give* them to her. Please take them."

Tears welled in the woman's eyes. "I don't know what to say. I'm sure the lass will be thrilled. Thank you."

"You're welcome. And please tell Katie I hope she'll be back at school tomorrow."

Anna had hoped Katie would come after lunch, but she didn't. Despite Katie being on her mind, helping the children catch up on their reading and arithmetic made the day pass quickly. All but a couple of the boys seemed eager to learn, and the lessons helped the new scholars to not dwell on their tragic circumstances.

Charles arrived at the end of the day in an enclosed carriage, saying the temperature was too chilly for the open one. He helped Anna into the compartment then looked her in the eye. "Your father returned on the early afternoon train and I'm to tell you to come straight home."

Did Father's unexpected return have anything to do with her telling Lyman she wouldn't marry him? Was he coming to Geneva to have a talk with her? With telegraph lines being more available in the city now, Father could have been informed quite easily about the conversation..

Upon arriving at Mrs. Maxwell's home, she went directly to the parlor. Her father stood by the fireplace, studying the flames.

"Father, is everything all right?"

He offered a smile that didn't meet his eyes. "As right as possible under the circumstances. Your mother wired last night that the Millards left rather quickly. She also said things are uncomfortable living under another person's roof. She wants me to find a house to rent in Geneva." He glanced at a discarded newspaper resting on a sofa. "I looked for homes to let in the paper, but there's nothing available at present due to all the fire refugees. I'll ask around town tomorrow."

She sat in a blue velvet chair. "I don't find it uncomfortable here. I think Jerusha rather enjoys our company."

The skin between his eyes puckered. "Well, you know your mother. I'd rather have you three up here than in the city. It's not a pleasant place to be. And I can't see to rebuilding our home there until I get the business up and running so I can start making money again. I'm afraid if I can't find anything in Geneva, she'll insist we move back to the city.

Anna tensed. "But where would we stay?"

"We'd have to head way out west away from the city. Too far for me to travel for the business. We'd have no choice but to move in with the Millards."

Sour tasting bile rose in her throat. She had to do something—anything—to avoid living in the same house with Lyman. "I wonder if Jerusha knows of anyone who has a home to let."

Father frowned. "I'll ask her, but it has to meet your mother's expectations or it won't be worth investigating."

The next morning, Father surprised Anna by joining her at breakfast. She swallowed her oatmeal and took a sip of coffee. "What a pleasant surprise. I'm usually the only one taking breakfast this early."

He nodded. "I hoped to catch you before you left. I spoke to Jerusha last night, and she gave me the name of a family who intends to move into Milwaukee in a few weeks. She said their home is quite nice, although not as big as this one. As far as she knows they haven't sold the property and might be interested in renting it. I have a few things I need to do before it's late enough to call on them." He pulled a paper from his trouser pocket. "They live on Broad Street north of the depot several blocks. It's Victorian in style and sounds like something your mother would like."

Anna took a bite of her oatmeal and swallowed. "Is it large enough for us and a household staff? I can't see mother doing without at least a maid and a cook."

Father fingered his gray goatee. "It's a three-story home. Quite lovely from what I understand. I'm sure there must be accommodations for staff."

Anna reached in her dress pocket and took out Father's pocket watch. "I rescued this the night of the fire then forgot about it. Maybe having it with you will give you encouragement."

His eyes widened. "I thought it was probably a melted mess back there in the rubble. You remembered how much it means to me." He took the instrument and snapped it open. "It's still keeping time. Thanks, Anna." He closed the timepiece and tucked it into his pants pocket.

She reached in her pocket again and took out the photograph she'd found. "I also found this in your desk. I know the child is Callie, but I don't know who the woman is."

He stared at the picture, his eyes widening. "I'd forgotten about that photograph. That's a maid we once had. Her name was Maura."

Anna frowned. "Funny. I don't remember her at all. How was it she and Callie had their picture taken like that?"

"I don't quite remember. I think it was when your mother and I went to have our portrait taken and we took Callie with us. Maura was asked to come to watch her. The photographer was taken with them and took their picture." He handed it back to her. "Go ahead and keep it with you until we settle."

Anna returned the picture to her pocket, then took her last bite of cereal. "I'm glad I remembered it. I'll be praying Mother likes the house." She bid Father a good day and headed to the front hall. She almost wished Mother wouldn't like the house because she would bid the family adieu and stay on in Geneva. Free from Mother and the Millards.

When Anna arrived at the school, Mrs. Devine stood near the steps holding Katie's hand. The sight lifted her spirits.

Katie's smile greeted Anna as she approached the little girl. "Katie, you wore your new dress. It fits you perfectly."

The child pirouetted, causing her black and dark blue checked skirt to lift. "I love it, Miss Anna.

"One of me neighbors gave me black stockings her daughter

outgrew," Fiona said. "It was hard to get her to take the dress off last night after she tried it on."

Anna laughed and chucked Katie under her chin. "You don't want to wear the dress out."

Miss Fiona says I should write a thank you note to the lady who made my dresses."

"I think that's a grand idea. During our table time today, we can work on a note."

THAT AFTERNOON, Anna stepped into hers and Callie's bedroom. Callie lay stretched out on her bed wearing a dressing gown. Anna went to the window and raised the shade.

Callie stirred and rubbed her eyes. "Can't you keep the shade down?

"Not unless I want to trip over the furniture while I change my clothes."

Her sister sat up. "Were Mother and Father back when you came in? They went to see a house for rent."

"No, they weren't. I've been praying most of the day that mother would like the property."

Callie yawned. "What's wrong with staying here?"

Anna sighed and sat on her sister's bed. "You know Mother. She can only last so long when she isn't the queen bee. If they don't find a suitable home to rent, we'll end up at the Millards."

Callie's hand flew to her mouth. "You can't stay there. And I don't want to either, knowing what a disgusting man Lyman is. He might come after me like he does you." Her eyes widened. "Anna, I wish you'd tell them."

She bent to unbutton her boots. "I can't, and that's that. I'm praying Mother finds the house suitable and that will end the problem of Lyman—for now."

Callie stood and wrapped her dressing gown around her tiny form. "We need it to be forever, not only for now."

Footsteps sounded in the hall outside the bedroom door, getting louder and then fading as they passed by and headed toward the room their parents shared.

Anna's gaze locked with Callie's. "They're back. I guess we'll learn our fate at dinner."

ory hoisted a charred trunk he'd found onto his shoulder and stepped off a streetcar in front of the Northwestern train station. It hadn't yet been two weeks since the fire, but it seemed like a year. After days on end of hauling loads of debris to the lakefront, he needed to get out of there. Not only to breathe fresh air, but also to grieve. Since they had more volunteers than needed, he'd grabbed the opportunity of a free train pass from the mayor's office. It was time to head for Irish Woods.

A half-hour later, Rory settled in his train seat. He glanced down at his work shirt and trousers. Those and the other pair of pants in the trunk were filthy and probably stunk of smoke. He'd done his best to wash up, but Aunt Evie may insist he bathe in the barn before setting foot in her clean house. He closed his eyes and pulled his cap down over his face as a wave of exhaustion washed over him.

Instead of sleep, the same questions that had plagued him since the fire raced through his mind. Why had he been spared when all he held dear were taken? Was Anna still alive? Would he find Uncle Denis's farm? Was he doing the right thing leaving Chicago? Why had God allowed all of this?

He pulled a handkerchief from his pocket and dabbed his eyes. He had to stop tearing up. No one is ever impressed with a weeping man. *God, help me find Uncle Denis and Aunt Evie. They're all I've got now.* The train's gentle jostling, coupled with the steady rhythm of the wheels rolling along the tracks, lulled him into welcome sleep.

The conductor's shout, "Geneva, Wisconsin. End of the line," startled Rory awake. The train screeched and hissed to a stop. The passengers stood and began gathering their belongings. Rory tugged the trunk from a shelf overhead and followed an older man and woman down the narrow aisle.

By the time he stepped onto the platform, Rory's heart pommelled against his chest so hard he wondered if he should seek a doctor instead of Uncle Denis. He surveyed the mix of businessmen in suits and families being greeted by people that crowded around him. Everyone seemed to know someone, but not him. What if he couldn't find Uncle Denis or he couldn't find work? Next to him the train hissed as if taunting him. A Psalm he'd read that morning flowed into his thoughts.

*The LORD is my strength and my shield; my heart trusted in Him, and I am helped: therefore my heart greatly rejoiceth; and with my song I will praise Him.*

God would not let him down—even in His silence. He'd ask around until he found someone heading to Irish Woods and hitch a ride. He set out south down Broad Street and stopped at the first feed store he came to.

A man behind a cluttered counter looked up from writing in a large ledger book. "What can I do for you?"

Rory surveyed the store, disappointed it had no customers. "I've just arrived from Chicago and need a ride out to Irish Woods where me uncle lives. I don't see anyone but you here. I'll look elsewhere."

The man dropped his pencil on top of the ledger. "Cam O'Reilly is in back loading his wagon. He lives out that way. Go through there and you'll see him." He indicated a door at the back of the store.

A SHORT TIME LATER, Rory lurched toward the edge of the bench and grabbed the side of Cam O'Reilly's wagon.

"Should've warned you this here road is rough." Cam glanced through the waning light at Rory. "But it's quicker than the main road."

Rory let out the breath he was holding and forced a chuckle. "No harm done, but I think I'll keep my grip." As hungry as he was, he was grateful he hadn't eaten before he'd hitched his ride.

The driver took the horse and wagon onto a narrow road and a short distance down, stopped in front of a farmhouse. "I'm pretty sure this is Denis Quinn's place. Ya want me to wait until you make sure?" Rory was tempted to agree, but he couldn't take more advantage of the old man than he already had. "If you're sure this be Denis's house, then it must be so."

He leaped to the ground then hoisted his trunk from the wagon's back end and rested it on his shoulder. "You go on. I know your wife be waiting supper for ya. If it's not me uncle's place, then I'm sure whoever lives here can help me find him. Thanks for the ride."

The old man waved. "Good luck to ya." Rory watched the wagon rumble into the dusk, then turned and studied the white frame house in the twilight. Soft light glowed in the front window. Not a huge house, but far better than the tenement apartment he remembered Uncle Denis and Aunt Evie living in years ago. He strode toward the two-story structure. Off to his right, the outline of a sizable barn assured him that whoever lived here was doing quite well.

*Please Lord, let this be Uncle Denis's house.*

Before he reached the porch, the home's front door opened and a man stepped through, followed by a dog. He looked about the height of Uncle Denis.

"Uncle! Denis Quinn. Is that you?"

"Who is that calling me uncle?"

"It *is* Rory. I just came on the train." Rory dropped the trunk and it hit the ground with a *crack*. He trotted down the path.

The dog started barking and Uncle Denis grabbed his collar. "Paddy, quiet. He's family. Stay." Hurried footfalls clomped across the porch and down the steps.

"Thank God you be alive. I thought you were dead." Uncle Denis's long thickset arms curled around Rory and pulled him against his chest.

Rory's legs felt as weak as egg noodles, and he hung on to his uncle for fear of making a fool of himself by falling. "I'm alive, Unc. I'm here."

"What about the others? Are they?"

A mass the size of the moon that hung over their heads pushed its way through Rory's throat and exploded into a sob. "They're gone. All of 'em. If I'd done more . . . ". He inhaled his uncle's scent of farm and fresh air.

Uncle Denis pressed him tight to his chest. "Thank God in heaven, you be all right. I prayed at least one of you would make it. But there's been no word for days." The dog wormed his way between the men and whimpered. Uncle Denis released Rory and scratched the dog. "Crazy dog." Tears on his grizzled face glistened in the moonlight. "Your sister, too, and the baby?"

Rory nodded. "All of them, including the baby who was six years old now."

Dennis wiped his eyes. "How did you escape and no one else?"

Rory stepped back, grateful his legs felt strong again. "I live on the north side. Have been there since Da kicked me out two years ago." He bent and ruffled the dog's fur.

"Ah, your da mentioned you'd found a new church. I told him as long as you be worshiping the same God did it matter?"

Rory straightened. "I'd tried to see Da the day of the fire, but he wouldn't let me inside. He said what he always said. I was as good as dead to him." Rory punched his right fist into his left hand. A stinging sensation traveled his forearm. "I should have insisted, then I at least would have died with them."

His uncle tilted his head. "Now what would that accomplish?"

Rory shrugged. "I don't know."

The men fell into another hug. They'd never been a hugging kind of family, but right now Rory couldn't get enough.

"It's God's blessing that you're alive. Your Aunt Evie will be happy to see you. Let's go inside. I think she's got some stew left over from supper she can warm."

Rory raked his fingers through his hair. "She may not want me in the house until I have a bath."

His uncle's laugh filled the night air. "After all the smells we have on this farm, I doubt she'll even notice."

# CHAPTER SIXTEEN

*November 3, 1871*

$\mathcal{A}$nna slipped out the door to the second floor balcony that overlooked Broad Street and let the warm air caress her face. Any day the temperatures could drop and she wanted to take advantage of the afternoon sun. Below, women wearing day dresses and capes designed for spring weather strolled down Broad Street, some using parasols to block the sun, while road traffic bustled with farmers' wagons and an occasional carriage.

She dragged a wicker chair out of the shade and sat. Tipping her head back to let the sun's warm rays soak in, little by little, her body let go of the tautness. She felt a smile working it's way across her lips. If Mother caught her with sun on her face, she'd be hustled inside and lectured on how a lady never exposed her face to the sun. How could something that feels so good be bad for you? But Mother was napping and her afternoon naps were never shorter than an hour.

Had it only been two weeks since Mother approved of this lovely home and Father signed a year's lease? The past two days she'd taken off from volunteering at the school had not been days of leisure. For as little as they had to carry into their new home, Mother had kept both Callie and Anna hopping, insisting since they hadn't yet hired live-in help, the sisters needed to wipe down every stick of furniture the owners had left behind.

"Anna, come down and see who's here."

At Father's shout, Anna's eyes fluttered open and she peered over the balcony rail. "Patrick!"

All sleepiness gone, she dashed into the hall, letting the screen door slam behind her, and down the staircase. "Patrick is outside with Father and our carriage and Goldie! The train must have arrived early."

Callie appeared from the parlor, holding a feather duster. She waved the dusting tool in the air like a flag. "Yippy." Clouds of dust flew into the air.

Anna waved a hand and faked a cough. "Careful with that thing."

By the time they reached the front yard, Patrick had driven the carriage next to the side of the house.

Anna hurried over to Goldie. "Hello, girl. I was so excited to see you that I forgot to stop in the kitchen for a carrot." The horse bobbed her head and whinnied as Anna rubbed the center of the animal's forehead.

"So, you're more interested in seeing the horse than me or Patrick." Father climbed down from the carriage.

Anna laughed. "Of course I'm glad to see you. Did you want a carrot too?" She gave Father a side hug then looked at Patrick, wanting to hug him too. But such public display with a servant wasn't appropriate, even though he was like family. She hoped her smile was broad enough to show him how she felt. "Patrick, we've missed you."

"As I have missed you, Miss Anna." He made a slight bow and grinned.

"Yes, indeed, it is a good feeling to have Patrick and Goldie back with us." Father stared at the feather duster in Callie's hand. "I thought the new maid was to start today."

Callie made an exaggerated sigh. "She comes tomorrow. I don't know why Mother insisted I dust today when it will all be dusted again."

"Because it's always dusty in this town. Cleaning house is good for you, daughter." Mother came down the porch steps, the corners of her mouth seeming to fight working into a smile. "Hello, Patrick. I'd like a ride into town in a few minutes."

Anna bottled a groan. Typical Mother. No greeting, just get busy and fulfill her needs.

"Now, Eleanor, let's let Patrick get settled first." Father stepped over to Goldie and rubbed her neck. "The horse is a bit jittery from the train ride, and she needs to acclimate to the new stable. Can't your errand wait until tomorrow?"

Mother lifted her chin. "I need to have a fitting on the dress Millie is making before the day is out. I can't trust a small town seamstress like I could Lucy."

Father frowned. "I'm sure a fitting can wait a day. I insist we rest Goldie and let Patrick get settled. Either that or you can walk to town. It's only a few blocks."

He glanced at Patrick. "Go ahead as planned and get settled."

The driver nodded. "Yes, sir. He climbed up to the driver's bench and made a clicking sound, "Giddy up, girl. Time to see our new home."

The horse pulled the carriage down the drive and around the house.

Father crossed to where Mother stood. "Would it be too much to at least give our driver a pleasant greeting, Eleanor?"

Mother turned and walked toward the porch steps. A few moments later, the door banged behind her.

An ache filled Anna's throat. Never had she seen him speak up to Mother like he just did. She wanted to hug Father, comfort him, but held back. No one in their family ever displayed such emotion other than an occasional brief embrace and air kisses.

"Shall we go in?" Father looked at Anna. "Didn't you want to get a carrot for Goldie and bring it to the stable?"

Anna nodded. "Good idea."

"YOU CANNOT MONOPOLIZE Patrick the way you did Charles, even using him after we moved over here." Mother glared at Anna. "Jerusha is very nice, but I do not approve of the casual way she treats her help. Her ways have influenced you girls."

Anna returned Mother's hard stare with one of her own. "Patrick always drove me to the mission school, and this is no different. Tomorrow morning, he'll drop Father off at the train first, and then continue on to the school. He'll be home in time to take Callie to the seminary."

Mother's jaw hardened as she leveled her shoulders. "I received a wire from Hortense Millard earlier. You and I will be going into the city a few days from now to stay with the Millards and plan the wedding. Tell the teacher tomorrow you'll soon be unavailable."

All air left Anna's lungs. How foolish she'd been to think the wedding plans had halted.

"I think a Christmas wedding would be lovely," Mother continued. "I'd hoped for our own church in the city, but with that gone, it's either hold the wedding here or in the Millard's church."

The Millard's church reminded Anna of a cold, stony fortress. Not at all appropriate for a wedding. But on second thought, perfect for a marriage to Lyman Millard. "Maybe the Millards have changed their mind about me marrying Lyman."

Mother's hand flew to her throat and her eyes widened. "You may wish that, daughter, but—"

"I'm sure that's not the case."

Anna faced her father who stood in the entrance to the hall, his jaw muscle pulsing. How much had he heard?

He took a step toward Anna. "The Millards home was spared, but not his offices. Like me, he's pouring everything he can into getting his business running again. He ran into some problems and that's why he called Lyman home to help." He gave Anna a pleading look. "I'm sure over time you'll come to have feelings for Lyman. I can't think of a better man for my daughter to marry."

Anna closed her eyes. *I must stay strong. I must stay strong.* If she stayed in the room another minute she'd be telling him at least a dozen reasons why Lyman is about as suited to be her husband as a snake. Now was not the time. "I'm heading to bed. I'll see you in the morning." She would talk to Father later when they were alone.

# CHAPTER SEVENTEEN

The next morning, Anna and Father climbed into the carriage. Certain she'd not slept one wink all night, Anna's head felt like a vice was squeezing it at each temple. How could she rest when she felt as though she'd she'd lost the ally she had in Father. Now he was heading into the city and the five-minute ride to the depot was not enough time to talk.

Father shifted in his seat and faced her. "I'm sorry, Anna, for the way our conversation ended last night. I realize Lyman lacks personality, but he comes from a fine family." He paused and took in a deep breath. "Marriages aren't always made for love. In our case, your union with Lyman will benefit both families more than you can possibly know. Perhaps in time you'll come to have loving feelings for him."

Her hopes for swaying Father to her side tumbled. She offered him a weak smile. "There are things about Lyman you don't know."

He patted her knee. "We all have our faults. Lord knows I've got a few."

She gripped his arm. "You don't understand. The man is a personification of evil."

He gaped at her. "Surely, that's an exaggeration. I'd expect that out of Calista, but not my Anna. You surprise me. Such talk will not sway me."

Moisture welled in her eyes and she blinked it away. Where did the father go that always had time for her, took up for her when Mother was harsh? The fire had changed him like it did all of them. She'd do most anything to please him, but marrying Lyman was more than she could bear. "I'll pray about it."

"That's my girl." He patted her arm as the carriage rolled into the depot and stopped. "Patrick, don't bother to leave your seat. I'll let myself out." Father opened the carriage door and climbed down. He waved over his shoulder as he trudged to the waiting train. "See you all on Friday."

Anna gave Patrick directions to the school and they started out. As the carriage rolled through the neighborhood on the west side of the village, Anna's thoughts shifted to the mission school. She slid the small window at the front of the compartment open. "Patrick, have you heard about any of the children or people who worked at the mission? Did they all . . . perish?"

The bench creaked as Patrick angled his body toward her. "The mission school is gone as is Illinois Street Church. Reverend Moody is looking for a site to rebuild. Meanwhile, they've located a temporary storefront for services. I'm guessing when you say the people who worked there you mean one lad in particular."

"Yes, Rory, but also Miss Evelyn."

"I only had opportunity to attend the church service once since the fire because I've been staying at the Millard estate. I did see Miss Evelyn there. As for Mr. Rory, I didn't see him. But he lived in Kilgubbin and that neighborhood was spared."

"He was to visit his family in Conley's Patch the day of the fire. Someone told me the Quinn family perished." Anna's throat caught. "I fear he was with them."

A long silence fell between them then Patrick sighed. "That's very sad if it's true. He was a nice young man."

They came to Main Street and as the carriage rounded the corner to head west, Anna pressed her fist against her mouth to suppress a moan. She had to accept that Rory was likely with God. Memories of how her stomach had tingled whenever she saw him flowed into her thoughts. Not one day had gone by when her heart didn't ache for him.

A vision flowed into her mind of Rory alive and helping rebuild the city, then perhaps meeting a beautiful young Irish girl and falling in love. An ache filled her chest. To think him dead was far better than alive and in love with someone else. Yes. She had loved him and still did. And perhaps that would be enough for a lifetime.

"Here we are, Miss Anna."

She snapped out of her reverie and stared at Patrick standing next to the carriage, his hand outstretched. How long had they been sitting there? "I'm sorry, I was thinking about other things."

Patrick chuckled. "There for a minute, I thought I misunderstood your directions."

She accepted his proffered hand, and then reminded him of the time he needed to return.

Anna's shoulders slumped as she plodded toward the school door, her focus fixed on her feet. She had to push Rory from her mind and focus on the children.

"Good morning, Miss Anna." Katie ran up to her. "I have the fancy dress on today." The little girl slipped off her cloth coat and let it drop to the ground as she twirled. "The dress fits just right. Mrs. Fiona only had to shorten it a tiny bit."

Anna smiled. "Is there a special occasion that you are wearing such a pretty dress today?"

Katie nodded. "It's my birthday, and Mrs. Fiona said I could wear it."

Anna picked up the girl's coat and draped it over Katie's shoulders. "Well, happy birthday. I didn't know it was today. I have no present."

The little girl's eyes twinkled and she grasped her skirts. "This be my present." She dissolved in giggles.

Anna laughed. "So it is."

Mrs. Cleary stepped outside. "My goodness what's so funny?"

"I'm wearing Miss Anna's birthday present for me. It's my birthday, Mrs. Cleary." Katie twirled.

Was this the same frightened child from a couple weeks ago? Anna made a mental note to order a warmer dress from Millie for the little girl. She'd call it her Christmas present. If the child were even still around and hadn't already been adopted. She turned toward the shouts from the schoolyard. The boys played a game of tag, while the girls gathered in small groups, giggling and watching the boys. Father may think the prayers she promised him were about marrying Lyman, but in reality she would pray for courage and wisdom to defy his wishes and refuse to marry Lyman.

RORY SAT next to his uncle on the wagon bench as they approached the crest of a hill. His gaze swept the rolling landscape. Off to the right, the blue water of Geneva Lake glistened in the afternoon sun. Straight ahead, on the other side of Geneva, the spire of the new Catholic church poked out from the last of the fall leaves still displaying their gold and orange colors. Lake Michigan held a beauty all its own, but nothing could top this.

His uncle's old mare eased the wagonload of grain down the hill toward town. Uncle Denis waved a hand toward a road cut through the woods. "That leads to Maple Lawn, the big old mansion the Sturgis family moved into a few months ago."

Rory peered through the trees, but with so many around the home, even with most of the leaves gone, the mansion was well hidden. "I've heard of George Sturgis. Is that the same family?"

"A brother. There are several of them. I understand some are stayin' in a rooming house down the way until they can build their own house on the lake. They all got a bunch of *paisti*."

Rory grinned. "Aye. Children are a gift of God. I enjoyed the young ones when I worked at the mission school."

His uncle's eyes twinkled. "There's plenty of available lasses in the Woods. It won't be long before you be marrying one of them." He brought his focus back to the road. "Unless you already have someone special in mind."

Anna's beautiful face popped into his thoughts. He shoved his hand into his pants pocket and wrapped his fingers around her pendant. He'd put it in his pocket several days ago when he left for Wisconsin, and carried it with him ever since, in the hopes of seeing her here. She was someone he couldn't have then or now. If she hadn't perished in the fire, she could be with the soldier in the locket. Uncle was right. He needed to think about starting a family and not live on dreams that went up in smoke the night of the fire.

He released the locket to the bottom of his pocket. "Once I get me a job, I'll be interested in meeting a nice lass. This is a good place to make a home."

His uncle's lips parted into a slight smile. "You'll be starting the Quinn family over again."

By now they were passing the lake, only a couple hundred feet from the road. "Here's the house I mentioned where the Sturgises and another family be staying." Uncle Denis waved toward a white frame house with a wide porch. A pair of young boys chased each other around the yard while a little girl sat on the porch steps playing with a doll.

They moved past a collection of stores toward the mill. Movement flashed in the corner of Rory's eye and he turned as a woman approached the entrance to a seamstress shop and slipped inside. His breath hitched. Was he dreaming? From what little he saw beneath her hat, she had the same color hair and was the same height as Anna.

A memory of his and Anna's conversation about someday meeting up in Geneva popped into his thoughts. Should he ask to be let off? But he couldn't go inside a seamstress shop. Such a place was no-man's territory. He could wait for the woman to step outside.. He rested both elbows on his knees and stared at his boots. On second thought, the woman seemed taller than Anna. He'd been thinking about her too much. That's all it was. Wishful thinking.

# CHAPTER EIGHTEEN

Sunday morning, a bellyache woke Anna early. Her stomach roiled and she reached for the chamber pot.

A few minutes later she lay back down. No church for her today. And if Mother had her way, by next Sunday they'd be attending a different church. She'd allowed for one more Sunday for Anna and Callie to say goodbye to Jerusha since that was the only place they saw her anymore. Now this bilious stomach was going to stop Anna from going.

After a knock, Peggy Finn, their new maid, stepped into the room. "Miss Anna, time to get up—" She stared. "Are you okay?"

Anna pushed herself up against the headboard. "I have an upset stomach. Don't come closer. Please tell my mother I'm sick and to go on to church without me."

The maid made a small curtsy. "Yes, ma'am. Can I bring you anything? Maybe a cup of tea to settle your stomach?" She sniffed the air and headed toward the chamber pot.

Anna waved her away. "I'll take care of that. No sense you catching whatever I have."

Peggy paused for a second as if trying to comprehend a mistress who cared whether or not she was ill. She nodded and whispered, "Yes, ma'am." She turned and started walking toward the door.

Anna lifted herself up on one elbow. "Peggy, wait. I want to ask you something."

The maid turned.

"You live in Irish Woods don't you?"

Peggy nodded.

"Do you happen to know a farmer there with the name of Denis? Or maybe you've met a refugee from the fire the name of Rory Finn. He'd be about my age."

The young woman frowned. "I don't think I know anyone by those names, but I can ask my da tonight if he does."

She let herself drop onto the mattress. "Thanks. Rory worked at the mission school I taught at in the city. He spoke of having an uncle living in Irish Woods. I'm wondering if he escaped the fire."

"I'll ask tonight." The maid shut the door with a soft *click,* and Anna slid under her feather comforter and drifted into slumber with the dream of reuniting with Rory filling her thoughts.

A loud *crack* of wood hitting wood sounded. Anna bolted to an upright position. Mother stood in the middle of the room, her fists on her hips. "What is this about your not going to services? The only reason we're going to Jerusha's church is because you insisted we needed to say goodbye."

"I'm . . . sorry, Mother, but I'm sick."

Mother grabbed the end of the comforter and pulled it off.

Anna curled into a fetal position and clinched her jaw to keep her teeth from chattering. "Please, Mother. I have chills."

"What happened to cause you to fake being sick?

"I'm . . . not faking. Why would I do that?"

"That's what I'd like to know. Get up and get dressed."

Anna's stomach spun and she grabbed the chamber pot.

A moment later she raised her head and stared at her mother. "Believe me now?"

Mother threw the comforter over her. "Since you're not going, we'll be attending First Christian instead." She marched out of the room, taking no care to close the door quietly.

RORY LEAPED off Uncle Denis's wagon and waved at his uncle and aunt. "Thanks for the lift and for understanding why I want to attend the community church."

His uncle nodded. "I'm not sure I do understand, but you're a grown man, and I'm not going to stop ya. We're all the family we both have left. We'll wait here for you after our church is over. I expect yours will last about as long."

Rory winced. "My guess maybe a bit longer. But, I'll come to this corner as quick as possible."

The wagon rolled off and Rory walked at a fast pace up Madison Street. From what he'd been told the other day, he had about a half-mile walk. Faith Community Church sounded similar to Illinois Street. He'd give it a try. He also had another reason for going he hadn't mentioned to anyone—could barely admit to it himself. If the woman he saw the other day was Anna . . . perhaps she'd be there.

Many families approached the white clapboard church on foot, but Rory presumed if Anna were among the congregation, she'd come the way she always traveled—by carriage. He watched as a large landau rolled up and a matronly woman and two younger women waited for the driver to help them down.

"Jerusha." A young woman scurried up and waited for the older woman to climb out of the carriage.

"Good Morning, Emily." The older woman spoke loud enough for Rory to hear. "Did you and Robert have a good trip?"

Rory knew he should move away, not eavesdrop, but maybe one of them would mention the Hartwells.

"Oh, yes," The woman named Emily said. "We came straightaway to Geneva after hearing about that dreadful fire in Chicago. Charley spent a couple days down there, trying to rescue as much as he could of his belongings. Now he and my father-in-law are both in the city, and Eliza is alone. She was feeling under the weather this morning, so we'll only be here for morning services. Will you be home tomorrow? I'd like to stop over for visit and meet your guests."

Jerusha's smile dissolved. "I'm afraid you are too late for that. The family moved into the Thompson's house over on Broad. It all works out for the best." She turned to the younger women who came with her. "Maria and Sarah, we'd better get inside."

The four women walked toward the church's front door and Rory fell into step behind them. Inside, he surveyed the half-empty room. Several women about Anna's age sat in the pews, but not her. His thinking about her so much was affecting him to the point he was imagining seeing her like the other day? Maybe he was pining after a dead woman? A wave of despair washed over him, and he winced. He needed to think about God, not imagine things he had no way of confirming. Besides, more people were arriving. He'd sit in the back and watch.

By the time he trudged down Madison toward Main an hour and a half later, a mix of emotions spun out of control in his gut. Disappointment over not seeing Anna had given over to the joy of hearing a wonderful sermon about God having a plan for his life. But once back outside reality hit him. It was time to put the past behind him and ask God to show him what he was to do next.

Anna's growling stomach woke her. Had the sickness passed so quickly? She leaned across the bed and turned the alarm clock toward her. Almost noon.

Usually if anyone were downstairs, she'd hear voices through the floor, but this morning only the bedroom window's rattling from the wind broke the silence. Knowing Mother, now that she was in a crowd where she felt more comfortable, she was probably still at church socializing.

Anna flung off her covers. Maybe she could sneak downstairs and get some tea before they arrived home. If Mother saw her eating, she'd surely think Anna had fibbed despite having seen her lose the rest of last night's dinner.

*The chamber pot.*

She grabbed the pot by its handle and stared at its shiny clean insides. Peggy must have slipped in and taken care of it while she slept. Maid or not, that was above and beyond her duties. No one should have to deal with someone else's vomit.

Anna took her Bible from the nightstand and flipped through the thin pages, enjoying the familiar crinkly sound they made. She came to the verse she wanted and read.

*Thine eyes did see my substance, yet being unperfect; and in thy book all my members were written, which in continuance were fashioned, when as yet there was none of them.*

When she'd first come across this verse, it had confused her, but her Bible teacher at Illinois Street Church, explained it meant all her days were written in God's book before they'd ever happened. Ever since, she'd clung to that verse, finding comfort in knowing God was with her from before she was born. Nothing surprised Him. Not her mother's animosity toward her or her parents' plans for her to marry Lyman or even the fire. God never promised a life of ease, but He did promise to give strength during suffering.

She closed her eyes and prayed God would help her to help Katie and the other children. She then expressed her confusion as to how marrying an evil man like Lyman would be His will for her. "And if Rory is alive, you will lead me to him if that is your will. If it isn't, please give me the strength to accept you may want me to remain single and to devote my life serving at a school like Irish Woods.

# CHAPTER NINETEEN

Anna had just finished her lunch when Mrs. Cleary approached her. "Anna, can we talk for a moment?"

She glanced at Sarah, who sat with the children at an adjoining table. She'd looked forward to seeing her friend who was there for her volunteer time. Maybe this would only be for a minute or two. "Of course." She closed her lunch pail and waited while Mrs. Cleary drew a chair over to the table and sat.

The older woman gave her a look that someone might use with a child before they delivered bad news. "I think you should know since you've taken so kindly to Katie, I'm not sure how much longer she will be attending our school. Mrs. Devine says they can barely get by with feeding their own family, let alone one more. They're talking about sending the girl to some relatives north of Madison."

A deep pain sliced through her chest. Katie was the only bright spot in her day. One by one she was losing those she cared for the most. How much more did God think she could take?

"Anna? Are you all right?"

She blinked and looked at Mrs. Cleary. "I'm okay. How soon

is this to happen? Maybe I can find someone in town to take her in."

Mrs. Cleary rested a hand on her shoulder. "Here's a word of advice. It's always a good idea to not become too attached to our scholars."

Anna nodded. "I know. But with Katie's circumstances . . ."

The older woman's frown dissolved. "I didn't say I always follow my own advice. There've been several over the years I've favored. And in each case, the child left after a time. We just have to love Katie every day she is here."

"Perhaps my family could take her in until all avenues of finding her real family have been tried." She clamped her mouth shut. The words had flown out of her mouth without thought.

Mrs. Cleary's face lit up. "That's a wonderful idea. If your parents are as kind as you, perhaps they wouldn't mind a sweet child like Katie living with them."

Anna pressed her lips together. What had she done? If Mrs. Cleary spent one minute with Mother, she'd probably wonder if Anna were really the woman's daughter.

She must take back her words, say she spoke without thinking. But, Katie needed a place to live, and Mother wouldn't mistreat a child, even one she considered beneath her. "Maybe I can invite Katie home for the weekend on a trial basis."

Mrs. Cleary's eyes twinkled. "That's an excellent idea. We'll talk to Mrs. Devine when she comes for Katie. Of course, you need to check with your parents first. We'll not mention anything to the child until we know for certain.

After the children returned from lunch, Anna assigned them arithmetic problems. Soon the tapping sounds of chalk on slate assured the scholars were doing fine without her help. Big raindrops splattered against a nearby window. Anna shivered and rubbed her upper arms. What if Mother insisted Katie eat in the kitchen with the help? What if she treated the little girl the same way she treated Anna?

"Miss Anna."

She startled and turned. Joe Dempsey had his hand up.

Anna hurried over to the boy.

He gave her a gap-toothed smile. "I was afraid you couldn't hear, Miss Anna. I had to raise my voice real high."

Heat crept up her neck. "I'm sorry Joe. I was thinking so hard I didn't hear."

She made herself stay with the children until Mrs. Cleary announced it was time to close up for the day. A very long day.

Anna absently helped Katie get her arms into her coat sleeves then turned her around so she could look her in the eyes. "I want to talk to Mrs. Fiona a few minutes when she arrives. Why don't we wait for her inside?"

The little girl looked at her with trust in her eyes. Anna's heart squeezed. The poor child had been through so much. She never should have suggested the weekend visit. With Mother so unpredictable, it was a bad idea.

"Ah, there you be Katie. Teacher said you were in here."

Anna jumped and turned. "Mrs. Devine. I wonder if you and I could speak over there, just the two of us." She indicated the far corner of the room.

Anna led the woman out of Katie's earshot and lowered her voice. "I heard you're in need of finding another home for Katie."

The woman's mouth pulled downward and she nodded. "Aye. It's difficult enough keeping our boys fed, let alone another child. They're growing and need to eat to stay strong to help their da. Our only choice is to send Katie north to my sister and her family." She bit her lip.

"I'd like to bring Katie home with me for this coming weekend and see if she is comfortable there. I have to ask my parents first if it's okay, so please don't mention it to her yet." She paused and looked off, almost afraid to say more. She faced

Mrs. Devine. "If it works out, perhaps she can move in with us temporarily until someone from her family is found."

The woman clasped her hands to her chest. "Oh, Miss Anna, you've done too much for us already. The dresses and extra attention are surely more than we be expecting. But she mustn't be told this is a test to see if she be acceptable."

An ache swelled in Anna's chest. She was in it too deep to turn around now. "I agree. If my parents say it's all right, I'll only tell her it's for a visit. It will be fun getting to know her away from school."

The woman nodded. "Bless you. If your family says it's fine, I will bring a bag with her clothes on Friday morning."

Anna worked to return the woman's smile. If only she could take the girl to Jerusha's and let those women lavish their affections on the child. Was it too late to approach Jerusha?

Mrs. Devine glanced at the table where Katie waited then back at Anna. "You are a blessing to this child. I hope this works out."

*I hope so too.* "Pray that it does." Anna doubted if she'd sleep much that night for the prayers she'd be uttering.

"IT'S ENOUGH you insist on being with those ragamuffins all day long. Now you want to bring one home for Saturday and Sunday?" Mother stared at Anna as if she'd asked if she could bring home a notorious criminal.

"I know it may be an imposition, but the child is an orphan, and the family she's staying with can't afford to feed her much longer. Remember, she's a refugee from the fire, same as us."

Mother's brows rose. "So that's it. If you think you're going to fool me into thinking it's only for two days and then the child never leaves, you're mistaken, Anna Hartwell." She turned toward the stairs. "This conversation is finished."

"Think of how the people around town will see you for doing this. You've heard the nice things people say about Jerusha for her benevolence."

"Then ask Jerusha to take the girl in."

"Don't you want people to think the same of you?"

Mother took a step toward the stairs.

"If it were me, I'd rather have people saying nice things about me than thinking I'm haughty and unkind."

Her mother faced her. "Is that what people say about me?"

"You know how some are. They judge people without taking the time to know them."

She prayed Mother wouldn't ask for details. If so, could she lie this once for Katie's sake?

Mother drew in a long breath and exhaled. "All right, bring the girl home. But she goes back on Monday." She climbed to the landing and turned. "The orphan can have the small bedroom next to yours. She's your responsibility. You'll have to make sure she is clean and fed. Don't expect me, Calista, or Peggy to take care of her."

"Yes, ma'am." Anna turned away and swallowed her hurt. If someone overheard Mother, they'd think she were telling a child she could have a pet dog.

She took the stairs to her room, praying the whole way. She reached the hall and headed for her bedroom door.

Peggy, stood next to her door as she approached. "Hi, Peggy. I don't have need of your services right now. I'm going to lay down for a while."

The girl looked at her feet. "I didn't get a chance to speak with you this morning before you left. I asked my da last night if he knew of any farmer in Irish Woods named Denis. He did not nor has he heard of a man named Rory Quinn, but he's going to ask around."

Anna smiled her thanks. "Peggy, thank you so much. I know

it's likely wishful thinking that I'll find them. I appreciate yours and your Da's efforts.

A few minutes later she lay on her bed and closed her eyes. "Lord if I never find Rory I'll accept that as your will. More important is finding a good home for Katie, even if it means the family in Madison taking her in.

# CHAPTER TWENTY

Friday afternoon, Anna led Katie by the hand to the waiting carriage.

"Are we going in that fancy wagon, Miss Anna?"

Was the carriage fancy? Father always made a point of never buying top-of-the-line to not appear ostentatious. But, compared to the wagons the children came to school in, the carriage was fancy. "Yes, that's how I come to school."

Anna introduced Katie to Patrick, and the child grinned. "Hi, Mr. Patrick. I'm going to Miss Anna's house."

Patrick's eyes twinkled. "So you are, lassie." He bowed deep. "May I assist you into your seat?"

Katie giggled. "I feel like Cinderella."

"Then we should pretend we're riding in a pumpkin." Anna laughed as she settled next to Katie.

*Please, Lord, let Mother be in a good mood.*

When they arrived at home, Patrick halted the carriage in the drive. Her face hidden in shadow from the trees across the road, Mother's board-straight form came down from the porch, each boot heel hitting the steps with a solid *thump*. As she came closer, Anna's mouth fell open. She hadn't seen her mother smile like that since Richard died.

Patrick assisted Katie out of the carriage and Mother bent to look the child in the eye. "You must be Katie. I'm Anna's mother, Mrs. Hartwell. But that's quite a mouthful. Why don't you call me Miss Eleanor?"

Katie looked back at Anna as if seeking assurance.

Anna nodded.

"Thank you, Mrs. . . . Miss Eleanor." Katie ran her gaze over all three stories of the house. She pointed to the third-floor balcony. "Do you live way up there?"

Anna laughed as she stepped down from the carriage. "We live in the whole house. My room is on the second floor. You'll sleep in a room next to me."

The little girl's face brightened. "I like being next to you."

Patrick held up Katie's satchel. "Where should I take this, Mrs. Hartwell?"

"Anna can show the way." Mother offered him a soft smile. "Thank you, Patrick"

She turned and started for the house while Patrick looked at Anna and winked.

She took Katie's hand. If she'd known this was how Mother acted around little children, she would have brought a student home months ago. "Follow us, Patrick."

They stepped inside the house, and Katie's blue eyes grew as big as the buttons on her coat. She glanced into the parlor to her right and then left into the library. "Pretty."

To Anna, the furnished rooms appeared a hodgepodge of high backed chairs and settees—left by the owners when they moved—designed more for show than comfort. Yet to a child who literally had nothing but her little life, it must seem like a palace.

At the top of the stairs they walked down the center hall.

Katie pointed to a closed door. "Where is the family who lives there?"

Anna's heart squeezed. The only structures of this size Katie had seen were apartment buildings. "Only one family at a time lives in a house like this, and we're the family." They stopped in front of a door. "This is your room for the next three nights." She opened the door and stepped in to flick a gas lamp to life.

Katie ran for the bed and smoothed her hand over the pink quilt. "I'm to sleep here?"

Anna chuckled at the squeal in the child's voice. "Yes, and I'll be sleeping on the other side of the wall in my bed."

Katie scrunched her nose. "Where is the little girl who lives here?"

"What little girl?"

"The one whose doll this is." She picked up a rag doll that sat perched on top of the small pillow. "And wears those pretty dresses."

Anna followed the child's gaze to a pair of small dresses hanging in the open armoire. Millie must have had them delivered during the day.

"I'll be going, Miss Anna, if you don't need anything else." Patrick stood in the doorway, the child's small valise still held in his fist.

"Sorry, Patrick. I forgot you were there. Please, set the bag inside, and that's all we need."

She sat on the bed, then lifted Katie onto her lap. "This room was fixed up just for you. No other little girl lives here. The nice lady who made the other dresses I gave you made those for you."

Katie twisted and looked up at Anna. "I met your ma, but where is your da?"

"He's on the train that should be arriving at the depot in about a half an hour. You'll meet him soon."

The child's eyes widened. "He takes a train to work?"

She smoothed out Katie's skirt. "He works in Chicago and takes the train there on Mondays then returns on Fridays."

"Is the city back together again?"

She removed Katie's bonnet and ran her hand down one of the girl's braids. "Not yet. But many men are working to build new buildings and stores. Soon we'll have a brand new city."

"Then will my ma and da be back too?"

Her heart sunk. They'd already discussed several times how her family was in heaven, and she'd hoped the child finally understood. "No, honey. Only buildings can be rebuilt. When people go to heaven they stay there with God."

"Oh." Katie wiggled off Anna's lap and scampered to the open armoire. She took the hem of a periwinkle blue school dress between her thumb and forefinger. "They're so pretty. Do I have to give them back when I leave on Monday?"

She wished she had time to compose an answer that was assuring and positive. The child was so unassuming. "They are yours to take back to the Divines'. Isn't that wonderful?"

Katie lovingly ran her palm over the skirt of the dress she'd been looking at. "Yes, Miss Anna. Very wonderful."

How long would Katie be living with the Devines? There must be a perfect family in Irish Woods for her.

She'd adopt her if she could. Thoughts whirled in her head so fast she couldn't catch even one to toss aside. Why couldn't a single woman adopt an indigent child who had no apparent relatives? She could afford to care for her if she found a paying teaching job. Wouldn't one stable parent be better than having none at all?

Her heart was going to burst if she didn't calm herself. She glanced at Katie, playing quietly on the floor with the doll and yearned to shower her with a mother's love. Who knew better than she what kind of love a child needed. After all, she'd grown up not having any.

The next morning, Anna woke early and stretched. How could she feel so rested when she must have been awake half the night? Every time she closed her eyes a vision erupted of Katie and her living in a small house in Geneva. Was that God's plan for her? If so, a lot had to fall into place to make it happen.

She climbed out of bed, then went to the window and pushed the curtain back. Bright sunlight splashed over the backyard. Patrick came from around the carriage house carrying a water bucket for Goldie. Already, the pale blue sky gave promise of turning to a deeper hue of blue.

A soft knock sounded. Anna grabbed her dressing gown and slipped it on. "Who's there?"

"It's Katie."

Grinning, Anna padded across the patterned rug. She drew the door open a crack and peeked through. "Who's Katie?"

The child giggled. "Me."

"Me who?"

"Katie Hanrahan."

Anna swung the door open. "Good morning, Katie Hanrahan." She drew the little girl inside and Katie wrapped her arms around Anna's legs. "Good morning, Miss Anna."

"Did you sleep okay?"

"Yes, ma'am. The bed is soft. I like it."

Anna remembered the hard thing she saw Katie sleeping on at the Devines' and winced. She didn't blame the family. What else could they give a child that had been thrust upon them without warning? *All the more reason to explore adoption.*

Anna led Katie to the bed and lifted her onto the feather mattress. She crawled in next to her and tugged the girl close until they were cuddled against the pillows. "I thought later we can go over to the schoolhouse and you can play on the swings. Maybe some other children will be there."

Katie's eyes widened. "We're going back to my school? That's a long ride."

Anna laughed. "Not that school. There's one in town for the children who live here. But first we need to eat breakfast. Are you ready to get dressed?"

Katie stretched her arm across Anna and snuggled closer. "Ma and me used to cuddle in bed like this before church on Sundays."

Anna ran a hand over Katie's head. Never in her life had she ever snuggled with Mother like this. If the little girl wanted to stay that way for the whole morning, it was fine with her. She pressed a kiss to the top of the child's head.

Katie turned and looked up and wiped a tear from Anna's cheek. "Why are you sad, Miss Anna?"

She pulled her closer. "I'm not sad. I'm crying because I feel happy you are here this morning."

"Miss Anna, who sleeps in the other bed over there?"

She glanced at Callie's empty bed. "My sister, Callie. She's sleeping in a guest room this weekend to give us some privacy. You met her last night at dinner."

"What's privacy?"

She chuckled. "You ask way too many questions, young lady. Let's get dressed."

As Anna and Katie were finishing their breakfast of oatmeal and eggs, Callie wandered into the dining room wearing one of the new day dresses Millie had made. "Did you two get up with the birds?"

Anna laughed. "Almost. We're going to walk to the schoolyard. Do you want to come with us?"

Callie rubbed her arms. "In this cold? I'm meeting one of the girls from the seminary for lunch at the Lakehouse. That will be soon enough to get outside."

Anna sipped her tea and set the flowered cup on its saucer. "It sounds like you're making some friends."

Callie sighed. "They're all younger. But knowing them is helping me bide the time until my debut."

Anna stared at her sister. Every time Callie did or said something that showed she was maturing, she did or said something else to show she hadn't changed much at all. "How many times do you have to be told. Everything is burned to the ground. There will be no debut this year."

Callie squared her shoulders. "Since Mother and Father are so intent on you getting married, I'm sure they can arrange a debut for me. If I keep thinking it will happen it has to happen one way or another."

Anna glanced at Katie. Her face gave no hint that she understood Callie's words. She stared at her sister. "I'd thank you to not talk about the arrangement right now. Besides it's never going to happen."

Her sister shrugged. "I didn't say it would happen. I only meant they planned it."

"Planned what?" Father stepped into the room.

"Callie's debut." Anna blurted out her words before her sister could mention the wedding.

Father's attention went to his youngest daughter. "Calista, I thought you understood anything as frivolous as a debut will have to be put off until the city is rebuilt. Surely you won't mind waiting a year."

Callie's face crumpled. "Not all of the city was burned."

His eyes filled with regret. "There may well be a few decent locations, but with most families scattered hither and yon, and all the focus on rebuilding, it's simply not an appropriate time. Consider how it would look to those who have lost everything and have no means of rebuilding."

Callie pulled a pout, but she didn't protest. "I'm so bored, Father. If I paint another flower on a piece of china I think I'll pass out."

Anna couldn't help but laugh. "We could use extra help at Irish Woods School. Why don't you volunteer there? If you gave two days a week, it would be a huge help."

Callie crossed her arms. "I'll think about it."

Anna looked at her father and shrugged. "Katie and I are going to the school playground. If you have time later today, I want to talk to you about something."

# CHAPTER TWENTY-ONE

Saturday morning, Rory pulled Uncle Denis's wagon out of the gristmill and headed toward Main Street. His uncle had suggested he take his time coming back after the delivery and get to know the town.

On either side of Main Street, women hustled from store to store, some holding little ones by the hand and carrying a shopping basket over their other arm. He made a point of studying each one's face, especially those who were alone, but none resembled Anna. A lump filled his throat. He had to think about other things.

He guided the wagon through the main intersection, then pulled to a stop on the side of the road. Across the way and through some trees, Geneva Lake glistened in the bright sunlight. Off to the right, Maple Lawn Estate held court over the bay. Soon other swanky homes would go up and the new estates would need caretakers. He'd worked as assistant gardener for an estate on Lake Michigan a few years ago and loved it. He'd have to find out how to apply before others grabbed up all the jobs.

He gathered the reins and clicked his tongue. The horse got

the wagon moving and at the next corner they headed north up Madison Street away from the lake. Ahead, the village school came into view. A small redheaded girl, her back to him, swung on a swing while her mother pushed. Memories of his sister and her daughter flooded his thoughts. He palmed a tear from his face and turned the wagon around. Uncle Denis had mentioned a couple young women in the Woods that might catch his eye. The church he attended last Sunday would also be a good place to meet someone. He'd already promised his uncle and aunt that he'd attend their church tomorrow. He'd love to eventually take them to the other church, but he'd approach that idea with care. After what happened with Da, he'd not be so bold again. In time he'd surely meet someone as nice as Anna.

SUNDAY MORNING, Anna roused Katie early. Mother had surprised her by agreeing to attend Jerusha's church with Anna and Katie, and it would take awhile to get them both ready. Ever since Friday evening Mother had been like a different woman. Would she be the same today?

Two hours later, the family's carriage rolled up in front of the church at the same time as Jerusha's landau. Anna waved. "Katie, there's Miss Sarah."

Katie bounced on the seat. "I didn't know I'd see her here."

As soon as Patrick set Katie on the ground, she skipped over to the three women. "Miss Sarah, I'm staying at Miss Anna's house. I'm sleeping in a pink room."

Sarah's eyes widened, and she sent Anna a questioning expression. Anna sidled up to her and whispered. "Taking care of Katie is becoming too much for the Devines. I brought her home with me for a few days."

Sarah raised an eyebrow. "That's lovely, but I hope having

experienced your house won't make it more difficult for her to adjust back to the Devines' home."

Anna swallowed hard. Why hadn't she thought of that? "I'm hoping she can come home with me again next weekend. Maybe if she has weekly visits, it will help ease the disappointment." Anna lowered her voice. "I'm going to look into how I can adopt Katie myself."

Sarah pulled back and stared at Anna. "As an unmarried woman? How? What about the arranged marriage plans?"

"I've refused to marry him. I don't love him, and he's not a nice man. Jerusha took *you* in and raised you after your parents died."

"Dr. Maxwell was off at war, and I was already living in the house at the time. Jerusha was made my legal guardian. She never adopted me. Maybe you could do something similar."

Anna wanted to hug her friend. "Sarah, thank you. I never thought about that. Meanwhile, I need to find something fun for Katie before next Saturday."

"That's the day for the annual fall festival. It's held off Main Street next to the lake."

Anna grabbed Sarah's hand. "That sounds perfect. What happens there?"

"The farmers bring in their harvest of pumpkins, apples, and other produce and ladies make pies and breads. We have a big bon fire, and this year they're having a big tug-of-war contest between the men of Geneva and the men of Irish Woods." Sarah grinned. "I'm looking forward to that."

"Girls, stop your idle chatter. We need to get inside."

Anna hadn't missed Katie's startled expression at Mother's harsh command, nor judging by their faces, had the others standing nearby. Asking for three days of good attitude was too much to ask. She'd have to clear the plans for next Saturday soon. With Mother back to normal, the question was when should she bring it up?

"I SAID you could have the child here once. I never said she could come every week." Mother raised her chin and marched toward the stairs. "I'm retiring for the night, and you should too." Katie had been in bed an hour, and Anna hoped her mother's snippy tone hadn't echoed up the staircase and awakened the child.

"Has she been an imposition?"

Her mother faced her, the rigid expression that had been missing the past two days was back. "That's not the point."

"But has she?"

"Not in a direct sense, but it's uncomfortable. She has the other family, Anna. Let her stay there." Mother reached the stairs and placed a foot on the bottom step.

"That's only a temporary home for her. They can't afford to feed her and their sons. Katie sleeps on a hard cot. Can't you at least provide a place for her until an adoptive family can be found?"

"We're not adopting her." Mother climbed the rest of the stairs, her skirts swishing.

Anna scrambled behind her. Mother stopped and Anna nearly ran into her.

Katie sat at the top of the stairs in her nightgown, tears glistening in her eyes.

Anna's stomach knotted. If only they'd held the conversation in a closed room. She scooted around Mother and took Katie into her arms. "Oh, honey, it's not what you think."

The little girl sniffed. "I don't want to go back to the Devines'. I want to stay here with you, Miss Anna."

"I know." She looked up at Mother who stared down at them.

The corner of Mother's upper lip twitched. "Oh, let her

come. I can't say no, after seeing that face." She stomped the rest of the way up the stairs.

"Thank you, Jesus." Anna nuzzled the top of Katie's head. "You will have to stay at the Devines' for the week, but next Friday you'll come here again and we're going to the Fall Festival on Saturday."

"Promise?"

"Yes. I promise." Lord help her if an unavoidable circumstance makes her a liar.

# CHAPTER TWENTY-TWO

Friday afternoon, Anna arrived home with Katie in tow. Katie chattered the whole way about the tug-of-war set for tomorrow. The Devine boys were to compete for the Irish Woods side and Katie planned to root for them.

At the house, Anna opened the door for Katie and followed her into the foyer.

"Well, there are the girls I've been waiting for. It's about time you got home." Father entered from the parlor and squatted to his haunches to look Katie in the eyes. "I'm glad to see you again, Katie. Are you going to root for me at the tug-of-war tomorrow?"

The girl giggled. "Can I root for both sides?"

Father tipped his head back and guffawed. "Of course, you probably know some on the other team. You root for whomever you want." Using his knee for support, he stood and looked at Anna. "The village president invited me to be on the village tug-of-war team. I'm not sure what the others can expect out of an old guy like me, but I said I'd be glad to try. If the village president can take a pull at the rope, why not me?"

Anna laughed. "I wondered what that was about. The age range goes up to fifty and you're not that old yet."

"True, but with each year I am getting closer." He ran his palms over his amble stomach. And there's a bit more of me than twenty-five years ago."

She sniffed the air. "Peggy must be baking."

"Your mother asked her to make a couple of apple pies for tomorrow. I doubt Peggy's had time to fix anything for dinner."

"Pie would suit me." Anna smiled at Katie. "Shall we take your things upstairs and get you out of your school dress?"

At dinner, which turned out to be corn chowder, freshly baked bread, and one of Peggy's pies for dessert, Father expressed hope the family would be at the tug-of-war to cheer him on. He winked at Katie. "Except for Katie who has her own favorites to root for."

"I'll be busy helping at the bake goods tent." Mother picked up a sugar cube with a pair of silver tongs. "I'm not interested in watching men behaving like boys in such a dishonoring way." She dropped the sugar into her tea and stirred it in.

There went any hope of her nice side making a repeat appearance. Until then, Mother had been rather quiet and Anna had held out hope she'd stay that way.

Father's smile dissolved. "If it is so ignoble then why is the village president participating?"

Mother stared at her plate. "What would one expect in such a place?"

"I'll be there, Father." Callie scraped the remains of her dessert onto her fork. "I'm meeting my friends from the seminary. Before the competition we're going to help at the ladies tea tent." She gave Mother a pointed stare. "Maybe that will be refined enough for you, Mother. We'll be using the china we've painted."

Father's smile returned. "I'm glad to see you making friends and getting involved here, Calista."

She shrugged. "It's better than being bored. Soon things will be different. I've not given up hope the the debutante ball will happen."

Father stared at Callie as if she'd suddenly sprouted wings. "As you've been told before, Calista. This year's balls have been canceled. All energy is being poured into getting the city rebuilt. Hopefully by next ye—"

"Then my life may as well be over." Callie pushed her chair back and scurried out of the room. Her sobs faded as she mounted the stairs. A door slammed.

Father shook his head. "I really thought her coming out this year would be the furthest thing from her mind."

"Perhaps if you'd been home more, you'd know better," Mother said. "She's talked of nothing but ball gowns and debutante events. Then insisted, against my wishes, on ordering a new gown from the dressmaker. I wouldn't have allowed it except that she will be able to wear it eventually."

Father pushed the remains of his pie away. "I'm home as much as I can be, Eleanor. I have to make money to spend on those gowns, and the sooner I can get the business back up and running, the sooner I can start earning again."

His sloping shoulders gripped Anna's heart. The least they could do was to cheer him on tomorrow afternoon. "Remember, Katie and I will be at the tug-of-war, Father."

He reached over and tweaked the little girl's cheek. "That makes me feel a lot better."

Anna's face heated as her breaths came faster. When she was small, Father used to tweak her cheek the same way, especially after times Mother had been harsh with her. She looked away and gathered herself. She had no business being jealous of a needy little girl whose own father had perished.

Father and Mother wordlessly stood and went their separate ways—Father to his study and Mother to their bedroom suite. After Mother's footfalls sounded from overhead, Anna took

Katie's hand and led her toward the stairs. All of them, Callie included, were like a disconnected group of ghosts walking around in this beautiful house.

Inside Katie's room, Anna sat on the bed and took the child on her lap to unfasten her shoes.

"Miss Anna, can I ask you something?"

"Of course."

"Why do we need to go to bed early when the festival doesn't start until lunchtime?"

Anna chuckled. Katie was smarter than they gave her credit. She removed Katie's shoe and let it drop to the floor. "We need to be well rested for our busy day. The event isn't over until after the bon fire, which happens after sunset."

"I'm not sleepy. I don't know if I'll fall asleep so fast."

"I'll tell you a story after you're tucked in and that should help."

THE NEXT MORNING, a soft knock drew Anna out of her sleep. A quick peek at the darkened window told her it wasn't yet time to get up. Was something wrong?

Without grabbing her robe, Anna padded across the cold wood planks and opened the door a crack.

Katie clutched the rag doll in one hand and had the thumb of her other hand poked into her mouth.

Anna hunched down. "Katie, are you okay?" She felt the child's forehead. "You don't have a fever."

"I woke up and didn't want to fall back to sleep and miss the festival."

"It's too early to be up. Come lay next to me in my bed. Maybe you can fall asleep again."

She got the child settled under the comforter and then slid in next to her and pulled her close until they spooned together.

Soon, Katie's even breaths indicated that the child was asleep. Now it was she who was wide awake. There had to be a lawyer in town willing to help with guardianship. But first, she'd have to find a teaching job that paid. After she broke the engagement, she doubted Father would continue to give her an allowance.

Katie's breathing transitioned into a soft snore and Anna pulled the child closer. Never had she experienced such a precious time.

*Lord, is it wrong to pray that no family of Katie's is found? I know it's selfish. Please forgive me for even thinking that way. Let your will be done.*

# CHAPTER TWENTY-THREE

The next morning, Anna kept Katie occupied gathering the eating utensils and napkins, which Anna packed into a large basket along with a set of utilitarian white plates. The child couldn't stop asking questions about the festival.

"What if it rains?"

"What if it's too cold?"

"Will Mrs. Cleary be there?"

No one was happier than Anna when time came to leave for the event. She was fresh out of answers, although the child hadn't run out of questions.

Seeing the lake, Katie bounced on the seat cushion as Patrick turned onto Lake Street, which ran along the water's edge.

As they approached a clearing, several tents came into view. People carrying picnic baskets and sporting equipment seemed to be coming from all directions. Anna laughed and nudged her sister's arm. "Don't you just love being a part of a community like this?"

Callie shrugged. "We have our ways and they have theirs."

"These ways are much better. I hope we never have to leave."

Callie snickered. "Don't let our mother hear you say that. Looks like this is where we get off."

Patrick had stopped the carriage and was making his way around to the door to help them out.

Once everyone was out of the carriage, Mother picked up the large pie basket. "I'll take these to the dessert tent and meet the rest of you. Where will you be, Leonard?"

"I'm not sure until we get there. Why don't you come with us, then I'll be happy to drop the pies off?" He picked up a second basket that contained their lunch and led the way between the trees toward an open area. Already, many people had claimed their spots with an array of colorful quilts and blankets. He surveyed the scene. "I see a place over there. Follow me."

By the time Father returned from delivering the pies, the family's picnic had been spread out on a large blue blanket. Father said grace and they filled the plates.

Between bites of chicken and baked beans, Anna scanned the crowd. She'd been so busy with Katie, she forgot to ask the servants since Father had given them the afternoon off if they planned to attend the festival. She supposed they were with their friends from Irish Woods. Maybe she'd see them at the tug-of-war.

"Hello, Hartwells. It's so nice you are all here for our festival." Jerusha stood a few feet away, hugging a dark green blanket to her chest. She glanced at the woman with her. "I'd like to introduce Eliza Baker. Her husband Charles is our justice of the peace and also has a law practice."

Mrs. Baker nodded at all of them, then let her gaze linger on Mother. "Mrs. Hartwell, I have seen you at church and wanted to invite you to join us this coming Wednesday when we plan to collect goods to send to the fire sufferers in Peshtigo. We ladies pack the boxes, and then have lunch afterwards."

Mother raised her chin. "I prefer to do charity work for the displaced people in Chicago. Surely our disaster was far greater than the other one."

The lines on Mrs. Baker's forehead deepened into a scowl. "The town may have been smaller, but nearly all of it was destroyed. No one hears of the Peshtigo fire, and Chicago has plenty of volunteers and collections going on. We have to think of the others as well. Do consider joining us."

Jerusha gave Katie a curious look. "Anna, isn't this the girl I saw with you last Sunday at church?" She smiled at Katie. "Hello, dear, I hope you are enjoying the day so far."

Impressed at the deft way Jerusha redirected the conversation, Anna stood and helped Katie to her feet. "This is Katie Hanrahan, a scholar at Irish Woods School."

Katie stared up at the grandmotherly ladies. "My Ma and Da died in the fire."

Jerusha's face fell. "Oh dear, my child, I'm very sorry to hear that. Are you staying with relatives?"

Katie shook her head. "All my family burned. I'm staying with a bunch of boys and today I'm staying with Miss Anna."

Anna laughed. "She is temporarily staying with a family who has two teenaged sons." She locked gazes with Jerusha, hoped her facial expression was one the woman would recognize as a call for help.

"Anna, why don't you call tomorrow after church and bring Katie with you? I'm sure Sarah would like to see her since she helps at the school. We're on our way to the tug-of-war events. Eliza's husband is participating in the first contest."

Father pulled out his timepiece and checked it. "I didn't realize it was so late. I'm in the first heat too. Since you and Katie are my cheering squad, can you hold this for me?" He handed his jacket to Anna and rolled up his sleeves.

Anna laid the jacket over her arm. She quickly discussed cleanup arrangements with Callie, and then held out her hand to Katie and they headed toward the grassy area near the ice company land. She spotted Jerusha and Mrs. Baker and moved in their direction.

Jerusha waved as they approached. "There's room for two more on our blanket. Join us."

Across the field, men had gathered in two groups. Anna laughed as she took a seat on the blanket. "It's easy to see who the Irish Woods men are and who are the village men."

"Yes," Jerusha said. "I think our men will have a hard time against all those muscles."

Anna spotted her father and waved. He sent her a wide smile then spoke to one of the men. She respected her father for doing something he'd probably never done in his life. Mingle with people of a status lower than him. Another reason to like this town and its people.

The village men won the first match of best out of three. The second match teeter-tottered back and forth with Father's group taking an early lead. Then the Irish Woods men gathered their strength and pulled the rope until it slid through the hands of the village men and the match was over.

After a five-minute break, the teams gathered again for the deciding match.

"I think the village men are going to do it." Jerusha pushed to her feet and shouted encouragement. The Geneva men had pulled the Woods team almost over the designated line when the Woods team started to count and on "three," they pulled hard and dragged the village team over the line. Whoops and shouts came from the crowd on the other side of the grass.

Father approached the blanket and wiped his brow with his handkerchief. "We gave those guys a good fight." He studied his palms. "Got a couple rope burns, but it was fun, even if we lost." He flicked some grass off his trousers. "Your mother won't be pleased with my dirty pants."

"You were wonderful, Father." Anna handed him his coat.

"Maybe the younger village team will beat the Woods men. Are you going to stay and watch?"

"Wouldn't miss it."

A tall dark-haired man joined them, and Mrs. Baker introduced her husband. He and Father stood off to the side of the blanket and chatted. From what Anna overheard, Mr. Baker was one of the first residents in Geneva and had an interesting background. She was pleased to see Father getting involved. If only her mother would do the same.

Katie scrambled to her feet. "I see the boys I live with. I want to cheer for them."

"Then you should, little one." Jerusha patted a spot next to her. "Why don't you sit here so you can see better?"

Katie crawled across the blanket and sat next to Jerusha.

"Here comes Miss Fiona." Katie pointed toward the field.

Anna turned as Fiona Devine approached. "Hi Katie. She nodded at Anna. "I wondered if I'd see you here."

Anna stood. "We just watched my father's team lose, but they gave your men a fight."

She introduced Fiona to Father.

"Thank you so much for welcoming Katie these past two weekends." Fiona said. "It's all she's talked about during the week."

Father let out a hearty chuckle. "We enjoy having her. It's been a while since our daughters were small. I'd forgotten what a delight little girls are. So, you think your boys are going to beat the town boys?"

Fiona laughed. "Probably."

"Why don't you join us? We're staying to watch." Anna indicated the blanket. "There's plenty of room."

"Yes, please join us." Jerusha scooted over and pulled Katie onto her lap.

Fiona flushed, but sat beside Jerusha and tucked her gray

skirt around her legs. "Thank you ma'am. I've been standing ever since I arrived. It feels good to sit."

The men from both teams trotted toward their respective ends of the rope that lay across the grass.

At the announcer's shout, they picked up the rope and gripped it. None of the village men appeared as muscular as the Irish Woods team.

The announcer's voice cut into Anna's thoughts. "We've got a last minute substitution for Dylan O'Brien. The new man is coming on the field now."

"It's him!" Katie flew to her feet and ran onto the grass shouting something indecipherable. Anna started after her. She had to get the child off the field. Her petticoats tangled with her legs and she landed face down on the grass.

Katie shouted again, and this time there wasn't any mistaking her words.

"Uncle Rory!"

# CHAPTER TWENTY-FOUR

*ory?*

Her Rory? Anna scrambled to her knees and moved to stand, but her right foot had planted itself on her skirt. She wobbled back and Rory caught her by the arm. His strong grip tight, he pulled her upwards. In a moment she was on her feet, staring into a face she thought she'd never see again this side of heaven. "Rory, it's you. It's really you."

"Anna. It is me. I can't believe it's you." He started to pull her into an embrace.

"Uncle Rory, It's me. Katie." The little girl squeezed between them, her arms outstretched.

"Katie. My niece. My precious *neacht*." He scooped up the child and whirled her around.

Anna's thoughts spun out of control. Katie was Rory's niece? She swatted at the tears running down her cheeks and pressed her palm to her chest, willing her breaths to slow.

"I thought you were dead, lassie." Rory leaned back and stared into Katie's face, then pressed her against his chest and peered over his niece's head at Anna. Their gazes met and held.

"Both of you." He returned his focus to Katie. "If you're alive . . . your ma? Your da?"

"Their all gone, Rory," Anna said. "Katie is the only survivor. I had no idea she was your niece."

Rory set Katie on the grass and faced Anna. He ran his gaze over her. "It's really you, Anna." He reached over and wiped a tear off her cheek with his thumb, setting off the familiar flutters in her stomach. "I asked around your neighborhood, but no one knew about you or your family, and I convinced meself you were gone too."

Anna palmed away the tears still trailing down her cheek. "We took the train here the Tuesday after the fire. We're renting a house in Geneva since ours in the city is leveled. I . . . I thought *you* were dead too."

"How do you happen to be with Katie?" Rory hunched down and stared at his niece. "I can't believe I'm lookin' at you." He wrapped his arms around the child. "Praise be to God, you're alive."

"I've been helping at the Irish Woods school. She's temporarily staying with a family there and I brought her with me for the weekend."

"Rory, what's goin' on? They want to start the match." A man hurried up, his weathered face full of concern. "Uncle Denis." Rory stood. "This is Katie, Maureen's child. She didn't die in the fire." He glanced at Anna and grinned. "And this is Anna Hartwell. She is—was—a teacher at the mission school. I thought she died too."

Rory's uncle squatted and placed his hands on Katie's shoulders. "Praise be to God. I've seen you about with Mrs. Devine, but had no idea this child be my brother's granddaughter. I haven't seen you since you were a baby."

A man standing nearby shouted to the gathering crowd, "Rory Quinn found family he thought died in the fire."

Shouts of joy and applause broke out, and a man shouted, "Rory, you don't have to pull the rope. Go enjoy your reunion."

Rory laughed. "Thanks, but I still want to pull. I feel like I can beat anyone now." He looked at Anna and grinned. "I have so many questions, but I have to pull the rope first."

She returned his smile. "We're sitting over there. We'll wait." She indicated the blanket.

"Mind if I come with you?" Rory's uncle ran a hand over Katie's head. "Now that we've found our niece, I want to stay with her."

"Yes. Please join us."

Anna startled and faced her father. "Mr. Quinn, this is my father, Leonard Hartwell."

The men shook hands and they all walked to the blanket.

"Miss Anna, I didn't know you knew Uncle Rory. Why didn't you tell me?"

Anna playfully tugged at one of Katie's braids. "I didn't know Rory *was* your uncle, and I thought he had died in the fire."

"How do you know him?"

"I'd like to know that too," Father said. "You haven't stopped beaming for the past ten minutes."

Anna felt her face heat. Her father understood. He always had. "Rory worked at the mission school as a janitor and handyman. We've become good friends over the past year. The fire started in his parents' neighborhood and he planned to visit them that Sunday. I was sure he perished. I'd been told all the Quinns had . . . died."

Father sat next to Anna on the blanket. "The fire began quite late that day. Would he have still been there?"

"Probably not, but when no one heard anything about him, I thought he may have decided to stay at their place that night. He lived in Kilgubbin."

A knowing look crossed Father's face. "That's why the concern about that neighborhood the night of the fire. And now it's turned out he and Katie both escaped the fire and became separated from the others."

"Uncle Rory wasn't with us when the fire started." Katie looked from Anna to Father. "He came earlier, but Grand Da wouldn't let him inside. I asked why, but Ma told me not to ask so many questions."

Anna hugged Katie. "Sometimes it's best not to."

A whistle split the air. "Ladies and Gentlemen, we have witnessed the wonderful reunion of Rory Quinn and his niece, and Rory still wants to pull the rope." The announcer looked back at the lines of men. "Let's get this match underway."

The first round lasted less than a minute, the town men being no match for the Irish Woods men. Father chuckled. "Denis, I think the news of your nephew finding his niece has given your team extra strength."

"I think you're right," Mr. Quinn puffed his chest. "I feel right now like I could defeat those young men single handed." He tweaked Katie's cheek. "To know we still have Katie is an incredible feeling."

The second round went only a little longer than the first, and the Irish Woods men were declared winners.

Rory trotted over to the group and picked up Katie. She wrapped her small arms around his neck and held onto him as though he'd disappear if she didn't. "What a wonderful day this has turned out to be." He looked at his uncle. "Will Katie be able to live at your house with me until I find us a home?" He put Katie down and sat on the blanket between Anna and his uncle. Katie plopped in front of him, and he pulled her onto his lap.

Anna stared off. In her daydreams she'd already rented a cute little house for her and Katie, obtained a teaching job at the public school, and now the entire dream had disintegrated. She drew her trembling lower lip between her teeth. What was wrong with her? The man she loved and thought was dead was sitting next to her and he was Katie's own flesh and blood. Her prayers had been answered both ways.

*Lord, forgive me.*

"Miss Anna, do I have to leave my new dresses at your house?"

Anna startled and ran a hand over the girl's head and down one of the braids. "Of course not. They're yours to keep forever."

Katie grinned. "That's good, because I didn't want to go back to wearing that big old dress Miss Fiona found for me." She twisted around and looked up at her uncle. "Uncle Rory, Miss Anna gave me new dresses. My other clothes burned in the fire."

Rory stared at Anna and their gazes locked. "That sounds like something you'd do. Thank you."

Her stomach flip-flopped and she nodded, afraid if she tried to speak she'd blubber nonsense.

"Of course Katie can live with us." Rory's uncle grinned. "Best we plan for her to move in tomorrow. We need to warn Evie and make up a room for her. We can come for Katie tomorrow afternoon." He looked at Anna then her father. "Is that okay?"

An ache filled Anna's throat. It wasn't like she wouldn't see Katie again at the school. She pushed out a smile. "The afternoon sounds good. We should be home from church at noon. I'll have her things packed up."

"Where do you attend church?" Rory's question was so softly asked, Anna barely heard it.

"Faith Community on Madison Street."

He frowned. "I visited there a couple weeks ago, but I didn't see you."

The Sunday she was sick. "Oh, no. We came so close to finding each other. I didn't feel well and stayed home that week."

"Well, praise God we found each other today—or Katie

found me, I should say." He wrapped his arms around Katie from behind and tickled her. The girl dissolved in a fit of giggles.

Many times Rory had mentioned how much he missed seeing his niece since he'd been estranged from his father, but he'd never said her name. God had done a miracle and now he'd probably marry a nice woman from the Woods and raise Katie as his own.

Visions of Rory and a woman wearing a wedding veil standing in front of the reverend, their backs to her, filled Anna's thoughts. Her throat felt like a knife had cut it in two. The woman turned and Anna gasped out loud. *She* was the bride?

She pressed her palm to her chest She may have fallen in love with him, but he'd given no hint he felt the same about her. She needed to stop these silly daydreams. Regardless, now more than ever, she needed to break the agreement with the Millards. If she couldn't have Rory, she wanted no one else.

"Anna, aren't you coming?"

She jolted and glanced about. Everyone had stood and was staring at her.

Father frowned. "Daughter, you were really lost in thought. Stand up so we can gather the blanket."

By now, the sun had dropped behind the trees to the west, sending a chill through the late afternoon air. Anna rubbed her arms and looked at Rory. "Are you staying for the bonfire?"

He grimaced "I wish I could, but we still have farm chores" He gently gave one of Katie's braids a tug. "I'll see you tomorrow at church."

Everyone said their goodbyes, and Rory and his uncle left while the Bakers and Jerusha headed toward their carriages. Anna, Father and Katie walked toward the dessert tent.

"Rory seems to be a nice young man," Father said. "How come you never mentioned him before?"

Anna bit her lip. Surely he knew why. "You know how Mother would have reacted. If she knew I'd made friends with an Irish immigrant, she'd insist I stop working there before I became corrupted."

"You're quite fond of him, aren't you?"

Anna stared at Father. "What do you mean by fond?"

"I could see it all over your face, and his too. Is he why you've been so opposed to marrying Lyman?"

Heat singed her cheeks. He saw Rory's feelings for her in his face? A tiny glimmer of hope lifted her spirits. "I do care for him a lot, Father, but regardless I will not marry anyone as evil spirited as Lyman. He's a cruel man."

He grimaced and glanced at his feet. "It's just so difficult to believe." He looked up. "I just remembered someone I need to see. Have Patrick hold the carriage for me."

# CHAPTER TWENTY-FIVE

Sunday morning, Anna caught a glimpse of herself in the foyer mirror. The absence of dark circles under her eyes belied the fact she'd barely slept the whole night. During the bonfire the night before, she noticed many couples huddled arm-in-arm in the chilly air, watching the flames. She'd blinked tears away, missing Rory more than when she'd thought he was dead.

Later, when she crawled in bed, she'd sobbed into her pillow and cried out to God to relieve the pain. Before dropping into a fitful sleep, she'd made up her mind. She'd try again with Father before he left for the city and insist the arrangement with the Mallards be broken. Now that he'd seen for himself the feelings she and Rory had for each other, he'd agree.

When Anna walked into the entry hall, Katie stood by the front door peering out one of the side windows with Father beside her "Why is it taking Mr. Patrick so long?"

Father chuckled. "He has to make sure Goldie is hitched to the carriage correctly. You wouldn't want the horse to break loose and leave us stranded in the middle of the road, would you?"

The little girl giggled and shook her head. "I can't wait to see Uncle Rory again."

Anna came next to Katie and pulled her to her side. "You had a wonderful blessing yesterday. And today will be even better. Time always seems to move slowly when we're looking forward to something good." She led the child away from the door. "Let's wait over here."

Truth be told, she was as excited as Katy to see Rory. Of course, Mother would expect her to sit with the family, but why couldn't she and Katie sit with Rory? The lines between classes were practically non-existent in Geneva. No one, except Mother, would be shocked if they shared a pew.

"Miss Anna. Patrick's outside now." Anna snapped out of her reverie as Katie tugged her by the hand toward the door. How had everyone else gone outside without her noticing? She had to stop what her granny used to call woolgathering.

The moment Anna stepped into the sanctuary behind her family she spotted Rory sitting almost where she'd imagined. He waved at Katie, then caught Anna's eye and held it a moment. Her stomach dipped and fluttered. She looked away and took a step toward the pew Father had selected.

Katie tugged Anna's hand toward Rory's pew. "I want to sit with Uncle."

Anna glanced at Rory's expectant face then at her Mother who stood waiting by the family's pew. She released Katie's hand. "Go sit with your uncle. I'll join you in a minute."

She approached Mother and whispered. "I'll sit back there so Katie can sit with her uncle."

Mother's mouth twitched. "The child doesn't need you now that she has one of her kind. Sit with us."

"But I want you with me too." Katie's high-pitched voice filled the small church. Several people turned and stared.

Heat crawled up Anna's neck. She hadn't realized the child

had come with her. She looked at her mother and whispered. "Best I sit back there than cause a commotion."

Mother's gaze bore into her. "I suppose so. The girl has no manners."

Anna glanced at Katie. One look at her told Anna she'd heard the remark. Hopefully sitting with Rory would soothe the wound. "We'd better hurry before the service starts." She led Katie to the back and gently nudged her into the pew. Katie sat next to Rory and snuggled up to him.

Anna sat and arranged her skirts. Maybe she could get a live-in nanny job somewhere or join one of those covered wagon trains heading west. Away from everything.

"What you said about our possibly meeting up in Geneva happened, and what a blessing that's turned out to be."

At Rory's whisper, she turned. He'd leaned across Katie, and his handsome face was only a few inches away. She sent him a knowing smile then faced the front. If she looked into those blue eyes any longer, she'd lose all common sense.

If the sermon was something Anna should have heard, she had no idea. Even with Katie sitting between her and Rory, every nerve in her body was aware of his nearness. At the choir director's words, "Everyone stand for the closing hymn," Anna stood. Rory lifted a sleeping Katie as he pushed to his feet.

As though sensing Anna's stare, Rory offered a crooked smile, sending a delicious sensation through her body. She bowed her head as the reverend began to pray. Only a few petitions in, her mind drifted again. Rory and Katie needed each other. They were all they had, save their Uncle Denis and his wife. She had to leave them to themselves to heal and move forward within their Irish community.

*Lord, why did I have to fall in love with a man I can't have?*

By the time the prayer ended, Katie was awake, but was in no hurry to leave Rory's arms, nor was Anna in any hurry to leave Rory's presence. She was more than happy to wait for others to file out ahead of their row.

"I don't believe we've met before." A man in the row behind them stuck his hand out to Rory. "I'm John Stevens. I run the general store on Main Street."

Rory grinned and set Katie down to shake the man's hand. "Pleased to meet you. I've only been here a couple of weeks. Rory Quinn."

The man glanced at Katie and Anna. "And this is your wife and daughter, I presume."

Anna glanced at Rory, surprised to see his face as red as hers felt.

"This is my Uncle Rory," Katie piped up. "My daddy went to heaven during the fire. And this is my teacher, Miss Anna."

The man's face reddened. "I'm so sorry. Leave it to me to put my foot in my mouth."

Anna found her voice. "An easy presumption. We just learned yesterday that Rory had survived the fire and Katie has family here after all."

By then the pews had emptied and they said their goodbyes. Outside, Anna turned to Rory. "It's a beautiful day. Our house is only a few blocks' walk. Why don't we go on foot?"

His dimples deepened. "I'd like that."

She told her parents they would meet them at home and she, Rory and Katie started out down Madison Street.

Rory moved Katie to Anna's left side, putting Anna next to him. Anna took Katie's hand.

His arm brushed against hers, sending a delicious shiver up to her shoulder. "I'm sorry for that man embarrassing you back there."

Anna chuckled. "It looked to me as though I wasn't the only one embarrassed."

He laughed and studied the ground as he walked. "I guess we all were, except for Katie. I like how up here no lines seem to be drawn between classes. At least, not to the same extent as Chicago.”

“I like it too, although my mother thinks it’s deplorable.”

“Would we ever have a festival in the city where the wealthy joined with the Irish—or Germans or Poles for that matter—in a tug-of-war?”

“I doubt it, except for church activities.” Anna fought the urge to slip her hand around Rory’s arm as she would if she were walking with a man of her social status. “When we stayed at Mrs. Maxwell’s the first couple of weeks we were here, I was surprised at how familiar she acted with her help. But, I suppose with all the families from my neighborhood and others like it, planning to build here, some of that will change.”

“I hope not. Tell me about your work at the Irish Woods school.”

Anna explained how she came to work at the school and that her job didn’t please her mother, especially when the Millards had visited.

“Why is she so insistent that you stay home to entertain that family’s son? Is he a friend from your childhood?”

She had to tell him the truth. Keeping it from him the whole time they’d known each other was wrong. “You could say that.” They came to the schoolhouse and Anna looked at Katie. “Why don’t you play on the swings for a few minutes while I talk with your uncle?”

“Okay.” The child took off running.

Anna drew in a long breath and looked up at Rory. She had to say it. “Mother wanted me to spend time with their son because I’ve been betrothed to him in an arranged marriage ever since I was a baby.” She grimaced. “He and his mother were here to plan the wedding.”

# CHAPTER TWENTY-SIX

Rory felt like he'd swallowed a live coal. He stared at Anna. She was waiting for a response, but no words came. This Lyman Millard fellow was a stranger, but he wanted to give him a good left hook to his jaw. He had no right, of course. Nor would it be the Christian way to settle things.

He swallowed against a hard wad in his throat. "I guess it's time to say congratulations."

"Isn't congratulations said for good things?"

He dug his fingers into his trouser pocket and pulled out her necklace. "I wanted to give you this today. I found it in the mission school rubble after the fire. I presume the young man in the picture is Millard."

Anna's eyes widened. "My locket." She took the jewelry and snapped the locket open. "This is my cousin who died in the war. It's the only picture I had of him." She pressed the pendant to her chest. "I'm so grateful you found it."

Rory let out a lungful of air. "Me too."

"A small touch of joy in the middle of a difficult conversation." She brought her gaze to Rory. At the pain in her eyes, he jammed his hands into his pockets to keep from wrapping his arms around her, protecting her from more hurt.

He ran his tongue over his dry lips. "When is the wedding?"

She studied the ground. "It was to be the Tuesday following the fire. I thought with much of the city in cinders, the plans would be postponed indefinitely." She stared off and blinked several times. "Mother is bent on a New Year's Eve wedding." She brought her gaze back to him. "I have no intention of marrying Lyman Millard. He's a cruel man."

It was all he could do to keep his hands in his pockets. "Why would your parents insist you marry him? I don't understand."

"They haven't seen the side of Lyman I have seen."

She pulled a handkerchief from her dress pocket. "I've been asking God to intervene, but so far He hasn't." She dabbed at her eyes then looked up at him. "I can't believe God would have me marry a hard-hearted man who has no love of Him. Scripture says we aren't to be unequally yoked."

Rory frowned. "Aye. That's true. If you refuse to marry Millard, what happens to you?"

Anna sighed. "I'll probably be disinherited. I've been stashing away a small sum each week from my allowance. It's hardly enough to rent a room, even in this small village." She gestured toward the schoolhouse behind her. "I've thought about applying here for a teaching position. If that doesn't work out, perhaps I could hire on to be a nanny. I have no desire to return to Chicago."

Rory's heart swelled. He hadn't known but a few women of privilege, but Anna was unlike any of them. None would be willing to work as a servant to get out of an arranged marriage.

He glanced over at Katie playing on the swings with another little girl. Why did things have to be so complicated? He faced Anna. "What do you mean by his being cruel?"

She opened her mouth then shut it. "I'd rather not say, but I'm not exaggerating."

Whatever he'd done, it must have been bad. "I'm willing to help any way I can."

For the first time since the conversation started, her eyes brightened. She rested her hand on his arm "Thank you. It means a lot. We'd better start walking. Your uncle will be arriving, and my family will want to have Sunday dinner soon."

He moved his arm until their hands connected and he gave it a squeeze. "I'd do anything for you, Anna." It felt so right and natural to be holding her hand.

Her eyes misted over and he longed to kiss her right there in broad daylight. He let go of her hand and called for Katie. Soon they resumed walking toward Anna's home. To someone unaware of their situation it probably looked like a young married couple and their daughter. If only that were true. Almost from their first meeting at the mission school, Rory had loved Anna. Could he stand by and let her marry such a man as Millard, as cruel as she said he was?

*Help me, Lord. Show me what I should do.*

# CHAPTER TWENTY-SEVEN

nna flicked the gas lamp on her nightstand and checked the time. Two o'clock. She extinguished the flame and punched her pillow into a puffy mound. The second night in a row without sleep. If her brain didn't stop spinning like a tornado, she'd be in no shape to help the children tomorrow. She touched the locket that had hung around her neck since Rory returned it on Saturday. The way he'd held onto it for her touched her heart more than anything anyone had given her of much more value. The relief she saw in his face when she assured him the man in the locket was her cousin had only buoyed her determination to get out of the marriage arrangement.

She punched her pillow then turned it over. How could she nod off when ways of escaping her trap kept racing through her thoughts? And when they stopped, she rehearsed her conversation with Rory and the couple moments he held her hand. It felt so natural. For a moment she was sure he was going to kiss her, but he didn't.

During their walk from the playground, he mentioned a man from Irish Woods who worked as a caretaker for the Maple

Lawn estate. He told Rory come spring there'd be an opening for an assistant caretaker and Rory hoped to get the job.

Anna turned over on her back and stared into the blackness. He had already been assured of a job cutting ice once the lake froze over. Rory's work ethic had always impressed Anna, but seeing the joy in his eyes while he spoke about cutting ice, she appreciated him even more. Wasn't that how she'd felt about her work at the mission and helping out at the school now?

A verse that spoke about working as though for the Lord and not for man, popped in her head. She may as well give up on trying to sleep and look it up. She climbed out of bed and took her Bible to the sitting area next to the window then flicked on a gas lamp.

A half-hour earlier than her usual departure time, Anna found Patrick in the stable putting Goldie's halter over her head.

His brows shot up. "Miss Anna, did you tell me you wanted to leave this early?" He moved faster, maneuvering the bit into Goldie's mouth.

"I didn't plan to leave now, but since I'm awake and dressed, I thought I would. Don't rush." She rubbed Goldie's nose. "Good morning, girl." She stepped back to allow Patrick room to finish connecting the horse and carriage.

Lines deepened around his eyes. "You always were a goer, Miss Anna. "I'll have the carriage rigged and ready in a few more minutes."

During the ride, Anna forced herself to mentally plan the day's lessons and not think even one minute about Rory. They arrived at the school, which didn't give off the usual appearance of being warmed and ready for the scholars. But then she was earlier than usual. She asked Patrick to wait until she got inside before leaving and made her way to the door.

She gripped the door handle and pushed. The door didn't move. Mrs. Peavey always arrived by seven o'clock. Anna knocked and paused then knocked again. She looked back at Patrick who waited by the carriage and shrugged. After knocking a third time, she withdrew the key Mrs. Cleary had given her from her reticule, then unlocked the door and pushed it open. Chilled air slapped her in the face.

She waved at Patrick. "Teacher must be delayed this morning. I'm okay now. No need to wait."

He lifted a hand then got the carriage headed back to the road.

Anna lit a gas lamp affixed to the back wall then hurried toward the potbelly stove, rubbing her arms as she crossed the room. The days were growing shorter and they'd soon need a fire started early every day. Perhaps she could volunteer to do that, or at least share the duty with Mrs. Cleary.

Anna had finished starting the fire when a child's familiar voice filtered in from outside. Did Rory bring Katie this morning? Her stomach tingled and she pressed a palm against the sensation. Her feelings for him couldn't be denied. But even if she was released from her betrothal, there was no guarantee he'd want to be with a high-society woman. There were probably plenty of attractive women living around Irish Woods who would soon catch his eye.

She headed for the door and stepped outside. Six-year-old Jane O'Dell climbed down from her father's wagon. Jane was always the first scholar to arrive as her father had to be at his job by seven-thirty.

The little girl ran up to Anna. "Morning, Miss Anna."

Anna hunched down to the girl's eye level. "Good morning, Jane. Did you have a nice weekend?"

Before the child could answer, a wagon pulled by a large brown horse rolled up and stopped. Mrs. Cleary climbed down and waved her husband off. She scurried up to Anna. "I'm glad you came early. I was held up when our bull broke through the fence and I had to wait for Mr. Cleary and our handyman to round him up." She frowned. "Is everything okay?"

Anna nodded. "Yes, I got the fire going and the room looks the same as when we left on Friday."

The older woman chuckled. "I meant is everything okay with you. You usually don't arrive until closer to eight o'clock."

She yearned to confide in Mrs. Cleary, but best she keep her plans quiet. "I woke up earlier than normal, and Father isn't returning to the city until next Monday, since Thanksgiving is this coming Friday. I have good news, though. The man I was looking for was at the rope pull and he is Katie's uncle. She's going to live with Rory and his uncle Denis.

Mrs. Cleary's eyes twinkled. "That's wonderful news. What a great way to start out a new week."

A half hour later, while Anna stood outside the door, greeting the children as they arrived, Denis Quinn's wagon appeared down the road. Anna's stomach made the familiar dip as the wagon drew closer. A sturdy looking woman wearing a gray cloak over a dark blue work dress held the reins. Next to her sat Katie, her little arm waving back and forth like a metronome. "Hi, Miss Anna. Aunt Evie brought me to school."

The wagon came to a stop. Anna approached the pair. "Good morning, Katie. You look like a happy little girl." She turned to the woman. "I'm Anna Hartwell, the assistant teacher."

The woman grinned and absently touched her well-worn bonnet. "Evie Quinn. Rory has spoken of you. We're all very grateful for your taking care of Katie the past few weeks." She glanced at the little girl. "There was a lot of celebrating at our house last night."

Katie beamed. "We had chocolate cake and ice cream. See, Miss Anna, I have a family now. Just like you."

Anna's heart squeezed. If only the girl knew how much Anna yearned to have a family like Katie's.

# CHAPTER TWENTY-EIGHT

*One Week Later*

As soon as Anna returned from school, she went straight to her room and plopped into the sitting area chair. She opened her Bible and read words about confessing sin. then hung her head.

Every morning since last Monday when Evie Quinn dropped Katie off at school, the child couldn't wait to tell Anna about what Rory had done for her the night before. On Monday, he read to her from the Bible followed by a bedtime story. On Tuesday he took her on a horseback ride with her sitting in front of him on the saddle, his strong arm holding her close. On Wednesday they took a walk to the lake and talked about her ma and da. On Thursday, they planned to help Aunt Evie prepare for their Thanksgiving dinner. And, today she heard all about Thanksgiving and how Uncle Rory took her to town on Saturday for new shoes and on Sunday, they attended church and were sad that Anna wasn't there.

How was she to tell the child she attended her mother's

preferred church to keep a semblance of peace, and had convinced herself it was better to not see Katie and her uncle and sit with them until she was officially a free woman?

As much as Anna was thrilled for Katie, she had to confess her jealousy to God and ask for forgiveness. It had started at the festival and she hadn't been able to overcome it. To be jealous of a little girl who'd lost both parents in a deadly fire was despicable. "Father, forgive me and give me joy at Katie's finding her family and Rory finding his niece." She continued her prayer in silence until the sound of a ringing bell announced dinner.

What she needed was to fast and pray, but to do so would only draw attention. She stood and crossed to the mirror to make sure any sign of tears was gone then headed for the door.

A few moments later, Anna helped herself to a small serving from the platter of roast beef as it came around, followed by a tiny mound of mashed potatoes.

Mother scowled. "Is that all you plan to eat, daughter? Your father paid good money for this food. Show him some respect by taking more than a bird's helping."

Anna glanced at Callie's plate. If hers was a bird's share, then her sister's was no more than a gnat's. Of course Callie's excuse had recently been she had to fit into the debutante gown Millie was making. To point out the obvious difference would make her look childish. "I'm not very hungry."

Mother snatched up her glass and water sloshed over the edge. She dabbed a corner of her napkin at a spot on her dress. "I hope you're not ill because you and I are taking the train into the city on Wednesday to meet with the Millards."

Anna winced and looked at Father for support. He was cutting his meat and seemed not to hear. She looked at her own plate. "I won't be free until Saturday."

Mother let her napkin drop, and it slid off her lap onto the floor. "You're only a volunteer. I'm sure the children can make do without you. What do those ragamuffins need besides reading and arithmetic? Anyone can learn to keep house or cook without more than that."

Callie gasped. "Maybe with education those children can better themselves. Katie is as smart as a whip. Doesn't she deserve to be educated?"

Anna covered her smile with her hand, loving Callie's boldness. "Katie *is* smart. She received an A on her last arithmetic test."

"Her station in life won't allow her to be more than a domestic. That's the way things are." Mother signaled the maid for a clean napkin.

Father held up his hands in surrender. "Ladies, ladies. Let's have a little peace." He looked at Mother. "Eleanor, I don't think travel into the city is a good idea just yet. The rebuilding is happening at rapid speed, but with all the workers moving supplies and materials about and the streets a muddy mess, the city is far from hospitable. In another couple weeks, a lot of retail stores will be open in temporary quarters."

"I heard that the Field-Leiter store is going to open in a building owned by the Singer Company." Callie's eyes brightened. "I can't wait to shop there again."

"It's a building that escaped the fire and Singer can't use it." Father fingered his goatee. "Really, the city's not yet a place for ladies."

Mother shrugged "All right, but we're going to have to work very hard to put plans together and get a dress made for Anna in time for the wedding. The nuptials cannot wait much longer."

"Why does the wedding have to happen so fast? And why can't Millie make her dress right here in Geneva?" Callie pushed her half eaten plate away. "I'm sure Anna doesn't mind waiting if the wedding is held later." Looking quite pleased with herself, she glanced at Anna as if for approval.

"Hortense Millard's seamstress has offered to make Anna a dress, and we should take advantage of the offer. It doesn't matter what Anna wants, Calista. What matters is that this marriage has been planned for years. The joining of our families has to happen or—"

"Marriage is supposed to happen after a couple falls in love." Anna pushed her chair back and threw her napkin on top of her half-eaten food. She glared at her mother. "I will not be a pawn in your drive to add to Father's portfolio." She jolted to her feet and stomped out of the room. As she reached the stairs, someone gripped her arm from behind.

"Anna, please come with me."

She faced her father. Worry lines had sprouted around his eyes.

She tugged at her arm, but his grip was tighter. "I refuse to return to the table. I am not a child, and will not tolerate being treated like one."

"Then perhaps you should stop acting like one."

She jerked her head back and stared into her father's dark eyes. "I'm sorry for the temper tantrum. It was childish. But, I have a responsibility to the school, and I refuse to take time off to shop for something I don't want."

"Let's step into the library."

Anna felt her shoulders relax and she took a deep breath. "Okay. But I'm not changing my mind."

She followed her father across the hall and into the library. He shut the pocket doors and gestured toward an upholstered chair. "Please sit." He moved to the chair's twin, positioned on the other side of a lamp table, and waited for Anna to arrange her skirts before he sat.

He pressed his lips together and stared straight ahead.

The pendulum on the mantle clock ticked off the seconds. Anna plucked at her skirt, lifting it and letting it fall. Almost a minute had passed, she cleared her throat. She had better things to do than sit here while Father stared off. "Father, I—"

"Anna, I know you don't have romantic feelings for Lyman. And you do have them for Rory." Father ran his tongue over his lower lip then drew in a long breath before looking at her. "But, with your becoming a Millard, it's likely our two companies will merge, and eventually Lyman will be at the helm. You'll never want for anything."

Heat filled Anna's stomach. "Is money all you think about? The Bible says the love of money is the root of all kinds of evil."

Father pursed his lips. "I'm certain God didn't mean we should never have money. Think of all we can do with wealth. Give to charity and foundations."

Anna looked toward the window. She should tell him about Lyman's hurting her. Would he believe her? Would he become her defender? But he'd known Mr. Millard for years. And men stuck together. Mother didn't believe her, so why would Father? She faced him. "Please understand. Lyman is not someone I could even grow to like, let alone love. He's not a nice man. I've decided to break the betrothal and live on my own here in Geneva."

Color drained from Father's face. "You can't mean that. How would you pay your living expenses? As much as you enjoy your work at that school, you're not being paid."

"I'll apply for a teaching job."

His eyes widened. "Where? At the Irish Woods school? That teacher can't be making much. Without transportation, you'd have to live out there."

"I can drive a carriage. But, I was thinking of the school in town. If I took a room, the town isn't that big. I can walk everywhere."

Father wrung his hands. "I wish you'd pray about this, Anna."

"I've been praying about it—for weeks. If you force me to

marry Lyman, I'll disappear and you'll never know where I've gone."

Had she really said that? Is that what she wanted? To leave everyone—Rory, Katie, the children—and disappear?

*Please, Lord, don't let it come to that.*

"I'll talk to your mother." Father stood and left the room, sliding the doors shut softly behind him.

# CHAPTER TWENTY-NINE

Father left the next afternoon for Chicago and wouldn't return for over a week. He'd promised to talk to Mother about ending the arranged marriage, but, when Anna returned home after school, Mother never mentioned it. Obviously, he hadn't spoken to her as he promised, and now she'd have to wait until he returned.

Anna had resolved to keep her distance from Rory until her betrothal was officially canceled and had done well until this afternoon when she stepped outside to wait with the children for their rides. Rory arrived as usual and Katie ran to him.

As she approached his wagon he climbed down, and gave Katie's braids a tug. "I want to talk to Miss Anna a few minutes. Why don't you swing until I call you?"

Katie scrunched her face. "Why can't I stay?"

Rory gave her a loving smile. "Wee one, sometimes grownups have to talk without little ears around." He gave her a hug. "We won't be long."

"Okay, as long as you don't have one of those talks that goes on forever." She giggled and ran across the grass.

Anna burst out laughing. "How many long conversations have we had with her around other than last Sunday?"

Rory's dimples deepened. "One too many, I reckon."

He leaned against the wagon and crossed his arms. "I have a job . . . starting Monday." His grin was so wide his dimples seemed deeper than ever.

"I thought you were going to cut ice when the lake froze over."

"I'll still cut ice. There won't be much work for me on the other job until spring. I'm going to be an assistant gardener at Maple Lawn. My friend, Dan, arranged an interview for me with Mr. Sturgis and we met this morning. Dan is going to train me. Then when some of the other estates are built, maybe I can get a job as head caretaker for one of them."

Anna grinned. "That's wonderful, Rory."

He nodded. "Dan gave me books about landscaping to read before I talked to Mr. Sturgis. The more I read, the more I knew this is what I am meant to do."

He pushed away from the wagon and stepped closer. "Most estates have small houses for their caretakers. I'll be able to make a good living and provide a home for Katie and me." He paused and looked at his feet. "For as much sadness as I've had recently, God is bringing me one blessing after another. A new place to live, a new job, reuniting with Katie . . . " He looked up and searched her face with his eyes. "And finding out you are alive and well."

Warmth washed over her. She ached to confess how she felt about him, but if he wanted more than friendship, he hadn't said so. Unless what he just said was his way of saying it. "And that's been my blessing as well."

His gaze settled on her mouth. Did he want to kiss her? Anna felt a flush rising to her cheeks. She'd never kissed a man before and would love for Rory to be the first. But not without a declaration of love. And certainly not out in the open.

He looked her in the eyes. "And soon you'll get that teaching job you want."

She chuckled. "I don't know about that, but I have news as well. My father agreed to talk to Mother about dissolving my engagement to Lyman."

His eyes lit up. "I've been praying that God would intervene for you. We need to celebrate."

She held up a hand. "Not yet. He said that Monday night and left the next day for the city. I haven't heard anything more."

"He seems to be a reasonable man. He's probably waiting for the best time. I'm bringing Katie to town tomorrow. If this warm weather continues, we plan to have a picnic near the lake. If it turns cold, we'll find a place to eat inside. I'm making the food myself—with my aunt's help. Would you like to join us? Spending those weekends with you is all she talks about."

She opened her mouth to decline, but shut it. Why not accept? She'd tell Mother she wanted to spend time with Katie. "I'd love to, but you must let me bring something for the meal. I make pretty good fried chicken."

Rory's eyes widened. "You can cook?"

She grinned. "The cook we had while I was growing up taught me to make chicken and chocolate cake."

He laughed. "Can you bring both tomorrow?"

"Both?"

"I was joking. But if you can, I love fried chicken. I was only going to make sandwiches."

"Anna, can you please come inside and help close up for the weekend?"

Anna startled and faced Mrs. Cleary, who stood on the school's porch. "I'll be right in."

When Anna stepped into the classroom, the teacher stood at the blackboard, washing it down with a wet sponge. "I'm sorry, Mrs. Cleary. I lost track of the time. Rory has wonderful news of a new job working as an assistant gardener at Maple Lawn."

The older woman faced her and offered a soft smile. "I'm not upset that you stayed to talk to Rory. I hated to interrupt, seeing how you two are sweet on each other."

Anna's mouth fell open. "Oh, we're just good friends. We both worked at the mission school."

Mrs. Cleary laughed. "Protest all you want, but I see smitten written over both your faces. Can you please set up Monday morning's reading lesson?

*Both our faces?*

Anna floated through her work, setting up the reading lesson, and a half hour later, when she settled in the family carriage, a memory filled her mind of Rory's gaze slipping to her mouth.

She rested her head against the seat cushion and closed her eyes. It was a good thing Katie was coming with them tomorrow. A very good thing.

nna turned the chicken legs then jumped back from the splatter.

"Anna Hartwell, what on earth are you doing? That's what we pay our help to do."

She wiped perspiration from her brow with the back of her hand and faced Mother. "I'm going on a picnic with Katie and her uncle. I said I'd bring chicken. Peggy offered to make it, but I wanted to prepare it myself."

Mother lifted a disapproving brow. "I suppose those people at the mission school taught you how to use a stove. And now you're cooking for a janitor." She stepped closer and looked Anna in the eyes. "I'll not have you spending time with a man like him. You are an engaged woman. I don't care if he's Katie's uncle and the child is along. It's not proper."

Grease popped from the frying pan and Mother's hand flew to her chin. She jumped back. "This place is not for you or me. It's dangerous."

Anna sighed. "I enjoy cooking, Mother. It feels unnatural to always be waited on and pampered. As for spending the day with Katie and her uncle, I'm going for Katie's sake. We'll be out in the open where the festival took place. Besides, he's not a janitor anymore. He'll be working as an assistant caretaker for Maple Lawn."

"Don't you see enough of that girl at school?"

"Not in a relaxed sort of way like a picnic. She's been through a lot and needs more attention than just being in school."

Mother huffed. "I think it's time for you to leave her to her own kind."

Anna squared her shoulders. "And what kind is that?"

"Stop waving that fork around before you hurt someone. You know what I mean. I forbid you to go."

Anna turned back to the chicken and lifted a golden crusty chicken leg onto a wire rack to drain. "I'm over twenty-one. You can't stop me."

"Until you are married, you have to obey me. If you don't, I'll have you out on the curb by the time you return."

"You do that, and I'll consider that means my engagement to Lyman is broken. Perfect." She lifted a chicken breast and set it next to the leg. "I have a picnic for a little girl to attend, and I'm going."

Mother muttered something under her breath and stomped out of the room.

Anna prayed that like the other times Mother had threatened to throw her out, it was all bluff. She hadn't saved enough money yet to live on her own.

RORY PARKED his wagon in front of Anna's house. "Wait here while I get Miss Anna, Katie. I won't leave the front porch, so you'll be able to see me."

She all but bounced on the wood bench next to him. "I'll be fine, Uncle Rory. I can't wait to get to the picnic."

He laughed as he climbed to the ground. He couldn't wait to get to the picnic either, but not for the food. Unless you counted how Anna Hartwell was a feast for his eyes. He mentally chastised himself. To think that way about a woman who was engaged to someone else, no matter the circumstance, was wrong. And to think that way about a woman he couldn't have, engaged or not, was wrong for his emotions.

As he climbed the steps to the porch, the home's front door opened, and Anna stepped out wearing a dark red checked dress and black boots. Her reddish brown hair beneath her bonnet framed her face, causing the green of her eyes to stand out. His heart pounded so hard it thundered in his ears. Nothing like taking the woman he'd loved from afar for the past year on a picnic to get his emotions going.

She grinned and touched the brim of her bonnet as if to make sure it was still there. "Good morning." She handed him her basket.

The aroma of fried chicken teased his nose and his stomach growled. "The chicken smells good enough to eat. Maybe we should sit right here on the porch and feast."

Anna laughed. "Suit yourself, but I'm looking forward to sitting near the water and sampling your cooking while you give mine a taste." She waved at Katie. "And spend time with my favorite girl."

Rory wanted to say he was spending time with his favorite girl, and it wasn't Katie—at least not his favorite grown-up girl. He held his words and offered her his elbow "Then we'd best be on our way."

Katie grinned as they approached the wagon. "Hi Miss Anna, I didn't know you were coming too until this morning."

Anna waited for Rory to help her onto the bench. Feeling her soft hand against his work-worn palm sent goose bumps flying up his arm. He reluctantly released his grip as she seated herself next to Katie. He climbed up to the other side of the bench. As much as he'd prefer Anna right next to him, no one could find fault in his taking her on a picnic as long as the little girl was with them.

Sensing being watched, he glanced at the house. Mrs. Hartwell stood on the second-floor balcony, straight as an arrow, arms crossed, her stony eyes fixed on them. He started to wave then thought better of it. The less time he spent with the woman the better.

ANNA TIPPED her head back and let the sun shine onto her face as Katie's continuous chatter faded into the background. It felt so natural to be with Rory and Katie. Almost like a family. A family she wanted so much and couldn't have.

"There's the lake, Uncle Rory."

Anna's eyes opened. They were approaching the intersection of Broad and Main, and the lake sat a block ahead, glistening in the sun, much as it had Anna's first day in Geneva. She glanced toward the far corner. Millie walked along the boardwalk wearing a dark blue-green dress, complete with a layered front and bustle. Anna smiled at the seamstress's ingenuity of wearing one of her new creations like a walking advertisement. As though feeling Anna's gaze, the seamstress looked over and waved.

Anna's breath hitched. Did Millie's brows rise a bit? Of course, Millie knew the situation about Katie and Rory finding each other. Anna hadn't mentioned her arranged betrothal to Millie, but Mother probably had. Would word get out that an engaged woman was seen in the company of a single man, not her fiancé? Rory kept the wagon moving toward the lake, and Anna buried her thoughts. This wasn't Chicago. Maybe she was too wary for her own good.

At the end of Broad Street, Rory turned right on Lake Street.

They clip-clopped along with the water off to their left and the sun high in the sky. Although not as warm as the day of the festival, as long as they stayed in the sun, they should be fine. Anna reached across Katie's shoulders and tugged her into the crook of her arm. The child nestled closer.

Rory brought the wagon to a halt and gestured toward a spot on the grass near where the tug-of-war had taken place two weeks ago. "How about over there?"

They soon had the blanket spread out, then settled on it and opened their respective baskets. Anna reached into hers and lifted out three plates, followed by three napkins and three forks. She placed a set in front of each of them. "You know I have chicken. What's in your basket?"

Rory grinned and lifted an apple pie. "This I didn't make. I left the baking to my aunt." He reached in his basket again and drew out a cast iron pot wrapped in a towel. He set it down and lifted its cover. "Not exactly Irish, but we have always loved them in my family."

She peered inside the pot. Although baked beans had been around a long time, Mother detested them, so they were never served at home. She had tasted her first baked beans while at college on the east coast and loved them. "They smell wonderful."

Rory grinned and his dimples deepened. He looked at Katy. "Do we want to eat now or play a game first?"

Katie and Anna said in unison. "Eat."

Rory laughed. "I guess that's settled."

Together they filled the three plates with chicken and baked beans.

"Shall we say grace?" Without waiting for a response, Rory held out his left hand to Katie, and his right hand to Anna, as she used to do with her students at the mission. She slipped her hand into his, loving the roughness of his hard-worked palm. With Katie's small soft hand tucked into Anna's other hand,

Rory prayed a blessing over the food while Anna prayed he didn't notice her trembling. She had to calm herself.

Despite Rory's raves about her chicken and her raves about his beans, Anna could barely get her food down. Mrs. Cleary's words about them both being smitten had entered into her thoughts and she couldn't shake them. If the woman was correct about Anna's feelings, could her intuition about Rory be considered correct also? Already full, Anna pretended to nibble at her beans, enjoying the way Rory went after a chicken leg.

Later, Anna watched Rory carry the leftovers to the wagon, admiring how he filled out his long-sleeved work shirt and denim dungarees. He probably didn't own a suit like Lyman would have worn today, or any other man in her family's crowd. Not that she cared. It must have taken great restraint on Mother's part that morning to not keep Anna in the house until Rory could return wearing the proper attire.

"Miss Anna, can I play with that little girl over there? She has a ball. Her name is Becky and she's nice."

A dark-haired girl about Katie's age stood a short distance away. A family sat on a blanket nearby. The mother waved and smiled and Anna did the same. "Only if you stay near her parents."

"We will." Katie ran toward the little girl.

"I see Katie found a playmate." Rory sat on the blanket. "Good. After a meal like that a guy needs to rest a bit."

Unsure of what she was supposed to do, Anna brushed brown leaves off the blanket. A few feet away Rory had stretched out on his back, eyes closed. A sudden sense of intimacy washed over her. Unsure if sitting there while he napped was appropriate, she moved to stand and her skirts rustled.

Rory opened his eyes and sat up. "Are you leaving? I was hoping we could talk."

She eased back onto the blanket. "I thought maybe you wanted to nap."

"I was composing what I want to say." He sat up and edged closer then looked her in the eyes. "Is it okay if I call you Anna instead of Miss Anna?"

In front of Katie he always called her Miss Anna, and in front of others, Miss Hartwell. Before, at the mission school he never called her anything when they were alone. The intensity in his eyes seemed to reach out and pull her closer. She nodded. "Yes, I'd like that."

His Adam's apple bobbed. "I've been trying to figure out my words, but nothing sounds right, so I'll just say what comes out.

Anna grabbed a fistful of her skirt. Whatever he wanted to say, it couldn't be good. But would he ask to call her Anna, if he were going to say something bad?

Rory cleared his throat. "The day at the tug-of-war when I saw Katie running up to me, it was like she'd risen from the ashes. Then you came across the field, your beautiful smile all over your face, and I couldn't believe my eyes. I'd decided you, too, had died and now there you were. It will forever be one of the best days of my life."

Anna chuckled. "And then I fell flat on my face."

He tossed his head back and laughed. "That you did, and you still never appeared more beautiful." He looked out at the lake then at her, his eyes warm, loving. "At that moment I realized my feelings for you had grown beyond friendship." He swallowed hard then looked down. "I don't know when exactly I fell in love with you. Maybe it was when you sacrificially gave your money to Mrs. Monahan the Friday before the fire. I don't know what you had intended to do with the money, but you gave it to her. That really touched me heart. I think though it was before that day, watching you with the children and discussing your faith with me. All of those things that make you who you are.

At once she felt warm and chilled, happy and sad. As much

as she was determined to not marry Lyman, a nagging fear her parents would get the best of her anyway, hung over her.

He brought his blue-eyed gaze back to her and smiled. "It's a terrible thing to be in love with a woman society says you can't have, but after the festival I determined if you felt the same as me, we could overcome everything. I was waiting for the right moment to tell you how I felt. Then I found out you are to be married."

"Rory—"

He held up a finger and whispered. "I have more. I don't even know for sure if you feel the same, but from how you've been with me since the festival, I sense you might. I love you Anna Hartwell. But even if you never marry Lyman Millard, I can't expect you to agree to spend your life with a man who cannot provide for you in the manner you are accustomed."

She wanted to pull him into her arms and kiss the daylights out of him, but she prayed for calmness instead and took his hand in hers. "If Father dissolves the marriage agreement with the Millards, you would have every bit as much a right to court me as anyone. I don't need fancy dinners and social events. I only want to be with you."

Rory squeezed her hand as a grin took over his face. "Are you saying what me thinks you are saying?"

She nodded. It was taking every once of strength to not fall into his arms right there in front of everyone who happened by. "I've known for some time now that I'm in love with you. To know you feel the same … Money makes no difference to me. I only want to be with you."

Rory let go of her hand and ran his palm over the tear that had been trailing down her cheek. "My sweet Anna. Are you sure? Living in Irish Woods isn't the same as a lakeshore mansion."

The touch of his calloused fingers against her soft skin sent a delicious shiver down her neck and into her already fluttering stomach. She tugged his hand away from her face. "I'm very sure. But, until Father can break the betrothal agreement, this will have to be our secret."

"I'm willing to wait." He lifted her hand and pressed his lips against it.

Everything around them faded. If his kiss to the back of her hand felt so soft and loving, what would a kiss on her mouth feel like? She'd asked him for patience, but would she be able to have any herself?

Rory released her hand and stood. "We'd better find that niece of mine and get into a game with her before I take you in my arms and kiss the daylights out of you."

Anna gathered her emotions and let him help her stand. If only there were a way to talk to Father that day and insist this betrothal be ended for once and for all.

# CHAPTER THIRTY-ONE

Despite two nights of only a couple hours' sleep each, Anna nearly bounced into the school room, certain the ridiculous grin she'd tried to erase was still there. "Good morning, Mrs. Cleary. The teacher shut the stove grate then dusted off her hands. "Anna, I'm glad you're here early. We need to talk before the children arrive."

Her serious expression and tone of voice cast a damper on Anna's mood and she wove her way between the desks toward the front of the room. As she neared Mrs. Cleary, dark shadows under her reddened eyes became visible. "Mrs. Cleary, is something wrong?"

She nodded. "Very wrong." She took a handkerchief from her pocket and dabbed her eyes. "My daughter-in-law's labor pains came Friday night, and they came hard." Her voice cracked. "She died, but the baby lived. The doctor says even though she's tiny, the baby should be okay. There's no one else to care for my granddaughter while my son works." She stared off toward the windows.

Anna's mind raced to digest the information. Just last week, Mrs. Cleary happily reported how well her daughter-in-law was feeling in her last month, and how the couple looked forward to their first child.

She stepped closer. "I'm so very sorry. Is there anything I can do?"

Mrs. Cleary brought her attention back to Anna. "Since I began teaching here, requirements for teachers have changed. Now, all teachers must have two years of training at a teacher's school. Since we've had no one with that background, I've been able to stay on." She took Anna's hand. "With your college education and experience you are well qualified, and I'd like to recommend to the superintendent that you replace me. Do I have your permission to suggest you take over here —permanently?"

Thoughts ricocheted through Anna's head. The answer to her prayer was coming in a most unexpected way. Father would be furious if she said yes without consulting him, but he already dismissed her this morning without giving her any time to hear her out. And already having a paying job would give her just the leverage she'd need to walk away from the marriage arrange- ment and Lyman for good.

"I know your circumstances are different, but you're a natural-born teacher and so good with the children. If you can't permanently take the position, perhaps you can take it temporarily until they find someone. My neighbor is watching the baby this morning, but I must be back home by noon."

Anna needed to think and pray, talk to Rory about it, but there wasn't time. "Of course, I'd love to have the position. This is so unexpected."

Mrs. Cleary squeezed her hand. "I've been praying all morning you'd say yes."

She rested her palm on top of Mrs. Cleary's hand. "Tell the superintendent I'd love to stay here as teacher."

"Thank you." Mrs. Cleary embraced her. "I'll stay the morning and prepare the children for the switchover. Knowing you will be staying will encourage them. So many have had such turmoil in their lives already."

Anna nodded. "I agree."

The outside door opened, and Sarah stepped through. "Good morning." She looked from Anna to Mrs. Cleary. "Judging by your faces, something is wrong. Should I step outside?"

Mrs. Cleary scurried up to the young woman. "Please come in. My daughter-in-law died in childbirth, and I have to care for my new granddaughter."

Sarah's hand flew to her mouth. "Oh no. I'm so sorry."

The teacher's body shook as a deep sob filled the room. "Anna will be taking over as teacher, starting today. We've not had time to set up for the day's classes."

Sarah gathered the teacher into an embrace. "How awful for you."

Mrs. Cleary stepped back. "It's good you're scheduled to help today. Anna will need you."

"I can't think of a better person to take over." Sarah glanced at Anna, a questioning expression on her face.

Anna felt a flush in her cheeks. She'd accepted so quickly and now would those words come back to bite her. "Thanks for your encouragement. I hope you're right."

Before teaching began, Mrs. Cleary told the class her grand-baby came early and she was needed at home to help care for her. The children began talking at once and it took all three women to get them quieted. Sarah worked with them on their reading and spelling while Mrs. Cleary went over her lesson plans for the week with Anna.

She'd have to work on the plans for future weeks at night. Wouldn't Mother enjoy that? Maybe she'd say Mrs. Cleary was taking a break and not leaving for good. But, that would be lying. Lying was never right.

By the time the teacher said her goodbyes and left a few minutes before noon, Anna's head spun. She'd only had to manage two grades at the mission. Now she had eight to deal with. The schedule Mrs. Cleary gave her made her dizzy. At least she'd had opportunity to observe for the past several weeks.

*Lord, I need your wisdom and strength for this. Please help me.*

At the end of the school day, Anna waved a child off with his mother as Rory drove his wagon into the schoolyard. Their gazes met, and his dimpled grin filled his face. He pulled the wagon to a stop and climbed out. He glanced around. "Is everyone gone?"

Anna pressed a palm to her quivering stomach and approached him. "Yes, only Katie and I are left until Patrick comes. She's over at the swing."

He took her hand and gave it a squeeze. "I missed not spending yesterday afternoon with you after church. But I didn't want to cause a stir by suggesting I give you a ride home when we had been together on Saturday."

His welcome words washed over her. "I felt the same, but you're right. It could have caused a fuss. Now I have news that will surely upset what little peace I have at home."

A deep V formed between Rory's eyes. "What's going on?"

Anna gave him a summary of Mrs. Cleary's circumstances. "And Mrs. Cleary asked my permission to recommend me as the new teacher here. I gave her permission but now I wonder if I should have waited until my parents were told about it."

His dimples deepened and he lifted his hands as if he were going to hug her. Then he let his arms fall to his sides. "When we prayed the other day for a teaching job for you, we didn't mean at the cost of another person's life. How can we rejoice over the opportunity when a woman died and left a child motherless?"

Anna nodded. "I've been troubled by that all day. Then there is the conversation I need to have with my father. I'd hoped to take a day off next week to see him about canceling the betrothal." She crossed her arms. "I'll have to explain to the superintendent that I need time off to put my situation in order with my family."

Rory's eyes twinkled. "And once you talk to your father, you will be a free woman."

"And probably disowned and homeless."

"Not if you marry me."

She stared at him. "Are you proposing, Rory Quinn?"

He laughed. "I guess I am." He looked around. "I don't see Patrick yet. Can we go inside? I'll help you lock up."

She couldn't help grinning. "I could use some help."

He told Katie he'd be inside and she should watch for Patrick.

Inside, Rory drew her to him and wrapped his arms around her. "I love you, Anna Hartwell. Like I said the other day, I can't offer you the life you be accustomed to, but I can offer you a life where you'll be loved and cherished by your husband all of his days."

Anna blinked. Words she never thought she'd hear. She touched his grizzled cheek, loving the feel of his whiskers. "I love you too, Rory. Yes, I will marry you. I just hope—"

"Enough talk." He brought his lips, soft and tender against her mouth. She wrapped her arms around his waist and the kiss deepened. This was the only man she ever wanted. And the only man she'd ever kissed or intended to kiss. It was well worth the wait.

Rory moaned then slowly drew his lips away from hers. He kissed the tip of her nose. "I know you need to officially end that marriage agreement before we can tell anyone, but knowing you want to marry me is enough for now." He pushed a wayward lock off her face, his fingertips brushing against her temple and sending a shiver down her neck.

Anna nestled her face against Rory's chest. Even through his thick work shirt, his beating heart pounded out a rapid beat against her ear. If only they could find a preacher right then and be married.

Rory nuzzled his face in her hair. "I can't wait to make you my bride."

A door slammed behind them and they jumped apart.

Patrick stood next to the cloakroom. "I'm sorry." He turned toward the door. "I'll be waiting outside."

The door shut and Rory looked at her. "I've put you in a bad position." He tilted his head and studied her face. "You're as red as a tomato. I must be too."

Anna shook her head. "More a pasty white."

"Will he tell your parents?"

"I don't think so. He doesn't like their strict ways anymore than I do. I'll talk to him on the way home." She walked to the teacher's desk. "I need to straighten up before I leave."

Rory helped her get the room set then before they stepped outside, he took her face into his hands, a palm against each cheek, and brushed her lips in a feathery kiss. "I know God will be with us in this, Anna. Just remember I love you with all my heart and always will."

Patrick's silence while he helped Anna into the carriage, all the while not looking her in the eyes, said more about how he felt than if he had spoken. Although she was never required to explain her actions to a servant, Patrick was different. Growing up, she'd spent more time with him than her own father. Did he disapprove of her being unfaithful to Lyman? After all, he knew nothing about Lyman's mistreatment of her.

She waved to Rory as the horse pulled the carriage onto the road. She leaned against the seat cushion and closed her eyes, then brought her fingertips to her lips. Her first kiss and it was everything she'd dreamed it would be, coming from the man she loved. Her chest tightened. What kind of person was she to be rejoicing over the love of a man when Mrs. Cleary and her family were grieving her daughter-in-law? The very death that was causing a family great pain had brought her joy beyond her imagination. She had to bottle her happiness and think of others. This was no time for celebration.

They were already nearing the hill and she had to say something to Patrick. She leaned forward and opened the window. "Patrick, can we talk?"

He angled his head but kept his focus on the road. "Miss Anna, you know I don't gossip. If you're worried about what I saw, don't be. I've watched you and Rory together for the past year and have known a long while you two are sweet on each other."

Heat filled her cheeks. "I didn't realize it was that obvious."

The driver chuckled. "It's kind of hard to disguise feelings when we're in love." He became silent for a few moments then called back over his shoulder. "I like what I see, by the way. I don't care for that Millard fella at all. You've got yourself a tangled mess to wiggle out of."

Anna blinked at the moisture in her eyes. "Thank you, Patrick. Pray for me."

They began the ascent down the hill into Geneva. "Praying I can do, Miss Anna."

FRIDAY MORNING, as Anna was setting up class notes to go over with the substitute who'd been hired to take over while Anna met with Father in the city, Rory stepped into the classroom.

She stood from her desk chair and grinned. "What are you doing here?"

He gave her a smile that made his dimples seem inches deep. "I don't have to report to work as early today and wanted to have a minute or two to talk. We never seem to do that when I pick Katie up after school." He walked down the middle aisle between the desks, his blue eyes staring straight at her. "You look beautiful today."

Warmth traveled up her neck and into her face and she looked away.

"And even more so when you blush."

Anna jumped. How had he come to within inches of her without her hearing his footsteps? She looked up at him. "I hate it when I blush."

He jammed his hands into his pants pockets. "I want so much to take you in my arms and kiss you, but after what happened the other day, I know I can't. Pretend that's what I just did." He glanced at the chair beside Anna's. "Shall we sit? Katie's on the swing, but it won't be long before the others arrive."

She sat and waited for him to sit before she spoke. "Rory, I'm scared. Up to now I was certain I could go to Father and tell him I will not marry Lyman under any circumstances, and that I intend to marry you. But now I feel as if all courage has left me."

He glanced toward the exit then took her hand and squeezed it. "Would you go through with that marriage arrangement if he refuses to accept your decision?"

She felt a tremble in his hand. He wasn't as calm as he made himself out to be. "I can't marry Lyman. Not the way he treats me."

"I know you said before he's always the perfect gentlemen around your parents. But, surely your father must know otherwise."

She shook her head. "He doesn't. I've tried to tell him, but whenever I start to, he waves me off and says I must be letting my nerves get to me. That I should think about the life of comfort I'll enjoy being married to Lyman." She pulled her hand away from Rory's grasp and pressed a palm to her stomach. "Just thinking about it makes me nauseated."

"I wish I could go to your father with you."

She bit her lip. Father did say how much he likes Rory and how he'll be a wonderful father for Katie. But for him to approve her marrying a man of his status was expecting too much. She gazed into Rory's handsome face, trying to memorize every detail. "Rory, remember that no matter what happens, I love you with all my heart, and always will."

The door opened and they both sat back in their chairs.

A tall thin woman stepped in. "Good morning." She looked from Rory to Anna. "I hope I'm not interrupting anything. "I'm Miss Goodnight, the substitute teacher for Monday."

Anna jumped to her feet. "No interruption." She looked at Rory who must have stood when the woman came in. "This is Mr. Quinn, the uncle of Katie, the little girl out by the swing."

Rory nodded. "And I be on my way to my job now. Thank your for your time, Miss Hartwell." He picked up his hat from where he'd placed it on Anna's desk and walked to the door.

Anna ached to run after him. There was so much more she wanted to say. She shook her thoughts away and offered the substitute a smile. "I'm so glad you're here, Miss Goodnight. You can hang your coat in the cloakroom. The rest of the children should be arriving in a few minutes."

The woman removed her bonnet, revealing dark hair pulled back so tight into a bun that it gave her face a pinched appearance. "I've never taught so many grade levels at once. I hope I can do it. I've had ten years teaching experience. Only stopped when I had to care for my sick mother." Sadness emerged in her dark eyes. "She's passed on now. I'm hoping to return to teaching as soon as there is an opening at the village school."

"I'm so sorry about your mother, but I'm sure you'll be fine here. The children are very forgiving with someone new. They have been with me." Anna walked around her desk. "It sounds like most of them are outside now. After you hang up your coat, you can see how they are called to begin the day."

Now she had to not only worry about what Father would say, but also if Miss Goodnight did such a wonderful job, would the superintendent want her to stay and Anna to leave?

# CHAPTER THIRTY-THREE

Monday morning, Anna swallowed a bite of scrambled eggs and prayed the food would stay down. All the while she dressed for her trip into the city, her stomach had churned. Mother never made her morning appearance before Anna left for school, yet there she sat across from her, sipping on tea. Hopefully, she would go along believing Anna was leaving early for school and not for the first train out to Chicago.

Peggy stepped into the room. "Miss Anna, Patrick asked me to tell you that you need to leave in five minutes if you're to make the train."

Mother set her teacup onto its saucer so fast the cup tottered. "Train? You're not going out to school today? What aren't you telling me?"

Peggy's face blanched and she looked from Mother to Anna.

"Thank you, Peggy. Tell him I'm coming." Anna set her napkin beside her plate and looked at her mother. "This came up at the last minute. I'm only going for the day to talk to Father."

Mother stiffened. "You have no time to be sized for your

wedding dress because of that infernal school, and now you take a day to meet with your father?" She pushed her plate of toast away and stood. "I insist you take a later train so I can go with you. After you and your father have talked, we can see about having you measured for your wedding dress. I heard that our own seamstress Lucy has set up shop in a brownstone in the unburned section. She's always been my first choice for you."

Anna wanted in the worst way to say that the only wedding dress she intended to wear was the one she'd wear when she married Rory. "I'm only going for the day. I'd best be on my way."

Her mother cocked her head. "You still haven't told me why you are going into the city."

"You'll learn soon enough. Goodbye, Mother." She stepped into the foyer and picked up her reticule without looking back.

Through most of the train ride, Anna couldn't shake the memory of the last time she'd been on a train, escaping the city. In the past month and a half, her life had completely turned on its axis. Now, here she was traveling back to sever the last connection she had there. Returning to Geneva this afternoon would be a joyous ride, full of anticipation of marrying Rory and spending her life with him.

"I hear many folks are still living in half-destroyed buildings and makeshift tents."

Anna glanced across the aisle at the two men sitting there.

The man nearest the window shook his head. "You'd think the city could do something for them. The weather is getting colder. They can't exist that way once winter sets in."

"They are doing something, but there are more displaced people than shelters. I hear some are even living in the cellars of those mansions on the north side."

Anna wiped her clammy hands on her skirts. Were refugees living in her home's root cellar? Rory had told her he'd helped clear some of the rubble from the property and said that the only thing left standing were the chimneys. He said nothing about the cellar.

The train crossed the Chicago River and Anna's mouth fell open. She'd seen a few pictures of the devastation left after a Civil War battle, but this looked worse. All Father had talked about was the massive building effort going on and how already buildings were rising from the ashes. He must have meant only in a small area, not the whole. She palmed away a tear from her cheek.

The train hissed to a stop at the depot. Anna didn't move to stand. It had been so easy to block out the horror of the fire while she stayed in Wisconsin. She had to face reality, and she had to do what she came to do. Besides, she'd already telegraphed Father she was coming.

Two streetcars later, Anna stepped into the storefront for Pierpont Insurance as Father's directions stated. A narrow-faced man wearing wire-rimmed glasses looked up from what appeared to be an old kitchen table doing duty as a desk.

"May I help you?" He ran his gaze over Anna.

She clutched her coat at the top button, suddenly feeling exposed. "I'm looking for my father's offices. Hartwell and Tavish."

The man's leering smile dissolved. "Those would be upstairs on the second floor. The steps are outside to the left."

Anna found the enclosed stairwell and began the steep climb. How did Father manage these steps with his girth? Surely he was huffing and puffing by the time he reached the landing. The weight of her own skirts was causing enough problems for her.

As she reached the top step, Anna caught her breath then stepped down the long narrow hall, walking on the balls of her feet to stop the sound of her heels from echoing off the high ceiling. At the end of the corridor, she paused in front of a door.

A makeshift sign nailed to the wall announced she'd come to Hartwell & Tavish.

She tapped on the door then, without waiting for a response, opened it.

Her father looked up from a paper he was reading. "Anna, I was about to send a search party for you. Was the train delayed?"

She shook her head. "No, but I had to wait about fifteen minutes between the two streetcar routes. Are you sure we're still in Chicago?"

"It's quite different, isn't it?" He removed his glasses and rubbed his eyes. "I've heard war veterans say these conditions are worse than what they encountered in the aftermath of battle." He leaned back in his chair. "When I received your wire I was pleased to hear you were coming. How did you manage to take time from your duties at the school?"

"A former teacher from the village school is substituting." Anna sat in the only other chair and studied the sparsely furnished room. "Quite different from your office before the fire."

"Yes. But I must say everyone's spirits are high. We're determined to make the city strong again as fast as possible." He frowned. "And to build with steel and brick so the same thing doesn't happen again."

Anna swallowed, wishing she had a glass of water. Anything to wet her parched throat. "Father, I have a particular reason for coming. I purposely didn't tell Mother my plans until this morning because I wanted to talk to you privately."

He lifted an eyebrow. "It must be serious if you couldn't wait until Friday."

She drew in a long breath and brushed dust from her skirt. All the words she'd practiced for days had vanished. Best to just say it outright. "I will not be marrying Lyman Millard. I've fallen in love with another man, and I plan to marry him."

Father's jaw dropped and he gaped at her. "Fallen in love? With whom?" He held up his hand. "I know who. It's Katie's uncle isn't it?"

She felt her shoulders relax. "Yes, it's Rory."

"Then I wasn't mistaken when I thought I saw a spark between you."

"Our feelings were always there, but we both denied them." She hung her head and studied the weave of her skirt. "We've spent time together since the festival and have admitted our feelings. He loves me as much as I love him."

"You're caught up in the emotion of him being alive and learning he's Katie's uncle. I know you adore the child. You're probably seeing how marrying Rory would make you Katie's mother. That's it, isn't it?"

Anna's mouth dropped open. "No. That's not it. I had feelings for Rory before the fire and before I'd ever met Katie. Ask Patrick."

Father jerked his shoulders back and frowned. "What's Patrick have to do with anything?"

Anna sniffed and pulled a handkerchief from her reticule. "He's watched Rory and me when we visited most afternoons before I left for home. Patrick told me the other day he knew we had fallen in love just by watching us."

Father cocked a brow and leaned back and crossed his arms. "So Patrick is in on the scheme?"

"There's no scheme. Patrick didn't say anything about it until I brought it up."

Father flew to his feet and glared at her. "What are you doing confiding personal information to our hired help? That is not appropriate."

Ann bit her quivering lip. "You know Patrick and I have an affectionate relationship. He's been my driver since I was a girl. I would never say to the other help what I say to Patrick. He's a special friend."

Father's shoulders sagged and he sat in his chair. "Yes, I know he is. It's just that I worry for you, Anna."

She kept her focus fixed on Father's face. "I cannot marry Lyman feeling the way I do about Rory."

Father tapped his fountain pen on the desk. "If you marry Rory, you won't be able to live in the manner to which you've been accustomed. What is he? A farmer?"

"He just started a job working as assistant caretaker at Maple Lawn. He's learning how to work with plants and flowers. We hope as more estates are built on the lake, he'll be able to work as a head caretaker on one of them. I love the lake and the town and working with the Irish Woods children. Marrying Lyman would be like a death sentence. As for being able to have enough to live on, Mrs. Cleary the teacher at the school had a family emergency and had to quit. I've agreed to become the teacher at the school. With my income and Rory's from caretaking, we'll be fine. I don't need all those comforts you love so much to be happy."

He removed his spectacles and rubbed his eyes with the heels of his hands, then hooked the earpieces over each ear before he looked at her. The lenses made his eyes appear larger than they were. "My dear daughter, I do understand. Contrary to what you may think right now, I don't have a heart of stone. But, if you don't marry Lyman . . . " He stared off. "It will mean financial ruin for me."

Anna's chest tightened. She must have misunderstood. "I thought you saved all the necessary papers to document your investments."

Father rested his elbows on the desk and steepled his fingers in front of him. "We made the agreement with the Millard's after you were born that you would marry Lyman. We thought that by connecting both families by marriage it would help protect our investments and afford our children financial security." He pressed his lips together and closed his eyes. "Millard has had greater success financially than I, and now with this fire, your marriage into their family is needed more than ever."

Nauseated, Anna pressed her hand to her stomach and glared at Father. "How could you do that to your own child without knowing what kind of man Lyman would turn out to be?"

He heaved a breath. "As you know, your mother's and my marriage was by arrangement and the Millards' is also. It's the way our families have done things for generations. I'm sorry you can't follow your feelings for Rory. He's a nice man, but people like us have a duty to fulfill. You don't have to love Lyman—"

"I loathe him and the very ground he walks on." She folded her arms and leaned over, staring at the floor. "He has brutalized me. Actually causes bruises. If you don't believe me, ask Callie. She's seen them."

He narrowed his eyes. "If he has hurt you, he must have been provoked. I've seen your attitude about this arrangement. If you've shown the same attitude toward him...if you stop provoking him, I'm sure there's nothing to worry about."

Her mouth fell open. "I can't believe you're taking his side."

"The war proved to be costly to me," He looked off at nothing. "I took out a loan to buy the Wisconsin property and for the house I plan to build there. If the fire hadn't happened, I could have handled the loan and worked on building up my clientele. As it stands now, I can't afford to rebuild our Chicago home and build the Wisconsin one too. The Chicago property is valuable, but I'm only getting three or four cents on the dollar from the insurance company. They're all going bust with the large number of claims."

He caught Anna's eye and gave her a pleading look. "If you marry Lyman, our family will benefit, and I'll have financial backing. Otherwise I may lose the business all together, and my reputation." He drew in a breath and held it. "There's another thing. I haven't told you girls or your mother yet, but I've decided to run for ward alderman."

Anna blinked. First he's broke and now he's going to run for alderman? "You've never shown an interest in politics before. Why now?"

His eyes misted over. "It's a business decision. I have to keep my image up, get my name out there. Besides, it's time I get involved. I can use my business sense to help make sure such a fire never happens again." He peered at her through narrowed eyes. "Breaking it off with Lyman when everyone knows of the impending marriage could raise some eyebrows. Make it look like it's related to my running for office. Having the Millards as part of our extended family can enhance my chances of winning."

Anna squeezed her eyes shut. This couldn't be happening. He'd always been in her corner when Mother assaulted her with angry words. Yet, this wasn't the father she'd always loved speaking to her now. Marrying Lyman could only mean resigning herself to a life of pain, physically and emotionally.

*Honour thy father and thy mother: that thy days may be long upon the land which the* Lord *thy God giveth thee.*

She tried to push the commandment away. Would God want her to honor Father's wishes when the man he insists she marry is evil?

*Lord, is this what You want? I know you demand obedience, but I need to see a sign I'm to do this. You know Rory and I love each other and he is a good Christian man. Help me sort this out.*

A life without Rory and Katie was like a prison sentence. An ache filled Anna's throat. God knows the beginning from the end and maybe he will provide a way of escape. She could agree and still pray for a way to stop this charade.

She let out a sigh and slumped in her chair. Why did life have to be so complicated? God may promise a long life for honoring her parents, but without Rory there was no life.

"Father, I'm sorry for the predicament you are in. I realize that if I refuse to marry Lyman, I'll probably be disowned by you. I need to pray about this."

Father wiped the dampness from his eyes. "Thank you, Anna." He checked his timepiece. "I asked Lyman to stop in this morning. There is no way to reach him in time to stop the appointment. He should be here in ten or fifteen minutes. Just do your best to act like nothing is wrong."

Anna flinched. She wasn't ready to face Lyman as if everything was good and right. She stood and darted out the door. Her father's shouts for her to stop echoed in her ears, but she scrambled down the stairs and out onto the street.

She turned toward the streetcar stop, dodging around construction workers and businessmen. A streetcar rolled up as she arrived at the stop and she climbed aboard, paid her fare and fell into a seat at the back of the car.

Running did no good. The pain slicing through her heart came with her.

# CHAPTER THIRTY-FOUR

Rory stepped inside the Sturgis estate's greenhouse and inhaled the earthy aroma of fresh greenery and damp soil. He walked the length of the center aisle between flats of ground covers he and Daniel had started experimenting with, pleased at their growth since Saturday. It never ceased to amaze him how God had created nature with such perfection and how it all worked together.

Anna's beautiful face intruded on his thoughts. Since early morning he'd been praying that her father would accept her decision not to marry Millard. If she'd asked him, he'd have gone with her this morning, but he understood this was something she had to do on her own.

He looked up at the glass roof overhead. "Father, I have no proof—only an uneasy feeling about Millard. Protect Anna from him."

He fisted both hands and stabbed the air with a right hook. "Take that, you lousy excuse of a human being."

"I'm glad I'm not on the receiving end of that punch."

Rory spun around. Daniel stood a few feet away, his head tilted back, guffawing.

"You would never be on the receiving end of my fist, I can assure you."

His friend grew serious. "It sounds like someone did something bad to you."

Rory shook his head. "Not to me directly. I found out the other day Anna is to be the bride in an arranged marriage."

Daniel rubbed his chin. "And you were hoping she'd marry you."

"I never said—"

"It's all over your face whenever you mention her." He frowned. "Is she going through with the marriage?"

Rory rubbed the back of his neck. "She went into the city this morning to tell her da she'll not marry the bloke and that she wants to marry me."

"When will you know what happened?"

Rory lifted his shoulders and let them fall. "Probably tomorrow. The worst that can happen is she may get disowned. I've made arrangements with my uncle's neighbors to provide her a room if that happens."

Daniel crossed his arms. "Are you sure she'll accustom herself to living in Irish Woods? She's used to fancy homes and high society."

"Anna likes the simple things. When I'm able to get my own head caretaker position, we're hoping it will be on an estate with a caretaker house. She says that's all she needs. And God, of course."

Daniel's facial expression was less than reassuring. "Well, I hope it all works out."

"I'm sure it will." Rory picked up a bag of seeds. "God is watching over both of us, of that I'm certain."

# CHAPTER THIRTY-FIVE

Anna stepped off the train in Geneva. Several carriages and their drivers sat in the usual waiting area, but the family's new coupe wasn't among them. Had mother even received the wire Anna sent advising which train Patrick should meet?

She drew in a deep breath and walked toward Broad Street. Anna had only walked a half block when someone called her name. She glanced toward the road.

Patrick stopped the coupe next to her and climbed down. "Sorry I'm late, Miss Anna. You mother needed to do errands, and they took longer than expected. I came as soon as I dropped her off."

Anna walked toward the carriage. "I hope Mother doesn't have you scheduled for anything more. I'd like to go to Irish Woods to Rory's uncle's before I go home."

He gave her a curious look. "Do you know where the farm is?"

Grateful she did because of Katie now living there, she gave him the location.

Anna stared through the glass window at Patrick's back as

they rolled along Broad Street toward Main Street. Tears filled her eyes and she blinked. How, after weeping in silence over the two-hour train ride, could she produce even more tears?

Anna pressed her fist to her mouth and stifled a sob. She needed to gather herself before they arrived and she and Rory were together.

She silently prayed that Rory would have wisdom to help her decide what to do. As much as Father had infuriated her today, she still loved him and the last thing she wanted was to be the cause of his losing even more than he had already. But, if she married Lyman, she may save her father's financial situation, but it may as well be a death sentence for her. All too soon, Patrick drove the carriage into Denis Quinn's farm.

Rory stepped out of the barn, and strode toward the carriage, a smile never leaving his face. He was obviously expecting to hear good news.

Rory waited while Patrick assisted Anna out of the carriage.

She looked at him, working to keep her composure. "We need to talk privately."

A look of confusion crossed his face. "We can go in the barn. No one's there but a couple of horses." He took her elbow and guided her toward the barn. "You're shaking. Are you okay?"

"Not really."

Inside the barn, aromas of hay and horse assaulted her nose. They came to a halt in front of a stall, and Rory ran his loving gaze over her face. "I'm taking it that the meeting didn't go well."

Anna swallowed against the ache that had been in her throat since she left Father's office. She had to get her words out. "It was awful, Rory. I don't know how to begin."

He drew her into his arms and pressed her face to his broad chest. She inhaled aroma of the rich soils he worked with that day. Oh, how she'd come to love that scent, and had looked forward to breathing it in each day when he returned from work and she stepped into his arms.

"Just tell me. Don't think about the words."

She stepped back, so she could look him in the eyes. "I love you so much, Rory, but . . . A sob exploded from her throat and she hauled in a breath. I'm not sure I can marry you. I need help to decide what to do."

He squeezed his eyes shut and pulled her closer. "Doesn't he realize you aren't in love with Millard?"

"Love means nothing to a man whose own marriage is void of affection. It's a business deal. If I don't marry Lyman, my father will suffer financial ruin, and the family may as well be homeless."

Rory stiffened. "A lot of people are homeless thanks to the fire. He can build a new home."

She leaned back and looked into his eyes again. "Not if he doesn't have the money to pay for it. He isn't himself anymore. For as much as my mother has treated me horribly, Father has always done his best to do otherwise. I don't need all those trappings, but he's done as much as possible to make up for the way Mother treats me."

Rory's arms dropped to his side and he stepped back. The ruddy color on his cheeks a deep red. "So in other words, our plans are off and your wedding to Millard is on."

She pressed a fist to her mouth and turned away. "I've not yet agreed to the marriage. I wanted to discuss this with you. Help me decide what to do. You know I want you and you only for my husband. I've been praying the whole train ride and all I can think about is the commandment that says I'm to honor my father and mother. I've always tried to be obedient to God but if I refuse to marry Lyman I'm breaking that commandment."

He paced a circle then waved his arm in the air. "Your father still has his business. He's planning on building a house here on the lakeshore. I don't understand how he can say he's without money."

She palmed tears from her eyes. "The insurance companies are going broke with all the claims. He's only getting a few cents back on the dollar toward the claim for our home. By my marrying into the Millard family, there was something in the agreement that would merge many of the assets of both families." She let out a sob. "I'm only seen as chattel. Not a—"

Rory gripped both her shoulders and fixed his eyes on her. "Is that all you want to be Anna? Chattel in a business deal? There's something else you're not telling me about Millard. What is it?"

She studied her feet. "He's mistreated me at times."

"In what way?"

"He's caused bruises on my shoulder. I told Father, but he said I probably provoked him and it couldn't be the way he'd actually treat me after we're married."

Fire burned in Rory's eyes and she stepped back. Was he going to hurt her too? She raised her hands palms out in front of her face.

He dropped his hands to his side and drew her into a hug. "My precious Anna, I would never hurt you like that brute has apparently done. I can't stop you from doing as your father wishes, but we need to pray about what to do in the meantime."

She relaxed in the cocoon of his arms. "I know one thing we need right now is time."

"There's a proverb that keeps running through my mind about trusting God with all your heart, even when you don't understand the situation and he will show the right way to go. That's what we need to do right now is trust Him. But, please try to not be alone with Millard. If I find out he's laid a hand on you again, I don't know if I'll be able to keep quiet."

"I love you so much, Rory."

He brought his mouth to hers and caressed her lips with his.

The kiss deepened and she wrapped her arms around his waist and pulled him to her, returning his fire with her own. Oh, how she loved him.

They broke apart and he cradled her face in his hands as he ran his soft lips over her face, kissing away her tears, then each eyelid. He trailed small feathery kisses over her cheeks then reclaimed her mouth until he pulled away and trailed the back of his fingers over her cheek. "Anna, my Anna. I love you so much. I'm certain God will show us the way out of this."

He pulled her against him and ran his hands up and down her back before nuzzling her neck, sending a shiver down her spine and into her toes. He brought his mouth close to her ear. "It was inappropriate to kiss you like that when you're engaged to another man. But if Millard kisses you before the engagement is broken, I want you to remember the kiss you received from the man who really loves you."

"I can't imagine ever kissing him the way I just kissed you." She leaned back and brushed her fingertips over his lips. "I love you and only you, Rory Quinn."

He took her hand and kissed her fingers, then released his hold. "You'd better get on home before I carry you off to a justice of the peace."

Startled at the catch in his voice, Anna nodded. "Maybe eloping is the answer."

He chuckled. "In the end it may be the only answer. But let's give God time to work first."

They walked in silence, hand in hand, and stopped a few feet from the carriage. Rory gripped her shoulders in each hand and kissed her on the cheek. "See you soon." He opened the carriage door and helped her inside then glanced up at Patrick where he sat on the bench. "Take good care of her, Patrick."

The servant nodded. "You know I will.

# CHAPTER THIRTY-SIX

Anna heaved a sigh of relief at Mother's absence when they arrived home. She went straight to her room and stepped out of her dress, letting it puddle on the floor. Thankful nothing needed her immediate attention, she wrapped herself in a dressing gown, then lay on the bed and stared at the ceiling.

She pressed her fingertips to her mouth, straining to recall the feel of Rory's lips. She let her hand fall to her side. She turned on her side and drew her knees to her chest. Growing up, instead of rebelling against Mother's harsh treatment, she'd tried to be obedient even when she couldn't understand what was required of her. Always attempting to win Mother's affections, and always coming up short. Was that what she was doing now if she married Lyman? No. She would be doing it for Father.

The bedroom door creaked and her eyes popped open. A moment later soft light filled the room. Callie stood by the gas lamp. "I'm sorry I woke you. It's almost time for supper and I need to change." She crossed the room to her dresser and poured water into the ceramic basin. "Are you okay?"

Anna stretched. She had no appetite and could easily stay in bed until morning, but what would that accomplish? "I've been better. I took the day off school and went to the city to see Father."

Her sister's eyes widened. "Did you tell him you were breaking the marriage agreement?"

"Yes."

Callie sat on Anna's bed. "And by the looks of you, he must have refused to agree. Of course you're not going to marry that creep and marry Rory instead, right?"

"That's the hope but right now I'm going to act as though the Millard wedding is on. Rory and I decided on this together."

Callie opened her mouth and Anna held up her hand palm out. "Please. No questions, and don't breathe a word of this. Go along with whatever you hear me telling Mother." She swung her legs over the side of the bed and stood. "Dinner should be interesting."

A short time later, Anna entered the parlor and Mother turned from warming her hands in front of the fireplace. She glowered at Anna. "You'd better telegraph your father and let him know you are home safe."

"You heard about our conversation?"

"He wired saying you ran out on him and Lyman and he had no idea where you went. How could you be so rude?" She sat on the burgundy velveteen settee and picked up the writing box that rested there. "I'll wire the Millards first thing in the morning and invite them here for a Saturday evening dinner party to announce the wedding plans." She lifted the carved lid and took out a sheet of paper, and a pen and ink.

Anna gave a half-hearted shrug and dropped into a chair. "That's the weekend before Christmas. Can't we do this after the holiday?"

Mother dipped her pen and began writing. "The George Sturges and the Rumsey family are staying in Geneva, and your father has done business with both men. I've met their wives at society functions. We'll invite them." Mother surveyed the parlor. "The dining room is much too small. Perhaps we could move the table in here and extend it to full length. I wish we had our new lakeshore home built already."

Anna frowned. "Are you sure we can afford all this right now?"

"Whatever do you mean? We can afford whatever we want."

"According to Father, not until we are related to the Millards can we afford much of anything. Didn't he tell you?"

Color drained from Mother's face. "I have no idea what you are talking about. It's true our financial status will increase with the wedding, but we are certainly not poor." She scratched the pen across the paper. "We'll have to be sure to invite the Shelton Sturges family as well. I've never made their acquaintance, but your father said he toured Maple Lawn when he was here to purchase our property. And of course the Rumseys and the other Sturgis family."

Anna bottled a sigh. Was Father being truthful about how destitute they would be without her marrying Lyman? If he wasn't, then the decision was an easy one. And it wasn't to marry Lyman.

Mother dipped the pen's nib into the ink then scribbled an addition to her list. "There's no time for you to be fitted in the city. Millie has done wonderful work on our new dresses. She'll have to do. I'll have to get you an appointment with her immediately."

Anna sighed. "I am still the teacher at the school and I must be there every school day. Any fittings will have to occur after school."

Mother snapped her head up. "You can't possibly expect to continue at the school until the wedding day. There's so much to do."

"I can't leave the children without a teacher."

"What about the woman who took your place today?"

"She's not available after this Friday. She has family coming for Christmas and a grandbaby due the first week in January."

Mother blotted her list then lifted the paper and held it at arm's length. "That's the school's problem. Not yours." She grimaced. "I can barely see what I wrote. I'm going to have to get my eyes examined. I was hoping to avoid wearing those garish spectacles."

Anna walked to the window and stared into the inky darkness. How different she'd feel if they were speaking of her marrying Rory. A vision of wearing a wedding gown and walking toward him and the preacher in the little church on Madison Street filled her mind. *Please Lord, let it be so.* She faced her mother. "Mrs. Cleary wears glasses and she looks fine in them."

Mother stood. "Dinner is in half an hour." She crossed the room, her list in hand, and disappeared into the hall.

Anna turned and stared up at the crescent moon. "God, I'm still trusting you, please don't let Rory and me down."

# CHAPTER THIRTY-SEVEN

Thursday morning, raised voices floated down the back stairs into the kitchen where Anna ate a bowl of oatmeal. Peggy turned from the sink. "It must be very rewarding, Miss Anna, to teach the wee ones out there at the Woods."

"It is." Anna took a spoonful of oatmeal, wishing she could decipher the angry words from two floors above them. Father had surprised them all by taking the train out from the city the day before. Although they seldom agreed on anything, hearing her parents fight was rare.

A door slammed and footfalls down the back stairs became louder until Father burst into the room, his face red and his jaw throbbing. "Anna, your mother insists on taking the train into the city this morning. She can't be ready in time for the early train. Have Patrick take you out to your school then he can take us to the depot later."

"Why is she going into the city?"

He frowned and shook his head. "She's determined to find a proper venue for your wedding, and refuses to believe me that there isn't a church or other suitable place for such an event close to where we lived. She's as bad with this as Calista has been with the debutante balls." He accepted a cup of coffee from Peggy, took a sip then set the cup on the table. He added a couple sugar cubes and stirred them in. "I'm beginning to regret I was unable to agree to your request of the other day and be done with all this."

He glanced at Anna. "You can wipe that expectant look from your face. We are staying with the plan. There is no other way. I'm very sorry."

The bite of toast Anna just swallowed rose to her throat. She forced it down and stood. "Whatever God has willed, we shouldn't try to change even if it doesn't turn out the way you hope. I'd like to see the state of your financial situation on paper." She picked up her bag and walked toward the back door. "Have a nice day."

With her Father's sardonic comment that it was too late for him to have a nice day trailing after her, Anna strode to the barn.

Patrick looked up from hitching Goldie to the carriage. "Miss Anna, I was expecting Mr. Hartwell."

"There's been a change in plans. He and Mother will be taking the mid-morning train. You're to bring me to school then return for them." She stroked Goldie's nose and the horse nuzzled her hand. "Sorry, girl. You're already harnessed. The treat will have to wait until later."

RORY FINISHED HITCHING the horse to his wagon as Katie came out the front door. She skipped down the path and across the yard. "Why do we have to go to school so early, Uncle Rory?"

He lifted her to the wagon bench. "Like I said, I have to be at work early, that's why." Pressure filled his chest. Truth be told, he needed to have a moment with Anna. Maybe then he'd feel more assured she hadn't changed her mind about wanting to be his wife. He sat next to Katie and hugged her to his side. "Don't you want your old uncle taking you to school?"

She giggled. "Maybe Miss Anna will be there early and you can kiss her again."

A sinking feeling came over him. "When did you see me kissing Miss Anna?"

"Yesterday when you were talking to her in the barn. I was up in the loft playing. I didn't want you to know I was there, so I stayed quiet."

His heart sunk. "What did you hear us talking about?"

She scrunched her nose and shrugged. "I didn't understand the words, but I heard Miss Anna crying. Then it got quiet. I peeked to see if you went outside. That's when I saw you kissing her, and I knew she wouldn't be sad anymore. Is she going to marry you and we be a family?"

Rory prayed for the right words. "I don't know. God has to want it before it can happen. Meanwhile can you keep it a secret that you saw us kissing?"

Katie's face twisted. "I want her to be my ma."

"What I just said, Katie-girl." He pulled a handkerchief from his back pocket and wiped the tears trailing down her cheeks. "Nothing is certain right now."

She threw herself across Rory's lap. "I thought she was going to be my new ma and live with us. That's what I prayed for."

He rubbed her small back. "God knows better what's best for us than we do." He eased her into a sitting position. "Let's get you to school, so I can get to work."

Aside from an occasional sniffle, Katie remained quiet during the ten-minute ride. As they approached the school, the Hartwell coupe pulled into the turnabout in front of the building.

Rory pulled his wagon behind them. Patrick waved as he climbed down. He reached for the carriage door handle, and Rory's heart raced.

Anna stepped to the ground wearing a winter coat, her hands inside of a furry muff, her back to him. Patrick said something and she turned. Their gazes collided and intertwined. She raised her hand in a wave.

"Miss Anna. See. I'm wearing one of my new dresses."

For a moment he'd forgotten Katie was with him. When had she climbed out of the wagon?

The child unbuttoned her coat and pirouetted in front of Anna and her skirts lifted, revealing the leather boots Rory bought her last payday.

"So I see." Anna's gaze returned to Rory. Her smile didn't reach her eyes. "Good morning."

He nodded. "Hello."

"I didn't expect Katie so early." She began assisting the girl with buttoning her coat. "You shouldn't open your buttons in this cold air."

He glanced at his niece who remained next to Anna. "I have to be at work early. Anything I need to know?"

She took a step toward him and tipped her head to look up at him. "Perhaps. I suspect my father may be exaggerating his financial status. My mother continues to hope the wedding will be the end of January."

He pressed his lips together and puffed his cheeks. "Not a lot of time."

"Remember Who is in control. I asked Father for an accounting of his situation." She glanced toward the school door. "I'd best get inside to prepare."

"Have a good day." He tipped his cap.

"And you as well."

He gave the reins a shake, and the horse started moving. "God, You only have a bit more than a month to show us the way to go. If he has exaggerated, please let the truth come out. Nothing is impossible with You. Nothing."

# CHAPTER THIRTY-EIGHT

*A*nna stepped into the house, grateful the long day was finally over. She hung her coat on the hall tree and crossed the Oriental rug toward the stairs. She'd have an hour before Callie was due home and until then, have the bedroom to herself.

"I'm glad you're home. Plans have changed since you left this morning."

Anna whirled around as Mother came from the back hall. "I didn't expect you back from Chicago this early."

"I didn't go after all. The Saturday after New Year's Day, you, Calista and I are taking the train into the city. The Millard's driver will take us to their home and your father will meet us there. Lyman will present you with an engagement ring, and Saturday night, the Millards will host a dinner party to formally announce your wedding date." Mother paused and took a deep breath.

"What happened to plans for a dinner here?"

Mother stiffened. "Hortense offered their home for the dinner and their church for the ceremony." Her gaze flicked upward then back to Anna. "After all, that's always been our home and where both families are well known."

"It sounds to me like Mrs. Millard is in charge."

She gave Anna a tight smile. "She only thinks she is. I wanted it at their home all a long. The ceremony will take place at the Millard's church on February third, and a reception and dinner will follow at their home. It's the only way, unless we want to wait months and months for our home to be built."

"Being controlled by someone else hurts, doesn't it?" Anna stepped past her mother and walked to the stairs.

She reached the landing and Mother called out. "You should be thanking God for the blessings of marrying into such a fine family."

Anna faced her mother. "I doubt God would consider my marrying a man such as Lyman a blessing."

Mother tossed her head. "There are many young women who would happily take your place."

"I doubt the line to marry Lyman would be very long, Mother." Callie came down the stairs and stood next to Anna. "You never saw the way he tormented children younger than him, including Richard."

Mother waved a hand. "That's just mischievousness that all boys go through. It couldn't have been that bad or your brother would have told us."

Callie placed her fists on her hips. "Not if Lyman threatened to hurt him if he told."

"You're exaggerating."

"I'm not. Why are you forcing Anna to marry him?"

The skin around Mother's mouth grew taut. "They've been engaged since they were children. Whatever he did in his youth, he isn't like that today."

Anna narrowed her eyes. "No. He's worse. I didn't dream he physically hurt me during a recent carriage ride."

Mother's eyes looked like they might pop out of their sockets. "Lying won't stop the wedding. Accept it."

Callie scowled. "Even if Lyman hadn't hurt Anna physically, I think you and Father are cruel to force her to marry him when she loves someone else."

Mother snapped her gaze to Anna. "What is she talking about?"

Heat traveled up Anna's neck and into her face. "She wasn't to say anything."

"I can't bear to hear her crying every night before we go to sleep. Rory loves her and she loves him." Callie turned and ran up the stairs.

Anna avoided Mother's hard stare. She should never have confided in her sister.

"Rory Quinn? How could you have feelings for someone of his kind?"

The rigidity in Mother's voice grated against Anna's ears. "He's an honest, God-fearing man who treats me well and loves me. That's why I love him."

"When we go to the city for the engagement announcement, you'd better pack to stay with the Millards from then on. Your days at Irish Woods are over."

# CHAPTER THIRTY-NINE

Anna crossed her arms and stared across the foyer at her mother. "I can't leave the school without someone to replace me."

Mother waved a dismissive hand. "And I'm to trust you? "

"Even if I were marrying Rory, I wouldn't quit until a new teacher is hired. That's the best I can do. If I go back on my word to them, think of how it will reflect on our family name."

Mother's irritable expression dissolved. She held up her hands in surrender. "All right. But if I hear one word about you and that Quinn man being together, I'll . . ."

Anna waited for Mother to finish her threat. When it didn't come, she continued to her room. Behind her, Mother's footsteps sounded across the foyer's wood floor in the opposite direction.

When Anna entered their room, Callie was sitting on her bed and staring at her lap. She looked up. Tears streaked her face. "I'm sorry for telling about Rory. I couldn't stand to listen to her go on about Lyman as if he were Adonis."

Anna sat next to Callie and hugged her to her side. "That's okay."

Callie's eyes widened. "I can't believe that after you told Father, he's still making you marry Lyman. I thought he had a soft spot for you."

"If I don't marry Lyman, it will mean financial ruin for Father, and that will affect you and Mother. And if I marry Rory, I'll be banned from the family."

"But you'd have Rory to love you and Katie too." Callie threw her arms around Anna. "I think you and Rory should elope. Father is probably exaggerating about his financial situation."

Anna eased her sister's arms off her neck and leveled a gaze on her. "I also have the feeling he might be. I asked him to provide me written proof. We'll see what comes of that."

"How long are you going to act like you will go through with the wedding?"

"I don't know. It depends."

"I could never live with myself if you marry that brute and he hurts you again."

Anna walked to the armoire and opened the carved mahogany door. "I can handle myself now that I know what to watch for. God will protect me." She mentally repeated the proverb Rory had quoted to her the other day. She had to trust that something would happen to change the plan.

SATURDAY MORNING, Rory forced himself out of bed. He'd promised Mr. Sturgis to work all day, as Daniel had to attend a family baptism in Chicago.

His aunt stood at the cook stove when he came to the kitchen. She called over her shoulder. "I thought I'd surprise you with a good breakfast. Flapjacks sound good?"

His stomach rumbled. He hadn't had much of an appetite since the problem with Anna came up, and the fact he was even a bit hungry surprised him. "I can never turn down flapjacks. I have to leave in fifteen minutes though. Can you make them that fast?

She grabbed a spatula and a plate. "I heard you moving around upstairs and got a head start. Just don't inhale them." She set a platter of golden brown pancakes in front of him along with a crock of butter and a jar of strawberry preserves. "No maple syrup, but they taste pretty good with the preserves."

She sat across from him while he gobbled the stack. "It does my heart good to see your appetite returning. What's been bothering you, Rory? Aren't you happy about your new job?"

He shrugged and lifted a mug of coffee to his lips. "I'm not bothered by anything."

She huffed a laugh. "You can't fool me, Rory Quinn. You've been walking around here the past few days looking as if you've lost your best friend. Something's not right."

He took a swig of brew and set down the mug. "I thought I be hiding my feelings. What you said might be right—bout losing my best friend."

Her brows shot up. "Who?"

"Doesn't matter." He shook his head and stared off into space. "Unless prayers are answered there's a good chance she'll be marrying another guy."

"I thought it had to be about a woman."

He looked her in the eyes. "We love each other, but she's trapped in an arranged marriage. The wedding is scheduled for the first week of February."

Aunt Evie's chair creaked as she leaned back, never taking her eyes off him. "No one in the Irish community arranges marriages."

He dropped his fork on the remaining pancake, appetite gone. "We met at the mission school in Chicago. She's Katie's teacher now that Mrs. Cleary had to quit. She's trying to end the arrangement, but it's complicated."

"Does she love this other man?"

He shook his head. "She told her da she couldn't go through with the marriage and wants to marry me. But if she doesn't marry the man, her da says he will suffer financially." He rubbed his eyes with the heels of his hands. "She's struggling with the commandment that says we're to honor our parents. We're praying for God to intervene." He scraped his chair back and stood. "I have to leave."

His aunt flew to her feet and grabbed his arm. "In time the pain will go away. Next time look for a woman from your own kind. I've seen do-gooders come from the wealthy to help the Irish. They seem willing to cross the line at first, but it always boils down to us and them. Best to stay with your own."

"I supposed that's true about some, but not Anna. What makes it worse is that her intended has physically hurt her. I'm afraid for her safety."

His aunt's grip tightened, her nails digging through his sleeve. "What do you mean?"

"He bruises her and threatens to hurt her more if she doesn't do as he says."

She winced and let out a loud breath. "Rory, this is urgent. She may be in serious danger. You've got to help her."

He pulled his arm away and stared into her flushed face. "I want to, but what can I do but pray for her safety?"

She lowered her voice to a whisper. "While you're at work, I be doing some prayin' of me own."

## CHAPTER FORTY

The day after Christmas, Anna yawned as she hung up her fur-trimmed coat on a wall peg in the cloakroom, then removed her hood and hung it over the coat.

As she walked between the desks toward the potbelly stove, the skirts of her new cotton paisley day dress swished around her ankles. At her desk, she dropped her leather attaché case that held her lesson plans, then crossed to the wood box and lifted the lid.

She grabbed some kindling and stuffed it into the stove's mouth. She loved the simple task of lighting a fire each morning. She plucked a match from a box nearby and swiped the head against the striking surface. A flame flickered to life.

"Anna, I hoped you'd still be here alone."

She blew out the flame and whirled around.

Rory stood at the far side of the classroom, his hat clutched in both hands. A lock of hair fell over his forehead giving him the boyish look Anna had fallen in love with months earlier.

"Rory."

"Praise be to God, you look happy to see me. You were all I thought of yesterday, wondering how things were for you at home." His long strides brought him within a few feet of her. He searched her face with his eyes. "I hope you had a nice Christmas Day."

She ached to fall into his arms, but the fear of someone interrupting them held her back. "I suppose I did, but how can I be festive? I keep praying for a way to stop the wedding plans, but so far everything is right on course. So far Father hasn't provided me with the written proof of his situation. I have a feeling he was not completely truthful. We're to go into the city a week from Saturday to make the engagement official."

"I wanted to tell you the preacher's sermon last Sunday convicted me that I have to step in and fight for your honor and safety." He took her left hand and ran his thumb over her ring finger. "I know I could never afford a ring like the one Lyman will likely give you, but my love for you is worth far more than all the precious stones money can buy. I want permission to speak with your da."

She ran her hand across his grizzled cheek, enjoying the feel of his stubble. "My knight in shining armor. I love you for what you're willing to do. I keep thinking we have to wait this out. A engagement announcement doesn't seal the deal. There is still time after that."

"Do your parents still not believe how badly he treats you?"

"No, they don't."

He crossed his arms. "Then your father must be made to understand. When is he coming to Geneva next?"

"He left for Chicago this morning and I'm not sure when he's returning."

His muscular arm went around her waist and his gaze focused on her mouth as his other arm circled her.

One more kiss wouldn't hurt. She loved him so much. He leaned down and placed a short kiss on her lips.

The outside door flew open.

They turned in unison.

Katie looked from Rory to Anna. "Danny fell off the swing and he's bleeding."

Anna scurried toward the door. "I'll be right there."

"I'm coming with you." Rory's pounding footfalls followed her across the room and down the outside steps. He ran past her toward Danny Murphy who lay in the snow crying and yelling.

Rory was already on his knees and gently feeling along the boy's leg by the time Anna knelt beside him. "It feels broken. He'll need to have his leg splinted by the doctor. I pass the Murphy's farm on my way to work. I can carry him home for his da to take him."

Anna nodded. "Okay."

Rory glanced around the yard. "We need something to keep his leg stable."

"Mr. Quinn, there's some boards over by the steps." One of the fifth grade boys spoke up. "Want me to go get one?"

"Aye. And find me a couple old rags long enough to tie around the leg."

Anna cradled Danny's head in her lap and stroked his hair off his forehead. "Lay as still as possible. Mr. Quinn will get you fixed up, then he'll take you home."

A few minutes later, Rory had a makeshift splint tied around the boy's leg. "Okay, Danny, this may hurt, but I have to carry you to the wagon." He lifted the boy as though he barely weighed anything then looked at Anna. "I meant what I said before. Now get yourself inside before you freeze to death." He turned and walked toward his wagon.

"Miss Anna, should I go home with my brother?"

Anna glanced down at Aileen Murphy, one of the first graders. "I don't think you need to. Your da will probably be taking him to the doctor in town. Best to stay here."

The child ran up ahead to join the other children, and Anna rubbed her arms as she walked across the schoolyard. Never could she picture Lyman dropping to his knees and tending to a child like that—even an injured child. He'd be too afraid of soiling his trousers. She herded the children inside and got the fire going.

The day passed quickly despite Anna's thoughts swaying toward Rory's insisting on talking to Father and their morning kiss. What if anyone but Katie had come into the classroom and saw them together? The awkward situation had to be resolved soon.

At the end of the day, Mr. Murphy sat in his wagon waiting for his daughter. He waved Anna over. "I want to thank you and Rory for taking care of my son. I got Danny to the doctor. He is home and feeling better. I expect by next Monday he'll be ready to return to school on crutches. Maybe tomorrow you can send some schoolwork home with Aileen."

Anna told him Rory was the one to thank and she was glad to hear Danny would be okay. She turned to head back inside. Katie ran up to her and slipped her small hand into Anna's. "Auntie wants to talk to you."

Anna quirked her head. "Who?"

"Aunt Evie. Over there."

Anna's gaze followed the direction of Katie's pointing finger. A woman wearing a cloth coat waved at her from a wagon.

The woman had climbed down from the driver bench by the time they reached her. She held out a hand. "Evie Quinn. Do you have a few moments?"

The woman's calloused palm spoke volumes of their opposite ways. What must this hard-working woman think of Anna's pampered life? She managed a smile. "Mrs. Quinn, how nice to finally meet Rory's aunt. I don't have much time as I have to clear my desk and make it ready for tomorrow before my driver comes."

"Maybe we can talk while you work. It won't take long." She looked at Katie. "Sweetie, can you wait over by the swing? We won't be but a few minutes."

Katie scrunched her nose. "I'm always asked to wait by the swing. Just like this morning when Uncle Rory told me to wait there while he went inside to kiss Miss Anna."

Certain her cheeks must resemble the red apples everyone was storing up for winter, Anna wanted to crawl under the Quinn's wagon.

Mrs. Quinn laughed. "Katie, I think that was supposed to be a secret."

"Why? I want him to kiss Miss Anna. I want her to be my new ma."

The older woman gave the little girl a soft pat on the head. "Enough. Go to the swing."

The child skipped away toward the play yard.

Mrs. Quinn rested her hand on Anna's arm. "Children can be so outspoken sometimes. Rory told me about the feelings you two have for each other and the arranged marriage." She glanced over at Katie, then back to Anna. "That's why I wanted to talk to you. I'm very concerned for your life."

# CHAPTER FORTY-ONE

$\mathcal{A}$nna led her visitor inside, fearing the woman intended to warn her to not break her nephew's heart. Why else would she insist on speaking to her privately? She indicated her chair. "Mrs. Quinn, please have a seat. I prefer to stand when I'm sorting papers."

The woman's features softened. "I don't mind standing, and please call me Evie." Her voice carried a note of kindness.

Confused, Anna offered a tentative smile. "All right, Evie it is, but I really work better standing." She arranged the papers across the desk then began collating them.

"I want to talk to you about your being trapped in an arranged marriage with a man who is brutalizing you."

Anna snapped her gaze away from the papers and stared at Evie. "Rory shouldn't have told you."

Evie leaned forward and kept her focus on Anna. "Please don't be upset with him. I had to pry it out of Rory because I couldn't understand why if you two care for each other, you couldn't be courting. I'm glad I did."

Anna turned away as a sob pushed into her throat. She gulped hard and faced Evie. "I should never have let Rory know my feelings for him until I was out from under this situation. I'm sorry for hurting him."

Evie's compassion-filled eyes, as green as Rory's were blue, stayed fixed on Anna. She cleared her throat. "I'm here because I don't want *you* hurt."

Anna frowned. "I don't understand."

"My first husband died two years after we married." She looked away. "He was shot and killed by my brother."

Anna's hand flew to her mouth, but not in time to mute her gasp. "I'm so sorry. I'll pray for—"

"I'm not." Evie brought her focus back to Anna. "If my brother hadn't killed him, I may not be alive today. My husband beat me almost every day we were married."

Anna eyed the door. "I'm not sure what this all has to do with me."

"She stepped closer until she was inches from Anna and took her hand. "You need to hear my story."

Anna pulled her hand out of Evie's grasp and stepped back. "It was only a couple bruises that were due more to my clumsiness than anything." She picked up the stack of papers. "I really must finish before my driver arrives. Thanks for your concern, but Rory has exaggerated—"

"If you believe that, why won't you look me in the eye, Miss Hartwell?"

Anna forced herself to meet Evie's gaze. "I was clumsy. Fell back when we hit a bump in the road and whacked my shoulder against the carriage."

*Deceiver, dissembler, your trousers are alight!*

The phrase from a poem she'd studied in literature class taunted her as pressure rose in her chest. Isn't it okay to lie to protect one's reputation?

"Perhaps if you hear my story, you'll be willing to take my warning. I'll make it short."

She had little choice. Evie Quinn wasn't going anywhere. She held up her hands in surrender. "All right. I'll listen."

The earnest expression on Evie's face dissolved. "Before we were married, I sounded much like you, trying to convince myself the bruises were of my own clumsiness. But three days after our wedding, he progressed from pushing me into furniture to hitting me on my back and legs. The daily beatings continued the entire two years we were married. The bruises were always in places where they wouldn't show."

Anna's throat tightened. "It only happens once in a while."

Evie regarded her with a skeptical expression. She drew a handkerchief from her dress pocket and wiped her nose. "Trust me. If he's got it in him to do what he's done to ya so far, he'll likely do worse once you take his name. On our wedding night my husband told me the Bible said I was to submit to him and that meant he could do whatever he wanted."

A chill ran down Anna's spine. The same words Lyman had spoken. "Did your brother get arrested for killing your husband?"

"Yes, at first, but he wasn't charged because what he did was done in my defense." She paused as if searching for her next words. "I know it's hard to admit this is happening, and you'd like nothing more than to change the subject. But, Anna, your problem with Lyman isn't going to go away. It'll only get worse."

Anna bit her lip. "If I don't marry him, my father says he'll be ruined."

Evie raised a brow. "Would his fortune matter if you end up dead at the hands of your husband?"

"Lyman wouldn't murder anyone." Anna stared off. She'd seen the fiery anger in his eyes many times when he killed chipmunks and squirrels.

She turned and caught Evie's earnest gaze. "You've warned me now. I must get back to preparing for tomorrow. Thank you for—"

"If you decide to not marry him and you feel threatened, my home is a safe refuge. Even if you and Rory never marry, I'm here for you."

Anna's heart squeezed. A refuge of safety sounded wonderful. If only she could disappear and hide out at the Quinns' "Thank you, but God promises to be my defender and protector. I have to trust in Him."

# CHAPTER FORTY-TWO

The Monday after New Year's Day, Anna sat at the small table in the sunny serving area off the dining room with her oatmeal and a cup of strong tea. Outside the window, mounds of snow glistened in the morning sun. She hated winter when they lived in the city, but in Geneva, the season seemed different. Here things slowed down, unlike the city where people continued their feverish pace, pushing through the snow and cold. Besides, thanks to the sudden snowstorm that lasted from Friday night until yesterday, she was prevented from traveling into Chicago on Saturday for the engagement party.

Ever since Evie Quinn visited her classroom, Anna hadn't been able to shake the woman's warning out of her mind. The next day, she even came close to approaching Evie to accept her offer of protection when she brought Katie to school. Was this the help she and Rory had been praying for. She had to be sure before she made such a move.

"Well it looks like your father did what he was threatening to do." Mother tossed a copy of the *Chicago Tribune* on the table.

Anna rested her spoon in the bowl and picked up the paper.

"Why are you up so early, and where did you get the morning edition so fast?"

"It's from Saturday. Peggy gave it to me this morning. Look at page three, bottom right corner. He never mentioned it was to be in the paper. If that snowstorm hadn't stopped him from joining us over the new year holiday, I'm sure he'd have told us."

Anna opened the paper. A pen and ink sketch of her father's face stared back at her and next to it large black letters.

LEONARD HARTWELL TO RUN FOR CITY ALDERMAN IN SPRING ELECTION

She skimmed the article, which contained a quote from Father saying he wanted to help put the city back on its feet and make it even greater than it was before the fire. The rest of the two paragraphs held biographical information about him and his business accomplishments since coming to the city from London.

Anna closed the paper and tossed it on the table. "Don't you want to be the wife of a politician?"

Mother winced. "He should have waited until after the wedding and our homes are built. Sometimes it seems he's tucked us into this godforsaken place and he is going on with his city life without us."

"This is only temporary. Lots of people who lost their homes are living up here."

Mother waved a hand. "I know, he couldn't get out of the city because of the snow storm, but . . . "

Anna waited for Mother to finish her sentence, but instead she continued staring out into the cold as if lost in her own world. Anna sighed. "Father is sacrificing a lot for our well being. The least we can do is support him in his political aspirations." She stood. "I need to leave for school. See you tonight."

"Don't forget our appointment this afternoon at Millie's for your fitting." Anna yearned to answer that it would be a fitting for a dress she'd never wear, but she held her tongue for now.

Outside, she climbed into the sleigh for her morning ride to school. She tucked a wool blanket around her legs then stuffed her hands into her fur muff. The leaden sky suited her mood. The wedding she never wanted was coming up faster and faster.

Since their conversation the day when Rory came to the classroom, they'd only exchanged glances whenever he picked Katie up after school. Yesterday, she attended her church, since Mother's was canceled. She saw Rory and they smiled across the room at each other. She ached to speak to him, but Mother had herded her and Callie to the their sleigh, no doubt an effort to keep them separated.

By the time she arrived at the school, fat snowflakes swirled around the sleigh like small cotton balls. As she waved Patrick off, Rory drove a sleigh into the schoolyard with Katie sitting beside him.

"Good morning, Miss Hartwell."

Rory's accented words wrapped around her heart like they'd done since the day they'd met. She waved. "Good morning, Mr. Quinn."

He tipped his cap. "The snow is beautiful, isn't it?"

She studied the gray sky and the swirling flakes. "So much prettier than when it snows in the city."

Katie ran up to her. "Uncle Rory says we can take the sleigh out on the lake as soon as it freezes over solid. Maybe you can come too."

"That does sound like fun, doesn't it? But, I don't know what I'll be doing that day."

Katie gave her a gap-toothed grin. "I'm going to pray you come with us."

Anna caressed the girl's cheek. "Why, Katie, you've lost one of your front teeth."

"I didn't lose it. It fell right into my hand and I put it under my pillow and the next morning a penny was there. Miss Anna, what does the tooth fairy do with all the teeth she collects?"

She chuckled. "I have no idea. She must have quite a few by now."

"Uncle Rory says she uses them to build tiny houses in the fairy village she lives in." She ran off toward the play yard where several children were building a snowman.

Rory walked up. "I'd sure find a sleigh ride on the lake more fun with you beside me, Anna."

She stopped fighting the smile that pushed its way to her face. "And I would agree with that statement. Have a wonderful day, Mr. Quinn." She turned and scooted toward the door, hoping the sob pushing through her throat wouldn't escape until she was inside.

Later that afternoon, Anna stepped into Millie's, and the tiny bells over the door tinkled. The dressmaker bustled out from the back, carrying large sheets of paper. "Right on time. I just finished measuring your mother and sister and they've selected their fabrics." She held up the papers. "I've drawn up several designs for you to look at. Once you decide on the dress, we'll measure and select the fabric. "Come over to the table with me."

Anna followed and waited while Millie spread her sketches across the wood surface.

Millie pointed to one. "This is your mother's choice."

Of course, Mother would choose one that looked like something a queen would wear to her coronation. Anna shook her head. "I don't see any I like."

Millie stared at her. "For a bride to be I've never seen such a sour expression. Is something wrong?"

Anna shrugged and pointed to a dress that had simple lines with minimal lace trim. "That one is fine."

Millie's mouth turned up slightly at the corners. "I thought you'd choose it. What about this one instead? It might be a better compromise." She pointed to the third sketch.

Anna regarded the soft lace-trimmed layers of the ball gown

style skirt. She liked the modest neckline and that the train wasn't overly extended. "It's nice, but I prefer the other one."

"Well do we agree on my choice?" Mother marched up from the direction of the dressing room.

Anna drew in a deep breath. "Do we ever agree on anything, Mother? Your choice is too frilly and I don't care for the low neckline."

"It's the latest fash—"

"Anna has chosen this one." Millie held up a sketch.

Mother peered at the drawing. "I suppose it's all right."

Footfalls sounded as they approached from the back. "Did you make your choice already, Anna? I love the dress Millie designed for me."

"Yes. It wasn't hard to choose."

"Anna, I have some fabric over here for you to look at." Millie walked to a stack of bolts on a counter. "I'll show you what I think is most suitable, but the final choice is up to—"

The bells over the door tinkled as a woman who appeared to be several years older than Anna stepped through, gripping the top of her cloth coat at the neckline. A plain flannel skirt peeked out from beneath the coat hem. Her auburn hair framed her delicate features.

Millie glanced at the Hartwell women and whispered. "You didn't say there was another family member in the wedding party."

Anna shook her head. "She's not from our family."

"Oh. My mistake. She looks so much like Callie. . . May I help you?" Millie approached the woman.

"I'm looking for the Hartwells."

Anna stepped forward. "I'm Anna Hartwell."

The woman regarded Anna with an intense stare then glanced at Mother and Callie. She brought her attention back to Anna. "I stopped at your house, and the maid said you were here." She stared at the floor and wrung her red chapped hands.

Anna's heart warmed to her. Something awful seemed to be bothering her, but what, and why would she need to see them? And why did she resemble Callie so much?"

The woman raised her head. Tears glistened in her eyes. "I'm sorry to barge in on you, but I only learned this morning where your family was living."

Mother stepped forward. "If this is about employment, until we are in our permanent quarters we are operating on a small staff."

The intruder stepped closer. "I'm not looking for employment." She swallowed hard. "My name is Margaret Hart, and I'm here because you need to know that Leonard Hartwell is my father."

# CHAPTER FORTY-THREE

The woman's words tried to force themselves into Anna's mind. She must have misunderstood. She approached Margaret. "I don't know who you are, but you're mistaken. My sister and I are Leonard Hartwell's only living children. If you need money, I'll be happy to give you enough to get back to the city."

The woman fixed her gaze on Anna with eyes almost the same blue-green hue as hers. "You may be Leonard Hartwell's only known children, but I'm one of two girls Len Hart—also known as Leonard Hartwell—fathered. If the news article is correct on the date of your parents' marriage, he and my mother were married in Chicago two years before he publically married your mother.

A chill wrapped itself around Anna and she clutched at the locket around her neck. The woman must be one of those refugees from the fire who have been claiming relationships with the wealthy, hoping to receive financial reward.

She glanced at Mother whose face was as white as the wedding dress fabric lying on the cutting table. Next to her,

Callie stood unmoving, her mouth hanging open. Anna faced the imposter and placed her fisted hands on her hips. "Get out of here. Now. And take your malicious lies with you."

Millie scurried to the door window, muttering "oh dear" under her breath and flipped the 'open' sign over to 'closed.' She looked at Mother. "Mrs. Hartwell, you can be assured what I've heard today will go no further. I know when to keep my mouth shut." She hustled toward the back, her heels issuing a staccato beat. A door shut in the distance.

Her face set like granite, Mother marched over to the woman. "Now, see here. Leonard Hartwell has been married to me for twenty-four years. Our parents arranged our marriage while we were still children. Anna may have offered you money, but I won't hear of it. Bad behavior does not merit a reward. I suggest you get on the next train back to Chicago and find someone else to swindle."

Anna stared at Margaret. If the papers got a hold of the woman's lies, Father could wave goodbye to political office, and no telling how such a reputation would harm his business. Was she an answer to her prayers? "If this is true where is your mother?"

"Anna, don't engage her."

She ignored Mother's demand. "Margaret, please answer my question."

The woman pulled a worn handkerchief from her coat pocket and dabbed her eyes. "I'm all that's left of my family since my sister died of consumption some years ago. Our house burned in the fire, and my mother didn't make it out. I was staying with a friend that night, and we managed to escape. We've been living in a tent encampment near the lake." She blew her nose. "When I couldn't locate my father anywhere, I presumed he'd died in the fire too. He told us he worked for the Pullman Company, and I checked with them, but they said no one named Len Hart ever worked there."

She lifted her shoulders and raised her chin. Anger fired from her eyes. "He lied about his last name and where he worked." She pulled a copy of the Tribune from the bag she carried and held up the article about his running for office. "Then I saw this. The names were similar and there was no mistaking the sketch was my father's face. The people at the Tribune told me he'd temporarily moved his family to Geneva, Wisconsin. I thought if I approached you, we could confront him together. There's strength in numbers."

Margaret gazed at them with pleading eyes. "He's done you as much wrong as he did us. All the times he was away we thought he was on a sales trip, but likely he was with you."

She glanced around the shop and focused on the wedding dress fabrics of imported silk and tulle. "We had no idea he was a wealthy man."

Pressure filled Anna's chest. Father was often absent on business trips for several days at a time. He wasn't perfect, but to have another family? If he'd married Margaret's mother in Chicago before he married Mother, he would have had to have spent time in the city before immigrating permanently. She pressed her fingertips to her temples to offset the sudden headache then cleared her throat. "How do you explain my father being in Chicago when he didn't come to America with my mother and me until two years after my parents' wedding?"

"He traveled to Chicago as a single man to consider moving there." Margaret said. "He met and married my mother before he returned to England. She found out she was pregnant with me after he left. It was two years before he returned, and when he did, he came with a wife and child."

Anna shook her head. It had to be a con. "The man I know as my father would never do something like that. I think you're looking for a rich family to connect with now that your own family is gone."

Callie stepped forward. "How do you know that's how it happened? Weren't you in the dark same as we?"

Margaret rested her hand on the corner of a display platform. "I was until a couple years ago when I began to wonder where he went for so many days at a time. I followed him one day and saw him meet you, Mrs. Hartwell, in front of a restaurant. Then I saw you," she looked at Callie, "walk up and join them. You looked so much like my own sister. I went home and told my mother what I saw and she told me the whole story. Mother knew all along. But she never told me his last name was Hartwell and that he didn't work at the Pullman Company."

"We need to hear her out. Father has been gone a lot."

Mother stared at Callie. "Daughter, I should wash your mouth out with soap. Leonard Hartwell has only fathered three children, two of whom are standing right here." She sniffed. "Poor Richard, God rest his soul, is the third."

Margaret snapped her focus to Mother. "When did your son die?"

Mother sniffed. "When he was twelve. Eight years ago."

"My sister died about the same time."

Anna's mind raced back to when Richard died. If Father had lost another child at about the same time, no wonder his grief seemed prolonged. Wait. What was she doing, entertaining the thought that Father could be a bigamist?

Mother opened her reticule and took out a one hundred dollar bill. She approached Margaret and held out the money. "This is what you came for, isn't it? There will be more for you if you keep this pack of lies to yourself. Now go on and get out of here."

Margaret stared at the money as if it were poison. Mother withdrew another bill. "Not enough? Here's fifty more. That's all I have." She forced the bills into Margaret's hand and stepped back.

"Very well." Margaret whirled around and walked toward the door.

Tension eased from Anna's shoulders. She *was* lying.

At the door, Margaret turned on her heel and flung the bills into the air. "Keep your money. My next step is the papers. It's time the bigamist is exposed."

The door slammed hard behind her.

# CHAPTER FORTY-FOUR

Anna had to do something. But her feet refused to engage with her brain that was leapfrogging from one outrageous thought to another.

"I'm going after her!" Callie stormed toward the entrance. The door slammed behind her. Millie's sign wobbled back and forth then dropped to the floor.

"She's going to get a chill without her wrap." Mother's voice lacked its usual acidic tone.

Anna picked up the sign and rehung it. "I'd rather Callie be cold and catch Margaret than not. If the papers hear these horrible lies . . ." She started toward the back. "I'll take Callie her coat and telegraph Father. Maybe he can head her off before she gets to the papers."

She hurried between the rows of fabric bolts and turned at the end of an aisle. A table corner stabbed her in her thigh. She rubbed against the pain as she stepped into a narrow hallway. Without waiting for Millie to answer the knock on her sewing room's door, Anna stepped into the room and asked for the coats.

The seamstress was already on her feet. She hustled past

Anna. "They're in here." Millie entered a room across the hall and returned with the outerwear.

By the time Anna reached the front of the store, Mother was gone. She scanned the shop and was about to step outside to see if Patrick still waited there when the door flew open and Callie rushed in, her cheeks flushed.

"Mother had Patrick take her home. She said you're going to send a telegraph to Father. I'm going with you."

Anna handed her sister her coat and shrugged into her own wrap. "What about Margaret?"

Her sister grimaced. "I looked in several stores and ran north on Broad toward the depot. She seems to have vanished. If she publicizes this, Father will be ruined." She glanced at a wall clock. "The next train leaves in ten minutes. We'll never catch her without a ride."

Anna walked toward the door. "Let's go to the telegraph office."

Callie caught up with her outside. "How are we going phrase the warning so the telegraph operator doesn't start spreading rumors?"

"We'll come up with something."

Side by side, as they raced down Main Street, the women worked out a coded message—*Your old friend Margaret survived the fire. She's taking the train to Chicago to tell the papers about her family.*

Callie slowed as they neared the telegraph office. "Do you think Father will understand us?"

Anna picked up the pace. "I'm praying he won't because then we'll know it's all a lie."

"What if it's true?"

Anna stopped and stared at her sister's earnest face. How could Callie even think of such a thing? Bigamy didn't fit Father. He was faithful, honest, and devoted to his family. "It's not true."

"But he's always traveling on business, and what about those times he's claimed to stay at the hotel near the office when he worked late? It's uncanny how much Margaret and I look alike."

Anna's thoughts raced over all the times Father had told her he loved her and that he wanted the best for her. The countless times he'd called her the sunshine of his life. A man like that wasn't a bigamist. She stared at her sister. "The picture."

"What picture?"

"I found a photograph in Father's desk the night of the fire. A woman and a little girl. I thought the girl was you. I figured the woman was a maid or nanny we had that I'd forgotten."

Callie teared up. "She could have been Margaret's mother." She grabbed Anna's arm. "Sister, think about it. If her accusations get out, our family will be shunned. Father will lose business, and we'll be living in rentals much smaller than the one we're in now." She palmed tears from her cheeks.

Anna drew her into a hug. "Those that know him well would never believe it and will vouch for him. Mr. Millard will surely defend him. We'll survive this."

"I could never be as strong as you, Anna."

She hugged her tighter. If she only knew how much her feet felt like clay at that moment. "God gives us whatever we need when we need it. He will for you too."

When the sisters arrived home, they found Mother pacing the parlor, suddenly appearing at least ten years older. She stopped and looked directly at Anna. "Did you telegraph your father?"

She startled at the evidence of spent tears streaking her mother's face. "Yes, and we used a coded message so the telegrapher wouldn't be tempted to spread gossip."

Mother visibly relaxed. "I was worried you wouldn't think to do that. But it would serve him right if you hadn't."

A sinking feeling washed over Anna. "You talk as if Margaret isn't lying."

Mother stiffened. "Of course, she's lying, but I warned him

running for office will bring people to our door looking for handouts. Your father will have to pay her off. She wouldn't take what I offered. She's probably angling for much more."

Anna relaxed her shoulders. The whole thing was making her to not think straight. Mother was right. It was all about money.

"I asked the telegrapher to have someone bring us any answer he sends back, no matter the hour." Anna removed her coat and hung it on the hall tree next to Callie's. She stepped into the parlor and sat on the settee beside her sister.

"Mother, have you ever had even a hint something like what that woman said was true?" Callie asked.

Their mother stared off at nothing. "Calista Hartwell, how dare you speak of your father like that. Of course not."

Callie didn't flinch. "What if he doesn't work as hard as he says? That would give him time for another family."

Mother walked to the window and stared out. "I asked Peggy to have dinner ready as early as possible. She should be calling us to the table soon."

The idea of eating nauseated Anna. She exchanged looks with Callie and pointed upstairs. Her sister nodded and they rose to their feet together.

Anna started for the entrance hall. "We're going to freshen up before Peggy calls us."

The moment they stepped inside their bedroom, the sisters fell into each other's arms. Anna didn't know who shook the most. "It can't be true, Callie. But why didn't she answer your question? Defend Father?"

"Maybe she didn't like me asking such a direct question."

Anna stepped out of Callie's embrace. "I feel sick."

"What if we don't hear back from Father tonight?"

Anna walked to her dresser and poured some water into the basin. "Then neither of us will get much sleep."

"Anna, I thought of something a minute ago. If it's true, maybe the Millards won't want you marrying their son."

She blinked at her sister. "I know. I thought of that too. But then maybe Rory won't want to marry me either."

Callie stared at her. "Why?"

"Because if it's true that means I'm a bastard."

Callie gasped. "Anna, stop cussing like that."

She shook her head. "It's not a nice word, but it's not cussing. That's what they call children born out of wedlock."

Callie threw herself on her bed. "That means I'll never be a debutante."

Anna huffed. "If only that were the least of our worries."

A short time later, Anna followed Callie and Mother into the dining room and the three women huddled together at the end of the long table, nibbling at Peggy's chicken and dumplings. After tea and picking at apple turnovers for dessert, Callie went upstairs while Anna and Mother sat in the living room, waiting for the doorbell to ring. At half past eight, somewhat relieved no answer had come, Anna set aside the needlework she was pretending to work on and stood. "It doesn't look like he sent a response. I'm going to bed."

Mother looked up from staring at an unread magazine and tossed it aside. "I may as well retire too."

Anna crossed the foyer. No answer was a good sign and she was going to get a good night's sleep.

The sharp ring of the doorbell pierced the air.

She rushed toward the entrance and flung the door open.

A young man who looked more a child than a grown man stood on the porch. "A telegraph message for Miss Anna Hartwell." He held out an envelope.

"I'm Miss Hartwell." She dug in her pocket for the tip she'd put there earlier and held it out. The coins flew out of her shaking hand and rolled across the porch floor. The boy chased after one of the coins while she grabbed up the other one.

Envelope in hand, she stepped inside and nearly knocked Mother over.

"Open it,"

She ignored the demand and stepped around her mother. "I think Callie should be here too."

"I'm here." Callie came down the stairs wearing a dressing gown, her long hair in a single braid.

Anna waited until her sister joined them, then slid her finger under the envelope flap and withdrew the single sheet of paper. She skimmed the words and handed the message to Callie.

Callie read out loud, "I met Margaret at the Northwestern depot. I'll arrive home tomorrow afternoon on the three-thirty train. Please have Calista and your mother at the house with you."

# CHAPTER FORTY-FIVE

Despite not having slept all night, Anna managed to get through the school day without breaking down. She'd thought she'd covered her distress well until Katie came up to her at lunchtime and asked what she had done to cause Anna to be sad. She assured the concerned child it had nothing to do with her and quickly changed the subject.

Arriving home, Anna stepped into a seemingly empty house and headed straight upstairs to hers and Callie's bedroom. No Callie. Grateful for the time alone, she dropped to her knees beside her bed and began praying.

A few minutes later, the door creaked open. "Sister, I'm scared."

Anna leaned back and twisted around. Her heart squeezed at the sight of Callie's reddened eyes. "I am too." She pushed to her feet and sat on the bed. "Come sit with me. I heard the train whistle a few minutes ago. It won't be long."

Callie plopped beside her and Anna drew her into her arms. The shaking girl pressed her face against Anna's shoulder and let out a pain-wracked sob. They rocked back and forth while

Anna searched for words of comfort, but none came. How could they when she needed comfort herself?

"How was it having to teach?" Callie squeaked out her words.

"Not easy, but God got me through. This whole mess will smooth out, little sister. It has to."

Callie sniffed. "How can it ever be right again when no one will want anything to do with us?"

"Maybe not with Father, but with us—"

"You said it last night. If he married Margaret's mother first, we're illegitimate. We can't deny the truth. If Margaret was lying Father would have said as much in his message. And how would he know what Margaret looks like to meet her at the crowded depot?" She took in a deep breath. "While you were at school, I made some inquiries with an attorney."

Anna gasped. "You didn't tell someone . . . "

"Of course not. I gave him a hypothetical situation and said it had to do with a friend in Chicago. He said the first marriage is binding. Period."

Anna's chest tightened, if it were true, she'd probably lose her teaching job. And, surely, Rory wouldn't want to marry her anymore than Lyman would. How ironic that what they prayed for might stop the marriage she didn't want, but also the one she wanted. Pressure built behind her eyes. Now was not the time for tears.

Outside the window, the bells on Goldie's harness announced Father's arrival. Callie stood. "Come, sister, let's freshen our faces." She went to her dresser.

Anna slumped against the headboard. Her eyes felt heavy. Sleep was what she needed. Precious sleep where she could escape to nothingness. Her eyes closed.

"Anna. Wake up." Someone was shaking her shoulder. She opened her eyes. Where was she?

Callie's face hovered a few inches away. "I can't believe you fell asleep. We need to go downstairs. Father is home."

She shut her eyes.

Callie shook her. "Come on, Anna."

She opened her eyes and rubbed them with her fists. "How long was I napping?"

"Whatever time it took for me to wash my face. I turned around and you were dead asleep."

She stretched. "Dead sounds good about now. I want my dream back. I was riding horseback in the mountains …" She glanced at Callie's startled expression. "Give me a minute to wash my face."

A few moments later, they opened the door, and angry voices filtered up the stairs.

"Leonard, how could you do something like run for alderman? All these years I've kept your dirty secrets. Lied when I knew you were with them and not on a business trip. And now because of your carelessness, you've caused us embarrassment."

"I thought Marcella and Margaret were dead or I wouldn't have run for office."

"After all I've done for you."

"You didn't keep my secret out of feelings for me, Eleanor, and you know it. You did it because you loved the lifestyle I provided you."

"What are you going to do now that Margaret is taking the news to the papers?"

"She assured me she wouldn't. I trust her."

"Why should she keep the news hidden? You lied to her, the same way you've lied to Anna and Calista."

Callie slumped against the bedroom wall and groaned. "It's true."

Anna shut the door. "I can't believe Mother knew the truth and never told anyone."

"You heard Father. She did it because he provided her the

fancy home and social status. I wonder if she doesn't have a secret or two of her own."

Anna's thoughts spun in her head like a child's top. "I'm not sure I can go down there and act civil."

"We have to, sister."

"I know. But first we pray."

Muffled shouts filtered through the closed door as Anna drew Calista into a hug and whispered a prayer for wisdom and strength. After she said "Amen," she released Callie. "Let's not let on we overheard and see what they say."

"Father is going to see our faces and know we've been crying."

She shrugged. "Why wouldn't we be crying? He needs to see how he's hurt us." She opened the door. Either they'd killed each other or called a truce. She motioned for Callie to come. "I don't know what the silence means. Let's make sure they hear us coming."

She walked to the staircase, letting her heels clip-clop on the wood planks. She took Calista's hand as they descended the stairs.

*Lord, I need Your strength.*

In the parlor, Father stood at the window facing the street, his hands clasped behind him. Mother sat on the settee, stiff as a board, a pinched expression on her face.

She cleared her throat and Father turned. He held her gaze, his eyes seeming to beg her forgiveness while his jaw throbbed as if it was ready to explode through his skin. Angry words pushed against the backs of her teeth, but she kept her lips tightly closed.

His gaze flicked from Anna to Callie. "I gather you two heard our arguing."

"Them and the household staff, I'm sure." Mother's words dripped with sarcasm.

"We both said things, Eleanor." He stared at his feet. "Girls,

I'm devastated you had to learn about my dalliance the way you did. I intended to tell you after you were grown, but I couldn't muster the courage."

"I'd hardly call another family with children a dalliance, Father." Callie's voice sounded shrill. "Who is legitimate? Us, or your other family?"

He gulped. "Calista, you are, of course. You carry my name."

Heat coursed through Anna's veins. Did he think they were naïve? "Who did you marry first?"

"I married Marcella four months before I married your mother. But I used Len Hart as my name, not my legal one. You two are my legitimate children."

Anna glared at him. "You were still Leonard Franklin Hartwell, and took marriage vows with the woman who is Margaret's mother. An attorney has advised us the first marriage is legal. That makes Callie and me illegitimate and your marriage to Mother a fraud."

He tipped his head. "No. My legitimate marriage is with your mother. The one that our parents arranged when we were children, just like yours and Lyman's will always be your official marriage."

Anna lifted her chin. "Are you insinuating that Lyman will father a few illegitimate babies in addition to children from his legal marriage? If he ever does marry. I'm certain once he hears about your other family, he'll call off our nuptials. Which is the only good that will come of this disastrous situation." A sob exploded from her throat. "You always made me feel as if I were the most important person in your life, and it's all a lie. I've never felt so betrayed."

Mother stared at her. "You must marry Lyman, Anna. If Margaret doesn't go to the papers, we can keep the whole sordid thing our little family secret."

Anna glared at her mother. "If you read the Bible, you'd see we are called to tell the truth and never lie." She faced Father.

"And a man is to have one wife. I'm not keeping anymore secrets. You were my refuge when Mother mistreated me. Was that out of guilt?"

Mother's eyes hardened. "Anna, you deserved that mistreatment. When you were born, you were the worst baby, wailing and fussing. I couldn't make you stop nor could your nanny. Then he'd come home." She indicated Father with a jab of her chin. "He'd pick you up and you were a different baby. All smiles and cooing. Always for him, and never me."

Anna gaped at her mother. "That's why you've been mean to me all these years?" It made no sense.

"I accepted having to put up with him being married to someone else before we married, but to take my own child's affection from me?" She looked at Callie and gave her a weak smile. "You were a delightful baby. Greeted me every day with the same pretty smile you have today." She looked at Father. "The most gratifying result of all of this is that your little pride and joy now hates you." She turned on her heel and left the room.

Anna moved to the settee and sat. "Please, tell Callie and me the full truth, Father. We deserve that much."

He remained standing in front of the window. "I met Marcella, Margaret's mother, when I came to Chicago to explore the possibilities of immigrating here. The Millards had just come over the year before, and I stayed in their home during those months. Marcella was a maid in the neighborhood. While on a walk, I met her in the park, and I was immediately taken by her beauty. We started spending time together, meeting on her days off, and fell in love." He moved to a chair and sat. "Being involved with a servant was not only incorrect behavior for a man of my stature, but I was to marry your mother in an arranged marriage as soon as I returned to England.

"I couldn't leave Marcella without showing her how much I

loved her, and decided to secretly marry her before I left. I planned to tell my parents what I'd done as soon as I arrived back in England, believing they would release me from the arranged marriage. But after arriving home, I never did."

Anna's sat up straight and jutted her chin. "I came to you wanting out of my arranged marriage, and you still insisted I marry Lyman. Father, how could you? You knew how much Rory and I love each other. Are your financial worries truly more important?"

He avoided her stare. "You have no idea how much it hurt me that day. I wasn't lying about the financial ruin." He stared at his lap.

"So," Anna said. "Why didn't you ask to break the arranged betrothal to Mother?"

Father sighed. "When I got home, the wedding plans were in place, and I learned we were to be married in a fortnight. I felt trapped—so I went through with it. I thought after we moved to America, I'd quietly have the marriage to Marcella annulled, but eight months after I came back to England, I learned Margaret had been born. And within a year after your mother and I married, you came along." He swallowed hard. "I've been balancing both marriages and families ever since."

Mother stepped back into the room, looking like she'd been to a war and back.

Anna faced her. "Do you realize that yours and Father's marriage isn't legal?"

Mother squared her shoulders. "Ours is his real marriage. We married in a church, using his legal name. The one to the other woman was in front of a judge. The lawyer you consulted has to be wrong."

"No mother. You're wrong. You're not legally married to Father, and Anna and I are illegitimate." Callie all but shrieked her words.

"Daughter, I should wash your mouth out with soap."

Father winced. "Please don't call yourself that. You carry my legal name."

Anna stood. "Our name might be legal, but our standing is not. As far as I'm concerned, I never want to speak to you again." She marched out of the parlor and up the stairs to her room where she threw up into the chamber pot.

# CHAPTER FORTY-SIX

The next morning, Anna entered the dining room.

Mother looked up from her tea. A plate containing an untouched piece of toast sat in front of her. Dark half-moons underscored her eyes. "I suppose you slept like a baby last night."

Anna grimaced. "Why would you say that? I barely slept at all." She walked to the sideboard and poured coffee from a silver carafe. "Why are you up so early?"

Mother's mouth turned down at the corners. "Your father tossed and turned half the night until I sent him to the guest room. By then it was almost dawn and I couldn't fall asleep." She sipped her tea and then set the cup down.

"I'm surprised you let him sleep in the same room after last night." Anna slid onto her chair and looked around. "Did Father take the early train into the city"

"That was his intention and I presume that's what he did."

Anna buttered her toast. "I wonder how long it will be before we know if Margaret went to the papers or kept her word. We should send Patrick out for today's *Tribune* as soon as they arrive on the train."

Mother stiffened. "I'd rather go myself than let Patrick see what is sure to be a front page headline."

Anna stared at her mother. "How do you expect to keep our help in the dark? If Patrick doesn't see it in the paper today, he will in time, or hear it through the grapevine."

"I'm hoping to explain it to the servants in a way that is softer than the papers will treat it."

Anna stirred cream into her coffee. "There's no way to make it not sound awful. You never answered my question last night. When did you know about his other family?"

Mother stared into her cup, her face void of emotion. After a few moments, she directed her attention toward a spot on the wall. "The first year we were living in Chicago. He was gone a lot and leaving me alone with you. He said it was because of setting up his business, but it went on longer than I thought it should. One day while you were with the nanny, I followed him straight to a little house in a poorer part of town. Marcella and Margaret, who was about a year older than you, greeted him. He picked up Margaret and asked how Daddy's girl was."

"He never knew you followed him?"

"Not until I told him that evening."

"You should have walked out on him."

Mother gasped. "Divorce?"

Anna shrugged. "Since the marriage wasn't legal, no need for that."

Moisture glistened on Mother's short eyelashes. "I know you won't understand, but I do love your Father. It wasn't immediate, but by the time we left for America, I loved him. When I found out about his other family, I was devastated, but I still loved him. I still do." She took a hanky from her pocket and dabbed her eyes. "Those first two years of our marriage while we were in London were the best years. That's why I've always said you'll learn to love Lyman."

Anna's heart squeezed. Even Mother didn't deserve what

Father did. Maybe that's what made her so angry. A nudge pressed against her heart to reach out to her mother. Was that from God? How could He expect that after the way the woman had treated her all her life?

*Please, God, no.*

But hadn't Mother been abused too in a different way? She made a move to stand and the pressure within increased. She placed her napkin on the table then looked across at her mother. Gone was the ramrod spine and stiff upper lip, replaced by a woman hurt and afraid. If the news hit the papers, Mother would lose her standing in Chicago society and the creature comforts she'd enjoyed all her life.

"Mother, I want to apologize for all the times I've talked back to you and resented you. I had no idea of the pain you've endured trying to keep Father's secret. I can't imagine what you've gone through."

"Thank you."

The softness in Mother's face switched to hardness as she leaned across the table. "Let this be a warning. Your father isn't the first man to cheat. Especially when they've been involved in an arranged marriage. Lyman will do it to you, and it's best to let him."

Anna rolled her eyes. "I doubt any woman would want the man. But it's not a worry for me anyway. I said last night the wedding is off, and I mean it." She picked up her toast from her plate. "I'll eat this on the way to school."

Friday afternoon Anna settled into the sleigh and tucked the blanket around her. As Patrick got Goldie trotting out of the schoolyard and onto the snow-packed road, Anna leaned back and closed her eyes.

She'd been grateful to have the school to come to each day

and for the children to keep her focused on them and not what was happening at home. She stayed in the classroom as much as she could, greeting and saying goodbye to the children from inside. She yearned to be outside in case Rory came for Katie but was afraid to look him in the eye. Surely their servants who lived in Irish Woods must have gossiped about the drama at the Hartwells. Now Saturday and Sunday stretched out before her. Would Father return from the city tonight? They'd not heard from him since he left.

"I think I better warn ya. There's been a lot of shouting this afternoon between your father and mother."

Anna startled and opened her eyes. They'd already descended the hill and were almost to downtown Geneva. "Isn't Father still in the city?"

"He arrived in town on the noon train." He guided Goldie up Broad Street.

Anna's heart sunk into her stomach. If Margaret had gone to the papers, Anna would never be able to work for any school, including Irish Woods. No one would want her, even Rory.

At the house, Anna let herself inside and paused to listen. They must have shouted themselves out. She stepped past the darkened parlor on the balls of her feet. Maybe she could make it upstairs without being seen.

"Anna, come in here."

She turned toward Mother's voice and stepped into the parlor. As her eyes adjusted to the low light, a pair of forms on the settee came into view—Callie and Mother. "I didn't realize you were in here."

Movement came from a chair on the other side of the room and suddenly a soft glow filled the room. Father stood next to the lamp affixed to the wall. "She did it, Anna. Margaret went to the papers after I begged her not to do it. It's only a matter of time before I'll be forced to give up my bid for alderman." He moved to a chair and sat.

"And what's worse," Mother said. "The Millards just sent a wire that your wedding has been called off. I know the cancellation is pleasing to you, Anna, but I hope you realize how all this is affecting your sister and me." Mother let out a sob.

Anna rushed to the settee and put her arm around her. "Mother, of course I realize." She glanced at Callie's grief-stricken expression. "The debutante ball is all Callie has talked about for months. I feel horrible. But I can't lie and say I'm heartbroken about the wedding. I wasn't lying about him bruising me. If I had decided to go through with it, it would have been for the sake of the family." She moved to one of the vacant chairs next to the settee.

"Now you're free to marry, Rory, Anna," Father said. "If this crisis did anything good, it's that you can marry the man you love."

Mother's skirts rustled. "How can you say that, Leonard? For our daughter to marry a common Irish immigrant is like saying he is as good as us."

"And you think our kind is good? We're nothing, Eleanor. Rory Quinn may be poor in the monetary sense, but he's richer than we are."

"Please tell me how?" Mother's voice was filled with sarcasm.

"He has God. More than either you or I have together."

Anna gulped. Was this her father speaking? "Where did you learn all this, Father?"

"The past couple days I've been reading the Scriptures and remembering some of what you've told me these past years. That, and the sermons we've been hearing at Mrs. Maxwell's church." He squeezed his eyes shut then pinched the bridge of his nose between his thumb and index finger.

Anna was about to speak when his eyes opened. He looked Mother in the eyes, then Callie, and then Anna. "I'm so very sorry for how I've hurt all of you. I don't deserve it, but I hope you all will forgive me." He let out a heavy sigh and stared at the ceiling. "Why is it that a man has to be brought to nothing before he realizes how much he needs God in his life?"

Anna glared at him. After lying to them all those years. It was easier to be angry with him than to so quickly forgive. How could she know he wasn't only pretending to be contrite?

"Forgive you, Leonard?" Mother's shrill voice echoed off the ceiling. "I've been too forgiving all these years."

Callie stood. "No, Father, I'm not ready to forgive you. You've hurt too many people with your lies." She stomped out of the room. Her receding footsteps sounded from the stairs. No one moved until an upstairs door slammed.

Father brought his gaze back to Anna. "I suppose you aren't ready to forgive me either."

She squirmed and stared at her lap. She was a sinner, like everyone else, and God had forgiven her. How could she withhold what He had so graciously given her? But Father had hurt her and the others—including Margaret and her mother—so much. She looked up into his eyes and saw regret. "My heart isn't ready to forgive you, Father."

His shoulders sagged and he slumped.

"But I'm reminded that we are to forgive as the Lord forgave us, and for that reason, I do forgive you. That doesn't mean we can carry on as if this didn't happen. I'm sure I'll be able to move forward, but right now, I need time."

His moustache seemed to droop along with his lips. He nodded. "I can't ask for more. What I did was terrible."

After an uncomfortable dinner where everyone ate in cold silence, Anna and Callie retreated upstairs.

Anna sat on her bed and waited until Callie settled on her own bed. "I'm not sure about you, but I never want to endure another meal like that."

"I agree. Maybe we should start taking our meals in our room from now on."

Anna picked up one of her pillows and hugged it to her chest. "I wonder how long we'll be living here."

"But, where would we go? We have to live someplace." Callie sniffed.

"Remember, Father said if I didn't marry Lyman he would be financially ruined. We may not be able to afford the rent."

Callie settled against the headboard. "The only good in all this is that you don't have to marry that awful man, and you can marry Rory."

Anna rolled her eyes. "How do I know he will have me either? Or that I'll be able to teach at the school—any school?

"No, sister. You didn't do anything wrong. Father is the one who will pay."

Anna stared across the several feet dividing their beds. "Neither of us did anything to be shunned from society, but we will. Mark my words. Right now, I just want to get through tomorrow and Sunday. Monday will come soon enough."

# CHAPTER FORTY-SEVEN

Nothing but prayer filled Anna's mind as Patrick drove her to the school on Monday morning. Part of her wanted to stay home, but while she still had the job, she had a responsibility to the children. To her relief, Father returned to the city Saturday morning, saying he had a lot to do to put his financial affairs in order and to drop out of the election. Anna, Mother and Callie moved about the house both Saturday and Sunday in near silence. Anna yearned to attend Sunday morning services but declined, afraid of seeing Rory and not ready to face him.

Now, she held an envelope in her hand. Patrick would drop it off at the school superintendent's office on his way home. The right thing to do was to inform the superintendent that she was willing to stay on as teacher, but in light of the recent information about her father, she understood if he would prefer her to resign.

As Patrick drove the sleigh into the schoolyard, a sharp icy wind whipped her in the face. She clutched her coat collar and pulled it tight around the hem of her hood. As uncomfortable as the January weather was, it was no match for the storm raging in the Hartwell household.

As Anna stepped down from the sleigh, Katie ran up, snow clouds flying from her heels. "Uncle Rory was sad you weren't here this morning. We came extra early so he could see you."

She ran her gloved hand down Katie's rosy cheek. "I'm sorry I missed him. I was late getting started this morning." Was he so anxious to explain that even if the news meant her betrothal to Lyman was canceled, he couldn't consider marrying her either? A part of her couldn't picture him being so judgmental, but why would he feel any different than other people?

"He said he'll see you after school. He's planning to be home from work early."

Anna frowned. Had he changed his schedule for her? She started toward the door. "Let's get inside where it's warm."

Grateful for the distraction of teaching, Anna threw herself into the day, always with an eye toward the door, expecting the superintendent to step in at any moment.

As three o'clock crept closer, a dark shadow of dread came over her. Who would arrive first? Rory, Patrick, or the superintendent? After the children had their coats on, she stepped out into the crisp cold and escorted a little boy to his dad's sleigh. Surprised the man didn't act any different toward her, she waved them off and turned to see Rory watching her from his sleigh. Their gazes collided halfway and seemed to weave together. She ignored the pull of his stare and walked toward the school door. At one time she was the one reaching down the social ladder to him, and now everything was upside down.

As she reached the steps, footfalls approached from behind. A hand gripped her elbow.

"Anna."

Heart pounding in her ears, she spun around. Rory stood inches away, his earnest gaze running over her face. Over his left shoulder Katie climbed into the Daleys' sleigh. "Why is Katie riding home with someone else?"

"Because I asked Tim to take her home. I want to talk with you."

Her mouth suddenly feeling as dry as a desert, she surveyed the empty turnabout. Every child had left. "I've been expecting the superintendent. We may be interrupted. And Patrick should be coming soon."

"I asked Patrick to let me take you home."

Her mouth fell open. "Why?"

"Superintendent Crawford is expecting us at his house soon. I told him I'd bring you." He nodded at the school door. "It's mighty cold out here. Can we go inside?"

It must be worse than she feared if Rory had spoken with the superintendent. "I've already doused the fire. The classroom won't be warm."

"We won't be long."

Inside, Rory moved to the front of the room and perched on a corner of her desk. He anchored his focus on her, and slowly the icicles of fear around her heart began melting. "Come over here. I want you nearby while I say what I came to say."

She took timid steps toward him. He took her hand. Delicious shivers raced up her arm. She should pull away from his grasp. What if someone came in the room? What difference did it make? Her job was probably gone anyway.

"Is it true about your father having a second family?"

Anna stared at her feet. Already the pressure behind her eyes was building. "Yes."

"Does Lyman know about it?"

"Yes."

"Is the wedding still scheduled?"

She shook her head. "The engagement has been called off because he c-c-an't marry someone like me."

Tears flowed down her cheeks. "I expect the superintendent will want my resignation. No one will want someone like me teaching their children." A piercing ache filled her throat, and she willed unsuccessfully for her tears to stop.

Rory handed her a handkerchief. "I was afraid of this."

She dabbed her eyes. "Afraid of what? So much has happened because of . . . I can't show my face anywhere anymore."

Suddenly she was in Rory's arms, her face pressed to his chest. She inhaled the scent of fresh soil.

"Oh, my sweet lass. Afraid you would be ostracized. And you deserve none of it." He nuzzled her hair. "Anna, you shouldn't be shunned for something you had no control over. I'm so sorry this has happened to you." He lifted her chin with his index finger. Their gazes met and she nearly melted at the love she saw in his eyes. "You, my dear, are more precious than rubies. A child of God who is engraved in His palm. And I love you more than ever."

She blinked. "How can you love someone like me? I'm illegitimate."

He chuckled. "You be forgetting you're first a child of the most high King. You can hold your head up. I'd be most pleased if you would agree to marry me." He leaned down and brushed her lips with his, tender and gentle.

"Really?"

Rory's eyes glistened. "You forget my world isn't upper crust. We understand people make mistakes, often at the expense of others. What your father did is not a reflection of who you are. You are still you, and I am still me. Now, will you answer my question?"

Rory still loved her and so did God. Why did she ever doubt? "Yes, Rory, I'll marry you." She slipped her arms around him and their hungry lips found each other and Anna sank into the spell of her future husband.

The kiss ended and they remained still, arms tight around each other. Rory brought his mouth to her ear. "I love you, my precious Anna, with all me heart."

"I love you, too, Rory."

His big hands gripped her waist and he lifted her off the floor. Suddenly she was spinning, her skirts billowing.

"She said yes!"

His shout reverberated off the rafters, mixing with Anna's giggles. He set her down and grinned. "We'll have to live with my aunt and uncle for a while, but I hope to get a job by summer on one of the new estates being built. Hopefully, the job will come with living quarters. Not near as large as what you're used to, but it will be ours."

Anna laughed. "I don't care where we live."

He kissed her forehead and then leaned back and looked at her, his eyes twinkling. "Anna Quinn has a nice ring to it."

Anna laughed. "Mrs. Rory Quinn sounds better." She stepped out of his embrace. "I still need to speak to the superintendent. You may not care if I'm not of proper birth status, but he might."

Rory tweaked her nose between his thumb and index finger. "You have no worries. I saw him in town earlier and asked if he heard the news about your father. He said yes, he planned to come here after school to assure you that the job is still yours if you want it."

Anna stared at him. "He discussed my employment situation with you?"

Rory's face reddened. "Well, I mentioned you and I were very close." He looked at the floor. "I actually said we'd probably marry soon." He raised his head. "I know that was bold of me, but I really didn't think anything changed between us. I'm sorry."

She should be upset for his interfering, but how could she be? "As my future husband, it is your business too. I'm not upset."

He looked about the room. "Now, if you're ready, we don't want to keep the man waiting."

# CHAPTER FORTY-EIGHT

On the way into town, snuggled under a blanket next to Rory, Anna closed her eyes and let large cotton-ball snowflakes drift down on her face. If that icy wind was still whipping about, she hadn't noticed. Not with the warmth that filled her heart ever since Rory proposed.

She opened her eyes and glanced at Rory's handsome profile. *Thank you, God, for your provision of this godly man for me.*

As if sensing her gaze, Rory faced her and smiled. He gathered the reins into his left hand then reached under the blanket and wove his fingers with hers. Tingles filled her stomach. Soon she would be able to cuddle closer to him, and with Katie at her side, they'd be a family.

In town, Rory stopped the sleigh at a two-story home near the Methodist Church and helped Anna step onto the snow-covered walkway. "Perhaps it be better if I wait here for you. I've interfered enough."

Anna almost insisted he come with her then changed her mind. "I'll only be a few minutes." She started toward the front porch, and the door opened. Mr. Crawford stepped out and greeted her with a smile. "Miss Hartwell, please come in." He looked past her and waved at Rory, "Young man, don't sit out here in the cold. Please join us."

Assured by the superintendent's welcoming manner, Anna relaxed. Inside, Mrs. Crawford served them tea in the cozy parlor then stepped out of the room.

"Miss Hartwell, I'm not going to act as though I don't know what has happened in your family. It's a tragic circumstance, and my heart goes out to you and your sister and mother. When I received your note this morning, there was no question that we want you to remain as the teacher at Irish Woods School." He glanced at Rory across the room. "I understand there may be a wedding in your near future. Like we did for Mrs. Cleary, we can make an exception to the requirement that the teacher be unmarried. Fine teachers like you are difficult to find. We'll be glad to have you for as long as you are able to teach."

Anna knew she was grinning like a child in a candy store, but she couldn't help it. Engaged to the right man and assured of her teaching job, all in the course of an hour or so. How could she not? But she had to remember when she arrived home to not make much ado about it. Not when Callie and Mother had hardly begun to pick up their own broken pieces.

A short time later, Rory walked Anna to her door, and they stood on the porch, staring at each other. He studied his feet a moment then looked up. "To think a few days ago, we had little hope of ever spending our lives together. God is good." He turned to leave.

"Rory."

He faced her and tilted his head. "Yes?"

"I love you."

A grin filled his features. "I love you too, sweetheart."

Anna all but floated into the house and removed her coat.

Mother stepped into the parlor, her face pale and drawn. "Why did Rory tell Patrick he could come home without you?

What gave him the right to order our help around? And where have you been?"

Anna drew in a breath and let it out slowly. "I needed to meet with Mr. Crawford to agree to be the full time teacher at the school if they still wanted me. Rory took me there."

Mother raised her head. "I suppose the man declined your offer. Too bad, since it looks like we'll be staying here indefinitely and money won't be easy to come by."

"I still have the job."

"I'm surprised. You still haven't said why Rory ordered Patrick to leave."

Anna pressed her lips together. "He didn't order him to leave. He told Patrick why he wanted to take me to see the superintendent, and Patrick agreed it was best for me to have Rory with me."

"How did Rory know about all this?"

Anna shrugged. "Father's dual life isn't a secret. It's been in all the papers. Our maids went home to Irish Woods and told their friends about it. You know how it happens."

"Well, I hope you don't think you're free now to take up with Rory. We have to work harder than ever to uphold our reputation."

Anna rested her fists on her hips. "How do you propose you're going to do that?"

Mother huffed and turned away. "I could kill your father."

Anna took a step toward her mother. The pull to comfort her was strong, but she held back. "I know. He's not treated any of us well. He has said he's sorry for what he did and knows he has sinned. I think he's remorseful. We all need to forgive him."

Mother spun around and glared at her. "Forgive that despicable man? Never."

# CHAPTER FORTY-NINE

By Friday afternoon, Anna felt as if she'd been put through a wringer. Each day, when Rory picked Katie up after school, they'd steal a few moments together. A delightful respite that fortified her for the stony silence at home.

They'd agreed to wait to let her parents know of their engagement until after Father returned from the city, but they hadn't heard a word from him for almost a week. Anna fully expected him to announce upon returning that they were paupers and he'd have to sell his properties.

Several minutes after she'd shooed the last child outside to meet his dad, the door opened and Rory stepped through holding his right hand behind his back.

She gave him a curious look. "What are you up to, Rory Quinn?"

He stepped forward and thrust out a bouquet of tulips. "Beautiful flowers for my bride-to-be."

She stared at the mix of blooms. "They're lovely but where did you find tulips in January?"

He puffed his chest. "In the greenhouse at Maple Lawn, of course. We forced some bulbs to see how they will look when they come up. We're working out wonderful landscaping plans according to Mrs. Sturgis' desires."

She buried her nose in the blooms and inhaled the scent.

"May I accompany you home this afternoon? We won't see each other again until Monday."

Anna laughed. "I plan to be in church on Sunday, don't you?"

"Yes, but that's with a lot of people around, and until the news of our marriage plans are announced, we probably won't be able to sit together."

Anna looked off then at him. "I think it's time to publicize our plans. Father is due home on this afternoon's train. All his wire said is that he had news and wanted me there after school. I think you should come in and hear what he has to say."

Rory scowled. "I don't know."

"He already knows we love each other. I told him weeks ago. And he said after the truth came out that I should marry the man I love—meaning you."

"But how will your mother feel about me being there?"

"She won't like it, but she's hurting, Rory. Now that I know a lot of her bad attitude is because of my father's actions, it's much easier to feel empathy for her. She knows she can't control me anymore."

Father was sitting in the parlor when Anna and Rory arrived. He stood as they entered and he smiled at Rory as he held out his hand. "Rory, I'm glad you're here too." The men shook hands then Father directed his attention to Anna. "Your mother and sister are upstairs. I've something to tell you and Rory that will please you."

Anna gave him a curious look. "After the past week I could use something pleasing." She moved to the settee and Rory sat next to her.

Father reached over to a side table and lifted a book that looked like a Bible. "The first day back in the city I decided to look for the new location of the Illinois Street Church mission and found it on the west side. I talked to Mr. Rollins, the director, and told him my circumstances, what I'd done, and how sorry I was and needed to ask God's forgiveness. I thought sure he'd send me away, but instead, he gave me this Bible and directed me to a passage about surrendering to the Lord in repentance. I prayed with him and have been devouring this Bible ever since."

Anna's heart felt like it was about to leap out of her chest. "That's wonderful, Father. God truly is a forgiving God when we repent and ask His forgiveness."

"I owe you a huge apology, Anna. I've told your mother and sister how I want to be a godly man from now on and asked their forgiveness. And I located Margaret and asked for hers as well. Now I'm asking yours."

Anna wiped a tear away and sniffed. "I already told you that I forgave you. I meant it then, and still mean it." She tugged a handkerchief out of her pocket and daubed at her eyes. "How did Callie and Mother respond?"

Father pressed his lips together. "At first they were skeptical. And I understand that." A grin spread across his face and his eyes lit up. "After I told them how I'd been reading the Bible and how its words convicted me that I need God in my life, they saw the difference in me. They've both forgiven me."

"They probably saw the change in your face as I'm seeing now. It's going to take time, but perhaps we can become the family we should have been all along."

Father nodded. "I've since learned that because I didn't use my legal name when I married Marcella I might be able to fight that marriage's legality, but because my first child came out of that union, it would likely be held legal over my marriage to your mother." He stared at his feet then lifted his head. "I told your mother I want to marry her again, this time for real, and I've rewritten my will to include her, you and Callie, along with Margaret."

"What did Mother say?"

"It took most of the day for her to agree, but she has. We applied for a license an hour ago. We'll be getting married Sunday evening right here in this room."

Anna drew in a breath and closed her eyes to give her thoughts time to catch up. Then she crossed the room to her father. His big arms went around her. "I'm so glad you are making things right with Mother."

He released her and stood back. "That's not all. I find that by selling the Chicago land, I can make enough money to still build the home on Geneva Lake. Construction will start come spring. I plan to make Geneva my headquarters and rebuild my business here." He looked at Rory. "I understand you're learning the gardening trade. How would you like a job as my property's caretaker after it's built."

A grin split Rory's face and he looked at Anna as if to see if she was okay with the offer. "I don't know sir. I'll have to give thought and prayer to it."

"Father, Rory asked me to marry him and I agreed."

Father grinned. "I'm glad to hear that." He looked across the room at Rory. "You definitely have my approval. I'll add a caretaker's house to the plans for the property. A fitting home for my daughter and her husband."

Anna looked from Father to Rory and back to Father. Things were moving so fast it was scary. "Rory didn't agree to work on your estate. He said he'll pray about it. We both will."

The light left Father's eyes. "I got ahead of myself. I thought after I approved of your marriage, that meant he accepted."

"No one asked me for my approval." Mother stepped into the room and glared at Anna. "Of what did your father approve?"

Anna fought to keep her tone soft. "My marrying Rory. We love each other, Mother." She went to the settee and sat next to her intended. "Now that I'm free, I plan to marry the man I love."

Mother's scowl dissolved. "I won't object. I can see how much you care for each other by the looks on your faces. Rory, I think you should join us for dinner, unless you have to be home soon."

Rory's brows arched and he glanced at Anna as if to ask if this was happening for real. Anna shrugged. "Can you stay?"

"Yes." Rory nodded. "Mrs. Hartwell, I'd be happy to stay for dinner."

After one of the happiest meals Anna had ever shared with her family, she walked Rory out. They went into the barn where he'd left the horse. She patted the mare's nose while he hitched up the sleigh, and then looked up at her fiancée. He drew her into his arms and kissed her.

"We'd better not linger out here in the cold. I don't want you sniffling on our wedding day."

Anna giggled, "Aren't we waiting until the end of the month?"

He hungrily kissed her, sending flutters whirling in her stomach. When they broke apart, he whispered. "With kisses like that, maybe we should make your parents' ceremony a double wedding."

"Maybe we should make a pact. No more kisses until our wedding."

He pulled her to him and pressed her face against his chest. "That's a fine idea. No more kisses until you are Mrs. Rory Quinn. But then, look out. I plan to kiss the daylights out of you, my bonnie bride."

EPILOGUE

*June 1873*

nna Quinn placed a bouquet of fresh cut daisies in the center of the dining table and smiled at their reflection in the polished oak surface. Rory not only had a knack for growing plants and flowers, but also for building furniture. Almost half of their house was filled with furniture he'd designed and built from the trees that once grew where the Hartwell home now stood several hundred feet away.

She walked to the parlor and peered through the windows at the sliver of Geneva Lake that peeked through the trees. Over toward the main house Rory knelt before a flowerbed, Katie, his ever-present shadow, beside him. Father's choosing to name the estate "Safe Refuge" had been a perfect choice. It was a safe refuge for the whole family. She closed her eyes and thanked God as she did every morning for blessing her so much. Her hand went to the locket that still hung from her neck as it had since Rory returned it to her. Only now it held a small picture of her on one side and one of Rory on the other, both taken at their wedding.

What joy it was to plan her own wedding without Mother's intrusions. Millie had made her the dress she'd first picked out and Callie was her only bridesmaid. Their tiny church was filled with candlelight at the late afternoon ceremony, after which only family and close friends joined them at the home on Broad Street for a light buffet supper before she and Rory stole away to a small rented cottage Mr. Sturgis had gifted them with for a three-night-stay.

A knock came at the front door and she snapped out of her memories and crossed through the cozy parlor to the center hall.

Mother smiled through the screen door. "Good morning. Is that sweet baby girl awake yet?"

Anna chuckled. "Mother, you know Maureen's schedule better than I. She won't wake up for another half hour at least." She opened the door and let her mother inside.

Mother strolled into the parlor. "Well, then I'll be here when she does. She sat on the primrose blue sofa. If you have something to do in town, I'll be happy to stay until you get back."

Anna couldn't help smiling. If someone had told her a year and a half ago her mother would change from a mean-spirited angry woman into the grandmotherly one who now sat in her parlor, she wouldn't have believed it. What a difference Mother's remarrying Father and asking God into her life had made. Not only on the inside, but outside as well. Gone was the severe hair style with all her hair pulled into a knot on the back of her head. Now, salt and pepper gray curls framed her face and she rarely frowned anymore. Of course, the nine-month-old bundle of joy sleeping upstairs hadn't hurt either.

Anna sat in an overstuffed chair across from her mother. "I wish I'd known you were coming I'd have made an appointment with Millie. I need another fitting. Callie's wedding will be here before we know it and I need to make sure my dress fits right."

Her mother gave her a curious look. "I thought you already had your dress fitted. The wedding is only a month away."

Anna patted her stomach. "I'm afraid by then I won't be able to button the dress. Millie is letting it out for me." She couldn't stifle her smile. "I'm expecting again."

Mother's eyes lit up as she clapped her palms together. "Another grandchild to spoil. How far along are you?"

Anna grinned. "Going on four months. I thought you'd notice I've been wearing roomier dresses lately."

"I just thought it was from having Maureen. Most women's bodies change after having a baby."

"Rory and I decided to tell the family tonight before we leave for dinner with Callie's new in-laws."

Mother looked off. "I so hope Robert's family is accepting of us."

Anna moved to the sofa and took her mother's hand. "I'm sure they'll be fine. Robert's parents know about our past and don't seem bothered."

"Thank God for that." Mother's eyes searched Anna's face. "They have God to help them in that way. I'm not sure about his two uncles."

Robert Unger's family consisted of three brothers who had made their wealth in boat building. Each of the uncles had purchased lakeshore land, two on the south shore and Robert's family on the north shore towards the village of Williams Bay. Callie and Robert had met the summer before when Robert visited their church.

"Have you thought about names for the new baby yet?"

Anna shrugged. "It's still early, but we think if it's a girl we'll name her Nora Eleanor. Her two grandmothers' names." She waited for the words to sink in.

Her mother's eyes lit up then she stared at her lap. "After the way I treated you. . ."

"That's all forgotten now, Mother. If it's a boy we'll use our fathers' two names together."

A screen door slammed, and Anna looked toward the kitchen and called out, "Katie, if you have mud on your shoes, take them off before coming in here." She shared a smile with Mother. "It's wonderful Rory has a job she can tag along and watch, but I wish sometimes he did something cleaner."

Katie appeared in the door to the dining room, her blue pinafore smudged. At least her black stockings hid what lurked on them. She grinned and raced across the Oriental rug, "Granny, I didn't know you were here." She climbed up next to Mother and snuggled into the crook of her arm.

Mother pulled her closer. "I haven't seen you for a couple days and it was time."

Katie scrunched her nose. "I was here. Where were you?"

"I took the train into Chicago with your grandfather, and I'm happy to be back in the fresh air."

A baby's happy babbling floated through the air, and Katie giggled. "Ma, the baby's awake."

Anna laughed and stood. "Looks like she is. I'll go get her."

After a diaper change, Anna carried her redheaded cherub downstairs and handed her to the child's grandmother. She sat next to Katie who was already entertaining Maureen with silly faces.

Anna arranged a small blanket over her shoulder then undid her dress buttons. "Let me get her fed before she loses her wonderful disposition. Then I'll find Rory and see if he needs my help with planting for a while, and the girls can stay with you, Mother."

She took Maureen and settled the baby against her breast. The child began to suckle. This is what she was born to do. To love and take care of her husband and children. God had surely given her everything she needed for life.

It is my hope that you enjoyed reading *Safe Refuge*.

Back in the early 1870s, the wealthy living in Chicago had discovered a beautiful spring-fed lake a short train ride away called Geneva Lake. When the Great Chicago Fire broke out in October 1871, the small village of Geneva, Wisconsin, and its beautiful lake came to their minds as a perfect spot for their families to stay while the city rebuilt itself. Soon, wonderful large homes, popped up on the shoreline. As more well-to-do people heard about the lake, additional large homes and mansions were built, and the area became known as the Newport of the Middle West.

Over the years, many of the homes, have become victims of the wrecking ball. Not wanting to have the legacy of my beautiful hometown and the lake be lost forever, I was inspired to write *Safe Refuge*. The family is fictional, but some of the people named in the book were real. However, the wealthy weren't the only ones who migrated to the area. Just before the fire, a new railroad line from Chicago to Lake Geneva opened. Irish immigrants were hired to lay the tracks. When they got to the end of the line, many decided to stay and lay claim on the rich farmland west of town. There, they raised their families in what became known as Irish Woods. Many of their descendants still live in the area today.

You may find it interesting that Jerusha Maxwell was an actual person, and was married to Phillip Maxwell, one of the town's founding fathers. Her home still stands today as an event venue called the Maxwell Mansion. I was two years old when my father took a job in Lake Geneva and we moved there from Ohio. His new boss owned the Maxwell home and we lived in the house's servant's quarters that had been repurposed as an apartment. My memories of living there are fuzzy, but I do remember much of those days. I had great fun there, including the home and Jerusha Maxwell in the story.

If you enjoyed *Safe Refuge*, I am planning two more novels that carry Anna and Rory's story forward into the next several decades.

Until next time, happy reading!

Pam

Pamela has written most of her life, beginning with her first diary at age eight. Her novels include *Thyme For Love, Surprised by Love in Lake Geneva, Wisconsin (a reissue of Love Finds You in Lake Geneva, Wisconsin)*, a 1933 historical romance set in her hometown, and *Second Chance Love*, a contemporary romance set at a rodeo in rural Illinois. Her novella, *What Lies Ahead*, is included in *The Bucket List Dare* collection, and another novella, *If These Walls Could Talk*, was published in May 2017, in a collection called *Coming Home: A Tiny House Collection*. Future novels include *Whatever is True*, a sequel to Second Chance Love.

**Shelter Bay**

**Newport of the West—Book Two**

Adventure girl, Maureen Quinn, isn't yet sure of her life's direction, but she knows she isn't cut out to be a bookkeeper for the town's undertaker. Wearing her stylish new bloomers, she suffers a bicycle accident in the middle of downtown and her long-time crush and fellow childhood mischief maker, Preston Stevens, comes to her rescue. He's back in the area and he couldn't have shown up at a better time. It isn't long before they become inseparable and she's sure he's the man God has for her.

Unlike his older brothers who are shackled to desk jobs at their father's financial services company, Preston yearns to see the world. What better person to do that with than Maureen? But after being expelled from Yale, because of a prank that brought embarrassment to the family, his dad has issued an ultimatum: Enlist in the military or join his brothers in the family business. He signs up with the U.S. Life Saving Service, a division of the Coast Guard, reasoning the time spent on the shores of Lake Michigan, keeping people safe, is far better than being stuck in a landlocked encampment. After his two-year stint, he intends to live out his dream of world travel before settling in Lake Geneva. But it isn't long before life-altering events occur affecting both his and Maureen's lives forever.

Returning to historic Lake Geneva for Book Two in the *Newport of the West* series, the Hartwell family saga continues through the life of Maureen Quinn, the daughter of Rory and Anna Quinn from *Safe Refuge*. Set mainly in beautiful Lake Geneva, *Shelter Bay* also carries the reader to the northern shore of Michigan and to the 1893 World's Fair in Chicago, also known as the Columbian Exposition.

**Tranquility Point**

**Newport of the West—Book Three**

Hannah Murphy is determined to make the summer of 1916, the best it can be before she heads off to law school in the fall. Like her mother and grandmother before her, she is inclined to "break the mold" when it comes to societal expectations of a young woman of means. Her mother was the first woman in town to wear bloomers, and Hannah becomes the first to ditch swim dresses in favor of a practical swimsuit that allows freedom to move through the water.

At the first gathering of the summer, she reacquaints with tall, handsome Ted Bauer, also an aspiring attorney. Ted, who is of German descent, had a huge crush on Hannah when he was in eighth grade, and she was in sixth. He's no longer the gangly boy she remembers and is quite appealing. With Geneva Lake as their backdrop, their summer romance escalates, until the dark cloud of the Great War can no longer be ignored. Although the U.S. has not yet joined the fray, people of German descent are seen with mistrust, and Ted enlists with the British Army to take the heat of discrimination off his family. With the future on hold, Hannah bids her fiancé farewell as he goes to war. Only God knows if she will ever see him again or if they will ever be able to recapture what they had those few short summer months.

Coming from Pamela S. Meyers in May 2021:

***Rose Harbor***

Book Four of the Newport of the West series.